THE NEW YOU SUR'

Daisy Waugh is a journalist and author. She lives in
London and has two magnificent children.

By the same author

WHAT IS THE MATTER WITH MARY JANE
A SMALL TOWN IN AFRICA

DAISY WAUGH

THE NEW YOU
SURVIVAL KIT

An Essential Guide to Etiquette,
Rites and Customs Among
the Modern Elite

A Love Story

HarperCollins*Publishers*

This novel is entirely a work of fiction.
The names, characters and incidents portrayed in it are
the work of the author's imagination. Any resemblance to
actual persons, living or dead, events or localities is
entirely coincidental.

HarperCollins*Publishers*
77–85 Fulham Palace Road,
Hammersmith, London W6 8JB

www.**fire**and**water**.com

A Paperback Original 2002
1 3 5 7 9 8 6 4 2

Special overseas edition published 2002

Copyright © Daisy Waugh 2002

The Author asserts the moral right to
be identified as the author of this work

A catalogue record for this book
is available from the British Library

Author photograph © Steve McDonough

ISBN 0 00 711906 2

Set in Giovanni by Palimpsest Book Production Limited,
Polmont, Stirlingshire

Printed and bound in Great Britain by
Omnia Books Limited, Glasgow

All rights reserved. No part of this publication may be
reproduced, stored in a retrieval system, or transmitted,
in any form or by any means, electronic, mechanical,
photocopying, recording or otherwise, without the prior
permission of the publishers.

This book is sold subject to the condition that it shall not,
by way of trade or otherwise, be lent, re-sold, hired out or
otherwise circulated without the publisher's prior consent
in any form of binding or cover other than that in which it
is published and without a similar condition including this
condition being imposed on the subsequent purchaser.

'I Will Survive'
Words & Music by Dino Fekaris & Freddie Perren
© Copyright 1978 Perren-Vibes Music Company & PolyGram
International Publishing Incorporated, USA.
Universal Music Publishing Limited, 77 Fulham Palace Road,
London W6.
Used by permission of Music Sales Ltd.
All Rights Reserved. International Copyright Secured.

WOT
By RAYMOND BURNS pka CAPTAIN SENSIBLE
© 1982 ROCK MUSIC COMPANY LIMITED

THE LUNATICS HAVE TAKEN OVER THE ASYLUM
By GOLDING/STAPLES/HALL
© 1981 PLANGENT VISIONS MUSIC LIMITED

For my old Dad
In Memory

ACKNOWLEDGEMENTS

Thank you Rachel Hore, Gabriele Grilz, Georgina Hawtrey-Woore, Amaury Blow, Nathalie Muller, Tilly Ware (especially for the buses), Imogen Edwards-Jones, Fiona McIntosh, Jay Pond-Jones.

Clare Alexander, thank you for all your help and kindness, and for being a magician. I can never thank you enough.

And Peter La Terrière, for your patience, generosity, chivalry, good advice and film industry Super NYou introductions, I definitely owe you a couple of sherbets. Thank you.

ARE YOU young, enthusiastic, self-motivated, target orientated, narcissistic, unreliable, with an excellent but casual personal appearance?

Then we want to hear from you! We are looking for like minded go-getters to help with the vital task of setting this country's agendas, forming opinions and feathering our own nests. We feel BAD about the homeless but we feel GOOD about our high-cost, super-hectic lifestyles. Want to join us? Have you got the SURVIVAL KIT? Send your CV, £22.95 (inc. p&p) and a recent photo to Pete G. at Unit 3a, 7 Overwood Street, London N1 7JQ. No time wasters please.

THE NEW YOU SURVIVAL KIT

Everything you need to begin:

1. A Back-Up Plan for Every Occasion
2. An Advanced Communications System
3. A Smart Uniform
4. Some Great Mates
5. A Big, Big Heart
6. An Amazingly Packed Agenda
7. A Quiet Self-Confident Delivery
8. The Members' Own Directory to What's Funny and What's Not
9. A Yes! Can-do Approach
10. BELIEF!!

NEW YOU RULE NUMBER ONE: Your new friends are busy people! They'll think nothing of cancelling you at the last minute . . . ten times in a row!! But look, don't waste your time getting angry. This system WORKS. Once you've learned the ropes you're gonna LOVE the flexibility it gives you. So remember, a NY commitment is nothing more than a 'pencilled option on mutual time'. OK? And if a better option comes up? Somebody's gotta be erased, baby! Organise a back-up plan!

A BACK-UP PLAN

7.30 p.m. Jo and her hardworking boyfriend Ed were meant to be meeting outside the Everyman Cinema in Hampstead in an hour's time, to watch an award winning *docufea* about the militant German girl rock band SCHREM! whose members were found dead in a hotel room in Wurzburg in 1986, after a massive post-concert drugs binge. Jo had read all the reviews and had formed her positive opinions about the film long ago. She was looking forward to it. She was looking forward to seeing Ed, whom she hadn't seen since before the weekend. They needed to talk, she thought. If for no better reason than to try to tackle the rumours.

She and her best friend Mel had discussed the worrying Word on Ed during most of Sunday. Not that Jo accepted it was anything more than jealous gossip (of which, she insisted, she'd heard not a whisper before Mel turned up that Sunday afternoon). It was true that Ed had recently become a little unreliable and a little too quick to take offence. But that, Jo said, was because Ed was clever. And because he was under so much pressure at work.

'He's no cleverer than most of the people we know,' Mel had snapped.

The fact was, said Mel, Ed's problem had nothing to do

with his intelligence or with his success (as a fashionable independent documentary maker) and a lot to do with his exaggerated fondness for cocaine. That was why he was always so broke, in spite of the fact that he earned a fortune. It was why he was often so ratty. It was why, said Mel – and Jo had to laugh – he'd had a bloody great boil on his neck the last three times Mel had seen him.

'I mean, let's face it,' said Mel, 'rumours have to start somewhere. I haven't had a decent conversation with that guy for ages. He's always in the bloody toilet.'

'Rubbish,' said Jo. 'It's irresponsible comments like that which get these stories going in the first place.' She didn't add, though she could have done, that the reason Mel and Ed hadn't had 'a decent conversation' for so long was because Ed thought Mel was an idiot, or a 'lightweight' to use his word. Too interested in who she was shagging and not, one suspects, interested enough in him.

Anyway, at 7.30 p.m. that ordinary Wednesday evening Ed called Jo at her office. She had been worrying about him so her voice sounded especially upbeat when she said, 'Hi Baby, howzitgoing? I'm just about winding up now so if you're OK with it perhaps we can hook up a bit earlier.'

But Ed said he was snowed under. Channel Foremost had suddenly brought forward the deadline for *Helsinki Pros*. 'Which means there's pretty much zero chance of me getting out of this place before midnight,' he said. 'Sorry.' He was obviously playing with his screen at the time. He sounded distracted.

'Well,' she said. 'I guess it means there's a lot of excitement about it, right?'

'Hmm . . . There's a *bit*-of-a buzz, yes. I think it would be fair to say.'

6

'Of course there is!'

'How about you then?' Ed asked (slightly unwillingly). 'Did you get the, em – Any news from Homeless?'

'Yup!' She sounded jubilant. 'It's definite. Just as soon as we've got the OK in writing from Channel Foremost. Can you give Geoff a bit of a nudge on that? Is he there now?'

'Sure,' Ed said carefully. Geoff was Ed's chief commissioner at Foremost and also, not in the least coincidentally, one of his favourite friends. 'Will do.'

Jo looked furtively around the room and leant closer to her telephone: 'Penny said if we get this account she's going to make me a partner.'

'I should think so. About bloody time.'

'Yeah, you're right . . . Listen, it's been pretty crazy over here. So don't worry about me. I'll probably take a bit of work home.'

'You're a star, Jo.'

'Of course I am!' It had sounded more brittle than she intended. There was a pause while they both smiled half-heartedly into their telephones.

'. . . Well look I'll let you get on. And Jo –' he said, putting a bit of emphasis on it this time. 'I'm sorry.'

Jo felt a wave of panic as she hung up. It was a highly valued aspect of their relationship that Jo and Ed never, *ever* complained about the other's work load. It went without saying that one of Geoff's deadlines took precedence over a cinema trip. But that hardly solved the problem of what she was going to do with herself tonight. It was unlike her not to have organised a BACK-UP PLAN. Jo hated nothing more than spending an evening on her own. It made her feel like a failure.

Under normal circumstances she wouldn't have hesitated to call Mel but after Sunday Jo didn't want to admit to her that Ed had let her down again. At half past seven. Anyway everything was going so well in Melanie's life at the moment it was quite irritating spending time with her. The evening loomed ahead, long and lonely. Unless she acted quickly she was going to have to spend it alone in her new flat. Which, though perfect for throwing small parties was a) quite boring when she was in it on her own and b) quite scary.

She lived in a fashionable street in Islington, favoured by people like Jo because of its lively, cosmopolitan atmosphere. But directly opposite her sitting-room window was a clearly disreputable minicab office, where waiting drivers loafed about smoking spliffs most of the night. Jo thought it was hilarious – when there were other people in the flat. But on her own the men made her feel vulnerable. She feared that one day one of them might want to . . .

She never allowed herself to finish the sentence, even in her head. It was pathetic and stupid and it was only because they were bla— West In— Afro–Carribeans. Whatever.

7.30 p.m. Jo's office, which half an hour earlier was bustling with thirty-three of the most forward thinking public relations experts in the capital, now lay virtually deserted. Top Spin, as the company was called, employed thirty-seven slim women and two fat ones (both secretaries), one West Indian post boy and three lean and well-dressed homosexual white men. At 7.30 p.m. there were just four women left. Jo didn't feel particularly excited at the prospect of spending the evening with any of them.

'Well,' she said loudly, '*I've* just been blown out. At half past seven! Anyone fancy a quick drink?'

She looked hopefully across the long thin office (open plan, clutter-free, bursting with natural wood and light; the ideal work space for modern, creative people). Silence.

It wasn't that she was unpopular. People liked Jo a lot. It was just that at Top Spin they tended to work hard. If they were still at their desks it meant they were still concentrating. They probably didn't even hear her.

'No?' said Jo, with courageous lightness. 'Oh well . . . Ali? . . . Rache?'

'Can't tonight,' said Rache. 'Love to but can't. In fact – Christ! I shouldn't even still be here!'

With the smallest, quietest sigh, Jo reached across the desk for her mobile telephone and her big fat contact book and headed for the company smoking room. Who could she call at such late notice, she wondered, without seeming like a loser? Who could she call?

Jessica of course.

At about the same time, in a pleasant but cluttered top-floor flat overlooking Parsons Green, Charlie Maxwell McDonald, thirty-three, was dolefully spooning baked beans onto a slice of stale toast. He'd had beans and toast for breakfast and lunch that day and again at two o'clock last night. But it wasn't his diet which was making him depressed that evening, so much as the knowledge that when he'd finished eating he was going to have to telephone his father.

Charlie's father, a retired and sickly general who lived with a housekeeper in a large manor house called

Fiddleford, in a rustic, distant corner of the South West, was not an easy man to talk to. He'd mellowed since his wife died eleven years ago but he was still a gentleman of eccentrically fixed and unfashionable opinions, too proud for his own good. Though he loved his son more than anything in his sad, slow life he could never hold a conversation with Charlie for longer than thirty seconds without inadvertently leaving an impression of his paternal disappointment. Charlie, though an excellent addition to the human race, was not an ideal general's son. He was too disorganised.

Until last December he and his twin Georgina had lived in the Parsons Green flat together. It had been bought six years earlier, out of a joint trust fund set up soon after they were born, and though they used to squabble occasionally (Charlie never bought lavatory paper, Georgie spent too long in the bathroom) they were generally very happy. They were, as twins are meant to be, the closest and sweetest of allies. Until suddenly, without even a whisper of warning, Georgina had left him.

It was eight months ago now; the weekend before the weekend before Christmas. She'd been down at Fiddleford, out hunting with the General, and it had been a beautiful sunny day. By noon the frost was still hard on the ground. Icicles hung off the bare trees and the cold air resonated to the sound of their horses' galloping hooves. There had been an incident. She was riding beside her father – both of them, flat out. Their horses, with necks stretched, nostrils flaring, ears set back, were heading full pelt towards a large fence. Something happened. The mare shied. Georgie was thrown through the air and her father heard the crack of her neck as she landed. She was dead long before the ambulance arrived.

Charlie and his father sorted through her belongings shortly after the funeral and ever since then her London room had lain empty and unused. The rest of the flat remained unchanged. Every picture, every piece of furniture, every bloody unused saucepan was only there because that was the way Georgie had arranged it. The place was still so full of her strong, warm, practical presence that Charlie, however drunk (and he drank a lot these days) had to brace himself each and every time he walked in. Though he hated to be there, Charlie couldn't bring himself to sell the flat. So now he had it to himself. There was no lavatory paper in the bathroom and no food in the fridge.

Charlie might have cut a sad figure, bent over a grimy saucepan in a flat still haunted with memories of his lovely twin. But he still had a great deal to be grateful for. The fairy godmothers had been unusually generous at his christening and he was blessed with more than his fair share of advantages, chief among them (with the exception of this evening) his artless ability, in spite of his sadness, to see the best of life and the best of whatever was dealt him.

He also had a singing voice that made women swoon and a warm-hearted, easy temperament which made everybody, male and female, want to befriend him. He was a natural athlete – excellent at tennis and an outstanding skier. Though he wasn't clever in the sense that Jo's friends were and his knowledge of the arts, pop culture and politics was abysmal, he had nevertheless managed to achieve what most people fail to do; an uncomplicated life for

11

himself which delivered to the world more pleasure than it took and which was unusually decent and enjoyable. For the past ten years he had paid his way – in the winter by teaching skiing in the Alps, and in the summer by singing in large pubs around South West London. He did both jobs exceptionally well.

What bewildered and upset his old father was his absolute lack of ambition. They used to squabble about it regularly, until the evening of the twins' twenty-seventh birthday when the General gave a speech, a résumé of Georgie's successes – her catering company, her respectable boyfriend, her outstanding horsemanship – and Charlie's innumerable failures. It was meant to be funny but it wasn't. Three quarters of the way through, Charlie's prodigal goodwill finally ran out. He quietly left the table, got into his car and drove back to London.

The General was ashamed. The following morning, with Georgina's encouragement, he apologised (something he had not done before) and the subject of Charlie's professional activities was never mentioned again. Then Georgie died. And Charlie was all the General had left.

But it wasn't the General who changed the rules, it was Charlie. Last April, he was sitting opposite his father at the Fiddleford dining-room table. They had already talked brightly about the new gardener, the state of the roof, the dogs, the horses, (never about Georgie, though there were photographs of her all over the house). Charlie had allowed his mind to wander while his father delivered his usual grumpy lament for the old nation, moaning about prisoners' colour televisions, immigrants' breeding habits, homosexual marriages . . . but the General had reeled it off so many times he wasn't even listening to himself. Perhaps

12

he noticed the boredom in his son's eyes, perhaps even the boredom in his own voice. Suddenly, for no apparent reason and with uncharacteristic diffidence, he turned the conversation to Charlie's singing.

'And do you usually,' he began hesitantly, 'er – tend to sing in pubs, or concert halls, sometimes? Perhaps?'

'Oh! . . . Well,' Charlie said when he'd recovered from the surprise, 'it's usually pubs, I suppose. Or winebars. Sometimes I might do a wedding.'

'How interesting. And it's usually . . . You find you're usually very much in demand? The landlords tend to ask you back again?'

'I have a couple of places I go to regularly, twice a week. And then, unless something comes up I normally have Thursday nights off.'

Charlie used to earn most of his income at the weekends but he'd given it up after Georgie died so he could spend more time at Fiddleford. Six weeks ago, to make up the money, he'd taken a part-time job at a mobile telephone shop. It was something he hadn't yet felt the need to mention to the General.

'Now – Isn't that splendid? And all the people come and listen to you play, do they? I suppose you're frightfully good . . .'

Charlie looked embarrassed.

'Well! I must come to London and see you one day! I should enjoy that very much! What fun! I can't imagine why it's taken me so long. Or would I be a ghastly embarrassment?'

Charlie felt sick. It was a horrible climbdown, from a man who'd wanted an officer for a son. That his father, who'd faced gunfire, whose shoulders had probably grown

13

distorted by the weight of all his medals, should now be forced to draw pride from a pub night singalong, was more than he could stand. Charlie felt ashamed, grief stricken, overwhelmed by pity.

'I've – er. Got a job interview next week,' he said suddenly. He was a bad liar. He was blushing. But his father was so pleasantly astonished he didn't notice.

'Anything interesting?' he said at last. He was pleased with how casual it sounded.

'Well . . . um. Yes, I think so. Friend of mine's setting up a sort of Internet company. He thought I might like to come in with him. I don't really know much about it . . . Something about computers, I think.'

'I should think,' said the General dryly. But Charlie watched as he absorbed the news. There was a long silence. The General stared down at his plate. His hands fiddled distractedly with the stem of his wine-glass, then he lifted his head and looked up at Charlie wearing a smile that lit up his entire face. Charlie had never seen anything like it. The General was born wearing a heavy scowl and the only time Charlie had seen it lift had been at Georgie's funeral, when he'd been crying.

'Well!' said the father. 'I must say that *is* exciting . . . Let me know, won't you, if there's anything I can do.'

So began Charlie's silly lies. His father seemed so happy Charlie couldn't resist encouraging him to dream. One failed job interview led inevitably to the invention of the next. Charlie began to invent a whole series of interviews, each one more complicated and more ludicrous than the last.

After the baked beans and stale toast, Charlie was going to call home to explain that the interview for Assistant

14

Manager of a senior citizens' adventure holiday camp based in Clacton-on-Sea had not gone well. They were looking, he would say, for somebody older.

Charlie hated lying to his father. The more the lies continued the more he longed to present his father with something he could be genuinely proud of. But with three failed A-levels, no degree, and only an intimate knowledge of off-piste Meribel to boast about, he was painfully conscious of how little he had to offer.

Jessica Caiplan was generally too lazy to organise anything in the evening that might keep her away from the TV. Which was why she was still, after all these years, Jo's most dependable fall-back companion, her number one, super-soother New You Essential, her fail-safe, first stop BACK-UP PLAN. The girls' bimonthly telephone conversations tended to be almost identical, always during the early evening, always initiated by Jo; Jessie – warm and slightly boring, making jokes about whatever rubbish she happened to be watching on the screen; Jo cajoling, faintly patronising, apparently casual but absolutely determined that her friend should do her duty, switch the television off and come out to play. Jessica always submitted.

Jessica did not dress like Jo or talk like Jo or think like Jo or work like Jo or know such exciting people as Jo. She didn't keep up with current affairs like Jo, and probably, thought Jo, couldn't even put a name to the Shadow Chancellor. But they had known each other for years. They had been best friends until Lower Sixth, when Jo peeled off with the other clever girls, to take extra classes for Cambridge entrance. The Cambridge thing had caused a rift. In the end Jo failed to get in anyway (her single most painful failure, though she'd gain a pound of fat before she admitted it). Jessica didn't go to university at all and there had been a few years of coldness between them, circa 1986–88, when Jo was at Manchester discovering underprivilege, and Jessie was working in a stationery shop in Bond Street learning the difference between embossed and engraved.

That Wednesday night Jo and Jessica arranged to meet at a crowded winebar off Fulham Broadway at just after nine o'clock. It gave Jo time to squeeze in a visit to the gym and it gave poor pregnant Jessica time to waddle, on this balmy August evening, from her chintzy house in Bloom Park Road without having to bother with driving.

The winebar was not an inspiring place. It had excellent air conditioning, creamy white walls and light-wood furniture, a facetious menu and, here's the thing, *live music on Wednesday nights*. It was part of a chain. It was the sort of place Jo normally took great pains to avoid. But Jessica, telephoned at such short notice, had said she couldn't think of anywhere better and Jo was so pleased she'd found someone to talk to that night, she didn't argue.

By the time Jo arrived Jessica had already been there some time. 'God Jess,' Jo said warmly, hurrying to wrap her in a tight hug, 'you look fabulous! You look – *radiant*. It's not fair! . . . I'm so sorry I'm late.'

The contrast between the two women, due to Jessica's expectancy, was even more marked than usual. Jo, with her lithe body neatly packaged in purple velvet hipster jeans and tiny grey T-shirt, looked like all happy, modern girls are meant to look. She shone with vitality. Her session in the gym gave her creaseless skin an extra golden glow. Her short dark elfin locks, subtly highlighted, were still damp from the shower. Her make-up was minimal and her only jewellery – a tiny silver heart, a birthday present from one of the girls at Top Spin – emphasised the smallness of her neck. She was lovely looking. She was ageless. In this light, she could have passed for twenty-three. Only her composure gave her away, and the subtle expense of her perfectly careless hair, clothes, wallet, shoes, key-ring, nails, skin . . . Jo was thirty-one. Highly employable. Admirably well-informed. Articulate. Intelligent. Financially autonomous. Infinitely *sortable*, as the old toffs used to say. She ate a healthy diet and all her teeth were her own. Any man would have been proud to introduce her to their friends. Ed should have counted himself lucky.

Poor old Jessie on the other hand had never really got to grips with the physical or intellectual demands of contemporary womanhood. She was plump at the best of times. She read the *Daily Mail*. She found David Hasselhoff attractive. And she giggled. Having systematically refused to attend to the lessons of her more liberated sisters it came as no great surprise when the first hurdle on the track towards independence sent her crashing to the ground. At only twenty-four, she'd married a boring man called Gerald, who wore a dark suit and did something despicable in the City. The doctors had said there was something, not exactly wrong but slightly feeble about Gerald's sperm which was why, nearly eight years later, his wife was only now pregnant with their first child. That night Jessica looked far from radiant. She looked bloated and drab and stoical, the way all but the most self-disciplined pregnant women will.

There was a moment of friction at the beginning of the evening, soon after the waiter arrived to take their order. Part of his friendly and efficient service included staring significantly at Jessica's bump and asking whether she wouldn't prefer to be seated in non-smoking.

'No,' Jessie said. 'Could we get some wine please?'

Jo was embarrassed. She thought Jess was being irresponsible about the baby and imperious to the waiter both of which, in her book, were pretty cardinal sins. She checked his name badge, smiled and said, 'Thanks, Michael.' They exchanged the briefest of glances and he bustled away feeling much better.

'Thanks, Michael,' Jessie mimicked.

'Oh come on, Jess,' Jo said uncomfortably. 'I'm sure he's a nice guy. He's only trying to do his job.'

Conversation moved on. They discussed Jo's career first, as they tended to. It was frantic but thriving. Especially exciting was one major new account – a pop concert in aid of Meals For The Homeless which, according to Jo, was 'going to be as culturally significant to the new millennium as Live Aid was to the eighties. And even bigger when you take into account the net audience. Because people are fed up. They're fed up with just standing by. They want to *help*. We've already got just about every big name in the industry showing an interest. Jess, it's going to be m-a-ss-i-v-e.'

'Oh!' said Jessie, clapping her hands in childish delight, 'you couldn't get Gerald and me backstage tickets? *Please?* I just – Gerald says the only thing he wants to do before he dies is to meet those girls from the Corrs.'

Jo smiled non-committally. 'How is Gerald?' she asked.

'He's fine. Quite sweet actually. When I see him. He

leaves lists of baby names on the kitchen table every morning but then by the time he comes home I'm usually already in bed . . . He's in Baghdad at the moment.' She frowned. 'I think. Or Burma. Somewhere horrid beginning with B . . . earning lots of money, which is a good thing I suppose. Especially as I'm so bloody useless . . .'

'No – you're – *not!*' said Jo assertively. 'For Heaven's sake, Jess. You're *growing a little person inside you*. Think about it! You can't *get* more useful than that!'

Jessica grimaced. 'Gerald's ridiculously excited about the baby.'

'Well, he would be. I'm not surprised!'

Jo said that Ed's career was also frantic and thriving. He'd just returned from filming a shocking documentary about underage prostitution in Helsinki, and it looked like Channel Foremost was definitely going to green-light the next project too, on an issue, said Jo, that desperately needed highlighting but which she obviously couldn't divulge, 'until Foremost was on board one hundred and fifty per cent'. She failed to mention Mel's unwelcome Word on Ed, though it was probably the thing uppermost in her mind. (Just thinking about it made her angry.) Nor, for fear that it made them both sound a) slightly less important and b) slightly corrupt, did she choose to be specific about the 'issue' so in need of Ed's exposure. It was a behind-the-scenes documentary about a Meals For The Homeless concert which promised, if you believed the PR, to be as culturally significant to the new millennium as Live Aid was to the eighties.

In fact, it was off the back of Jo's claim that Channel Foremost was definitely up for the documentary – and on that condition – that Top Spin had been awarded

19

the account. And of course it was off the back of Jo's promise to Ed of unprecedented behind-the-scenes access that Channel Foremost was apparently willing to let the project go ahead. Ed and Jo worked well together. This wasn't the first time they'd pulled off such a coup, but it looked set to be their most profitable.

Jo was updating Jessica on the recent successes of her annoying friend Mel, a self-employed lifestyle journalist, when she was distracted by the arrival of the *Wednesday night live performer*. She watched his casual climb onto the small platform directly behind Jessie's chair – and felt faintly irritated by it. There was something, she thought, a little defiant about how comfortable he looked. In such terrible clothes. He leant against a high stool which had presumably been put there for the purpose and set about re-tuning his guitar.

He was tall and pleasantly lean. But his clothes, Jo noticed, were at least ten years out of date. He wore close-fitting jeans which bagged at the knees, cowboy boots and a white T-shirt with the message I SKIED MONT BLANC across its front. His wrists were weighed down with bangles and his head and face were obscured by a large leather hat with corks hanging off the brim. His discordant strumming meant she had to shout to make herself heard. All in all, the sight and sound of him (ex-public school Fulham ski-bum) only fuelled her frustration with the world.

Or her frustration with Mel to be more precise, though she and the musician could not have been less alike. This is the thing. This, and Mel's criticism of her boy-friend, is the thing that was bugging Jo that night. On the strength of one of Mel's totally unresearched observations,

('Screenplays are the new novel. Every waiter in every restaurant in the city has got a screenplay on his PC. London is the new LA.') she had just signed a contract with a Sunday broadsheet to write a weekly column about the domestic and social agony of writing a screenplay herself.

'Apart from the fact that she doesn't know anything about film, and apart from the fact that she's going to be paid £750 a week for what will amount to about three hour's work – The *guaranteed* publicity,' Jo shouted, 'means she's definitely going to get the thing into development, even if it's complete crap –'

'I suppose it does,' said Jessie.

'Which I'm sure it *won't* be. And I'm pleased for Mel. I really am. I love her to bits. But the point is, when things like this are being commissioned by what was once supposed – ha! – to be a serious newspaper, the implications are – they're actually enormous. First and foremost that the British media has *completely* lost its grip on what constitutes news. Second of all – the point is – It's actually things like *Mel's column* that make people despair for British journalism.'

'I bet,' said Jessie indulgently. She wasn't really listening. 'Me too.'

'But the thing is Jessie – Listen. It gets worse.'

'Ooo! *Ow!* Crikey this baby kicks! . . . Sorry. Sorry, Jo. Go on.'

Jo paused to smile politely at her friend's stomach before continuing. 'The thing is – *Apparently* she's already been approached by the guys who did *Billy Elliot* – who I actually know quite well. They're really lovely guys. But it turns out, if you can believe this, they want to buy an

21

option on the *column*. Not the screenplay! On the bloody *column*. It *has* to make you wonder about the state of the film industry, doesn't it? I mean I'm happy for her. You know I am. I don't need to say it. But . . .'

'I never really liked Mel that time I met her,' said Jessie, getting the general drift. 'She seemed a bit pleased with herself if you ask me.' Which Jo hadn't. But at that, thankfully, the subject was forced to a close. Moments later, with no introduction, the opening chords of the musician's first song suddenly, and quite deliciously, reverberated around the room.

At first I was afraid . . .

'Oh fan*tas*tic!' said Jessie. 'I adore this song. Don't you?'

But as suddenly as he began, he fell silent again. Smiling lazily, he let his leather bangled wrist hang tantalisingly over the guitar strings.

I was petrified . . . sang one of the diners.

The guitarist looked at him and chuckled.

I was petrified . . . he sang.

The rumble of friendly impatience turned slowly into a round of boisterous applause as he began to sing on . . .

kept thinking I . . . would . . . never . . . live . . .

'Get on with it!' someone shouted.

'At least he's taken his hat off,' mumbled Jo to disguise the fact that she, like a lot of people in the room, couldn't help but return the singer's joyful smile.

'*Give* it to us!' yelled Jessica.

And he did. Suddenly his voice filled the room, soaring effortlessly over the racket of the scores of Fulham diners who had already taken it upon themselves to join in.

It turned out, Jo noticed, that he was very handsome without the hat. He had beautiful thick dark hair, a straight nose, high cheekbones, square jaw, strong chin . . . In fact, she found she couldn't take her eyes off him. The voice, the way his Adam's apple moved, the angle of his neck, his forearms, his back, the way his fingers caressed the instrument's strings, the way that white T-shirt hung off his chest, the rich, smooth, soulfulness of his voice, made Jo blush. Gave her goose bumps.

> *I should have changed that stupid lock*
> *I should have made you leave your key . . .*

The Fulhamites (estate agents, bankers, rugby players, boisterous, Tory-voting embarrassments every one) were beating their tables in exultation and the sound of shaking crockery and uninhibited merriment only seemed to spur the musician on.

> *. . . If I'd known for just one second*
> *You'd be back to bother me!*

They stood up.

23

. . . Go now Go!

The thumping feet and booming voices sent a shelf full of glasses at the back of the restaurant crashing to the floor. Everyone sang on.

Only poor Jo was too inhibited to join in. She was fixed to her seat, overcome by shame at the hearty mindlessness of her surroundings, filled with gratitude that Ed was not there to witness it – but still, inexplicably, with that grin fixed to her face. She simply couldn't stop gazing at him, at the incredible light in his dark brown eyes, those deep laughter lines, that smile, those voluptuous lips, the way the knees and feet moved in time to the music . . .

'Oh – my GOD!' screamed Jessie suddenly. 'I don't believe it! I didn't even notice without my contacts! It's Charlie! . . . Charlie! Over here!' He turned at the sound of his name and, seeing Jess, his face lit up with recognition.

'I'm pregnant!' she shouted, pointing at her belly. He nodded enthusiastically. 'This is my *friend.* Jo! You can see she's frightfully glamourous! . . . So, will you come and talk to us afterwards?' He looked across at Jo but she was so terrified that her interest was engraved on her normally self-possessed face, she could only glare at him. He winked at her; a friendly, flirtatious (unfashionable) wink – at which, to hide the fact that she was blushing, she threw herself into a phony coughing fit.

It took all the strength I have not to fall apart . . .

'I've got to go,' Jo said abruptly.

24

'What?' shouted Jessie. She was standing on top of her chair singing hard enough, Jo thought primly, to bring about premature contractions.

Just trying hard to mend the pieces of my broken heart . . .

'I've got so much work on at the moment –' Jo picked up her bag and stood up. 'D'you think,' she shouted, 'we can GET THE BILL?'

'For Heaven's sake! What do you want to do that for? He's going to have a drink with us afterwards! And there you were,' Jessie bellowed happily, 'thinking I didn't have any glamorous friends! I've known him for *ages*! Isn't he gorgeous?'

Jo didn't reply. Suddenly Jessie stopped dancing and examined her old friend more closely. 'You fancy him!' she said with a sly, victorious smile. 'Joanna Smiley –'

Jo Smiley winced.

. . . But now I hold my head up high! . . .

'You bloody do! That's why you're running away! Because you fancy him!'

. . . Go now Go!

Of course she didn't fancy him. What an absurd, embarrassing, humiliating, ludicrous bloody idea. She, Jo Smiley, confidante to some of the most – intriguing – young achievers in the land, did *not* – Just the thought of what Mel would make of him made her writhe. I SKIED MONT BLANC, for Christ's sake! What *millennium* did this joker think he was living in? Not that it was remotely relevant . . .

Walk out the door!

And perhaps that's exactly what she should have done. But just then he turned and happened to catch her eye. He smiled. And she found herself sitting down again.

At about the same time, in a newly appointed, £280-per-hour editing suite just behind Soho Square, Ed and Geoff were sitting in semi-darkness eating Chinese takeaway and wondering who would be the first to dare suggest calling it a night. Ed had greatly exaggerated the deadliness of his deadline to Jo. In truth he hadn't much fancied the thought of a cinema trip. He and Geoff had been 'in the zone' as they called it (work was going well) and Ed hadn't wanted to break off. Now they were both tired. But as much as he wanted a drink, he was unwilling to be the first to say so. It would be tantamount to admitting that Geoff's professional commitment was greater than his own, and that was more or less unthinkable. Except he really did want a drink.

In front of them a blurred picture of a pretty fourteen-year-old Helsinki girl's bruised and bleeding breasts filled a large television screen. After lengthy discussion Ed and Geoff had decided that the image, agonisingly beautiful, they thought, 'and yet strangely sexless', illustrated perfectly the girl's woeful tale. While she told her heartrending story, Ed and Geoff agreed, the screen would focus on them exclusively; as she told of the father who abused her, the pimp who was her dealer, the punter who beat her up, viewers would watch the soft movement of her breathing and the slow motion trickling of her blood. It was the sort of thing, Ed and Geoff thought privately, which won awards.

The fact that the blood was due to the antics of her pet cat who, scared by the television lights, had leapt onto the prostitute's chest a few seconds before they started filming, was not 'technically relevant', they both agreed. Because the bruises were real, if you believed her story, which neither of them honestly could, since – though they might rather forget it now – it was they who had more or less invented it. Whatever. The amazingly fortuitous arrival of the blood only served to highlight what was already a shocking tale. And a tale, needless to say, that needed to be told. Helsinki, the post-watershed Tuesday night viewers of Britain must understand, is not just, em, a very cold city quite near Norway. But a place where pretty girls with nice breasts are made to suffer. Constantly. At the hands of men.

'I swear,' said Geoff, his mouth full of Chinese, eyes still fixed on those bosoms, 'this sequence makes *me* feel a bit weepy. And God knows, after the things I've seen in this business, that's not easy.'

Ed said nothing but his silence was well-judged. It hinted at depths of sensitivity that even Geoff would never understand. It was also a perfect cue for Ed to say something along the lines of, 'Phoo! Don't know about you but I'm knackered. Fancy a quick drink, Geoff?'

He was preparing the way for it, sighing, leaning back in his swivel chair, crossing his hands behind his head, crossing his right foot over his left knee, 'Crikey!' he began, when his mobile interrupted him. He snatched it up with a businesslike flurry, said, 'Yup, yeah, hi –' in a dreary monotone. 'Hi, Mel,' though she had never called him before. 'What's up?'

Mel was at the Groucho Club with a couple of her newest friends and she sounded slightly drunk.

'I've got to *whisper*,' she said, shouting over the racket of the bar. ''Cause they don't let you use mobiles in here. You should see me. I'm actually having to crouch under the table!'

Ed had learned the power of the telephonic pause very early in his rise to glory. He waited coolly for her to get to the point.

But she wasn't that easily bullied. 'How are you, anyway? Haven't seen you for ages. How was Helsinki?'

'Fine,' said Ed. 'Fine, Mel. What can I do for you? I'm actually in the edit room right now.'

'Oh! Oh sorry. Well look – perhaps I should call another time. It's just – I've got a guy with me here – GREY McSHANE. OK?' Silence. But she knew he was impressed. 'He's just been telling me how much he'd like to meet you. And I think you two should hook up. What are you doing *right now*?'

Ed was thinking quickly. He knew exactly who Grey McShane was, of course. Only a very mad and pointless hermit, Ed thought, wouldn't know that. Grey McShane was a thirty-seven-year-old, gloriously handsome six foot four former tramp who'd been discovered six months ago, stinking of booze and filth, reciting his own poetry outside the King's Head pub in Islington. A fashionable author had taken a fancy to the cut of his jib and inveigled various of his fashionable friends to make a cult of him. The week before last McShane had infuriated them all by signing a one million pound recording contract with Phonix, the second largest record company in Europe. For four or five days it had been big news. 'He is a Sylvia Plath for our generation,' panted one of the Phonix spokesmen. 'His searingly honest observations on contemporary urban suffering hold a mirror to what has become a very new, painfully disenfranchised New Britain. He is the voice of a forgotten generation. A lost people. Grey McShane communicates for us all, with an agonising sincerity which makes us all here at Phonix delighted – and *humbled* – to welcome him on board . . .' His first album would be released some time in early December.

The timing meant Ed would probably have to re-jig his priorities somewhat but Grey McShane – There was no question. 'Yeah,' said Ed, 'sounds interesting, Mel. Thanks. So, er. Right. I'm just about finished here. Leave my name at the door.' (Ed had deserted the Groucho for a more fashionable media watering hole a couple of years ago; it was one of Mel's innumerable affectations that she hadn't moved across at the same time. 'I'll be with you in twenty minutes.'

'Nice,' she said. They hung up without saying goodbye.

Of course she'd forgotten to give his name to the Groucho reception. He had to wait for ten minutes while somebody went in to fetch her out and when she finally emerged it was obvious she was plastered. Her cleavage, he noticed – which was always pleasantly on show – was trussed up like a turkey that night. It reminded him of the Helsinki girl and he felt a wave of lust as she squeezed it against him. There was something about Mel, something grubby and pushy and highly sexed, which made her particularly attractive after midnight, and particularly repulsive before. Ed's stirring was a couple of hours premature, then. But he'd been suppressing his desire for blonde, nubile underaged prostitutes all afternoon.

'God, sorry, Ed,' Mel slobbered, running both hands down his back and kissing him briefly on his thin lips. 'Grey and I were having such an amazing conversation. That guy – I swear.' She pulled back so she could look at Ed more earnestly. He stared at her breasts. 'You are going to *love* him. He's so pleased you came. And you know what? I *think*,' she tweaked him infuriatingly under the chin, 'that a certain person is going to owe *me* one BIG dinner by the time this night is through.'

'Your lipstick's smudged,' he said lamely. But she didn't hear, or didn't care. With a flourish and a wobble she spun around and led him towards a table at the far end of the bar where Grey McShane, dressed in a large black coat similar and yet £1,365 more expensive to the one he had been wearing when he was discovered, sat hunched and glowering over a large tumbler of neat gin.

Ed, who used a facial scrub for men, and bought most of his casual but flattering clothes at agnès b in Hampstead or Notting Hill Gate, was good-looking in a bookish sort of way. He was tall, with long legs and sparkling blue eyes which promised to spot the humour, the irony, the truth and the bullshit, in everything they deigned to rest upon. (He wore contact lenses.) Mel had always found him attractive – until now. He looked feeble beside Grey;

insipid and soft and faintly repulsive. He was, it has to be said, hazily aware that the comparison reflected badly. He tried to brace himself. As he headed towards Grey he tried to make his step a bit more masculine.

'Grey, darling,' said Mel. Grey looked up blankly. For an instant it seemed he didn't remember who she was. 'This is my lovely friend Ed . . . Who I told you about.'

'Aye,' said Grey, still looking faintly confused. He offered a large, worn, desultory hand, which Ed took with matching though less heartfelt coolness.

'Grey,' said Ed, casting (brutishly) around for a spare chair. 'Congratulations on the contract. You must be feeling – bloody – pleased about that.'

'Aye. I must be.' He was drunk.

'He doesn't like talking about it, do you?' said Mel, draping a proprietary arm over one of his enormous shoulders.

'That's – not correct,' said Grey mildly.

'I was only joking,' said Mel.

'Ed.' Grey pulled himself together. 'It's a very great pleasure to meet you. Now, as you know, I've got a business proposition ta make you but first of all the lassie here wants a line of Charlie. Can you help her with that?'

For a moment Ed was lost for words – something which had happened only twice in his adult life. He was appalled, humiliated, angry that they hadn't even bothered to disguise why they'd called him over, angry with himself for falling for Mel's bait, angry with the bitch Mel for daring to set him up like this and yet still, torn. Unwilling to walk away. Did McShane have a genuine proposition? If he did, Ed knew he wanted it.

On quick and careful consideration he decided to ignore the question entirely.

'What are you drinking?' he asked him pleasantly. 'Looks like water.'

'Hard-ly,' slurred Mel. She might at least, thought Ed, have had the grace to look embarrassed. But she was too drunk. The fact was she'd only called Ed because her cocaine dealer, a charming contemporary dance student called Gary, had been arrested three days earlier and her BACK-UP dealer, quite inexplicably, had chosen this evening to switch off his mobile telephone. Calling Ed had been a BACK-UP in the last resort, and Mel had only been prepared to do it because of her desperation to impress McShane. She was now slightly regretting it because Ed, if you studied him closely, was actually looking quite pissed off.

'Can you help her with that?' Grey persisted. 'Come ta think of it – can you help *me* with that? I wouldn't say no to a little bit of cocaine myself.'

An easy smile. 'Of course I can,' said Ed. 'But first I want to get a drink.'

'Och, come on!' Grey laughed. 'Don't be so damn prissy!'

Again Ed calculated quickly and calmly. He could walk away. The guy was clearly an arsehole. But – there was no doubt about it – he would make great television. Important television. Relevant television. The guy had a story to tell, and he looked fantastic. If Ed walked away then who would get to do the documentary? *Somebody else.* God, what a thought. 'Fair enough,' he said, smiling again. 'Grey, why don't you come with me!'

'Oh no,' said Grey. 'Ladies first. And this young lady's

been gasping for it for hours, haven't you angel?' He smiled at her, or at her trussed up cleavage, a blurry, leery smile which she seemed to relish. 'Go on, darling. Off you trot.'

Ed passed over his wallet. 'You're a saint,' she said.

He watched her arse in its tight skirt, balancing precariously on a couple of hideous pin-width high-heeled boots and, for a brief moment, forgave her her loathsomeness. He plopped himself down in her empty seat. 'So,' he said smoothly, 'how long have you known Melanie then?'

'Oh, about –' Grey pretended to examine his new watch, 'three-quarters of an hour. Lovely girl . . . Do you happen to know, is she married?'

'She's not,' Ed said, stifling a smirk. 'Mel is – very much – a single woman.'

'So, she'll be up for it then?'

He looked at Grey. 'I would say so, wouldn't you?'

With a faint chortle Grey looked down at his glass. 'Aye,' he said, 'I would say so. Aye.'

They sat in silence for a while, Ed thinking bitterly about Melanie making free with his cocaine. Grey lost in a private world, thinking no doubt about the men he left behind him and the peculiar twists of fate that had brought him to this place.

'I got a call from Weetabix today,' he said suddenly.

'Oh yeah?' said Ed.

'The breakfast cereal.'

'That's right.'

'I know it's bloody right.'

'What –' said Ed carefully, 'did they want with you?'

Grey started to laugh. Ed smiled patiently as Grey's head and shoulders rocked silently back and forth, but he was longing for a drink and the man's heartfelt, private laughter was making him feel excluded.

'They want a poem about fibre,' Grey said at last. 'D'you know what fibre is, Edward?'

'Well, yes I do –'

'It makes you shit – Ah! Here she comes. Mel-a-nie. God, she's fuckin' sexy isn't she? Shall we be off to the toilet now then? I must say I'm looking forward to this.'

Ed found toilet cubicles very useful in his business. They were an excellent networking environment, especially if you were the one chopping out the lines. Drug spongers, even tricky ones like Grey McShane, tended to be at their most malleable while waiting to be given their ration. So it was while Ed was tipping the powder onto the cistern that he first brought up the subject of the documentary. Had Grey, wondered Ed, managed to take a look at any of Ed's previous work? No, said Grey. Had Ed read any of his poetry?

'Of course,' said Ed. 'Amazing stuff. Really – I don't get time to read enough poetry, but yours, it's, er. It's pretty compulsive stuff.'

Grey looked at him suspiciously. 'Which is your favourite?' he asked.

Clever Ed didn't hesitate. He quoted perfectly the first four lines, the only four lines he had ever read, of a poem that had been printed a week earlier in the *Guardian*:

> The stranger looked a bit miffed
> as I laid in the Proctor & Gamble-sponsored crevice.
> 'Fuck off you rich snorter,' I whispered.
> He dropped a Big Mac on my face.

Grey was duly impressed.

'You must have had a fascinating life,' Ed observed, allowing himself to relax just a tiny bit. Grey agreed that he had.

'Been in prison,' said Grey.

Fantastic, thought Ed.

'Been on the streets since I was seventeen.'

Ed nodded sympathetically. 'So, all this must come as quite a surprise.'

'Aye,' said Grey distractedly. 'But you can put out more powder than that, can't you?'

They were fat lines, fatter, in fact, than Ed usually made them. It didn't matter. He tipped out a bit more. 'Has anyone else approached you about doing a documentary?'

'No,' said Grey.

'But you'd be interested?' He rolled up a twenty-pound note and passed it to Grey.

'Aye,' said Grey, shoving the note up his nostril and bending over.

'Because we should get cracking pretty much right away if we're going to do it in time for the album.'

Grey stood up, wiped his nostril, passed the note back to Ed. 'Whatever you say,' he said. 'We can start tomorrow, for all I care. I've always wanted to be on telly.'

'I should probably talk to your agent,' said Ed.

'Aye.'

'Who *is* your agent?'

'Oh God. I don't remember. It's written somewhere. I'll give it to you later. Now come on, let's get back to your little friend. I feel like a fuck tonight.'

*　　*　　*

The same ninety minutes had passed no more comfortably for Jo. She was appalled by her own lack of cool. To redress the situation she forbade herself even a single glance at the attractive singer for the rest of his performance. Instead she sat with her back to the stage and forced poor Jessie to listen while she expounded loudly on various issues of the day, with especial focus on the media's treatment of asylum seekers. It was a subject about which she knew very little and cared, though you might never have guessed it, even less. Jo would never have dared to hold forth with such confidence in front of her other friends but pregnant Jessie was a perfect sounding board. An ignorant Tory-voter. A sitting target for setting right. Jessie didn't mind. She wasn't listening. She nodded distractedly throughout, beat the table in time to the music and wondered, as she so often did by this stage in an evening with Jo, why the two of them ever bothered to keep in touch.

'So when the tabloids whip up this obscene *hate-fest*,' Jo droned on, 'which bears absolutely no relation to the facts – because the facts are these people are *proud* people. They've come to our country out of desperation, not – ha! – because they actually *want* to sponge off Mr and Mrs Outraged from Tunbridge Wells . . .' But she lost her thread when the music stopped. Her fellow diners erupted into cheers and she was forced to look up at Him one more time.

'Thanks everyone,' Charlie mumbled into the microphone. 'Thanks very much. See you all next week, I hope.' With a smile and a wave he laid down his guitar and climbed off the stage.

'Charlie!' shouted Jessie. 'Over here!'

Poor Jo. Her determined efforts not to dribble while he sang had been utterly pointless. In fact she had been so

36

conscious of him that now, as he made his way over, she felt quite paralysed by her own confusion. She could feel the blood pumping in her ears and a sweaty, unfamiliar flush spreading across her cheeks. She couldn't think where to look or what to do with her hands. It was excruciating. It was entirely out of character.

Fortunately for her, neither Jessie nor Charlie seemed to notice. Jessie was bouncing up and down, then they were embracing each other, clapping each other on the back. Charlie was looking down with benign concern at Jessie's belly; asking when the baby was due, what sex it was and so on. Finally he turned politely towards Jo.

'Oh, God, *sorry!*' said Jessie. 'Here I am banging on about the baby, thinking about myself, as usual! Apparently people get terribly egocentric when they're pregnant did you know? Anyway this is Jo! Jo, this is Charlie. Charlie's one of my oldest friends. He was actually my first snog after I moved to London, weren't you Charlie?'

'Was I?' said Charlie looking pleased.

'Of course you were! God you were gorgeous! Can't think why we never took it any further, can you?'

'Because you decided you preferred – what must have been the second person you snogged after you moved to London. About two days later.'

'Oh yes,' said Jessie vaguely. 'Christ it all seems like a long time ago. Anyway sit down, Charlie darling. Get a drink. I've got to have a pee.' She turned to Jo. 'What you'll discover,' she said, 'is what they never tell you. You spend your whole bloody life on the *loo* when you're pregnant. It's *unbelievably boring*! Back in a sec.' She waddled away chortling and Jo and Charlie were left alone.

'So . . . you don't have any yet?' asked Charlie.

'Kids? *No!* God, no, not nearly! I'm still way too much of a kid myself!'

'Really?' he said, looking at her curiously.

'I mean,' she said quickly, 'I *feel* like too much of kid. Don't you?'

He shrugged. He didn't think it would be polite to disagree with her at such an early stage. Instead he turned to watch Jess negotiating her way around the tables. 'Doesn't look very comfortable though, does it?' he said.

'But I think most women find it's worth it.' She knew she sounded like a schoolmistress but she wanted to make it plain right away that, in spite of her previous comment, she did respect parenthood enormously. That she was serious. That she took women's pregnancies seriously. That she – to put it bluntly – that she was interesting. It was a strange way to go about it. But Jo was in turmoil. She wasn't thinking straight.

'Oh, of course. I'm sure they do,' he said hurriedly. 'I mean, what's a few extra visits to the lavatory compared to – er. In fact, sometimes it can be quite a nice break. Gives you a chance to take stock, you know. Stop talking for a while.' He smiled at her.

But Jo was not quite able to smile back. She could discuss clitorectomies *ad nauseam*, or the disturbingly high incidence of anal penetration during heterosexual sex in some parts of the developing world. She could talk happily about cystitis, Tantric orgasms, erectile dysfunctions, testicular cancer, and the official version of what constituted her own personal sexual fulfilment, but conversations featuring lavatories she found difficult. It was impossible, she felt, to be serious or light-hearted on the subject without

38

appearing faintly silly. On quick and careful consideration she decided to ignore his comment entirely.

'You're a very talented performer Charlie,' she said with a big bright smile. 'Really. Amazing. You've got a fabulous voice.'

'*Thank you!*' he said. 'Thank you very much.'

'Do you have an agent?'

'An agent?' he laughed. 'No.'

'No? Well you should get one. With that sort of charisma. On the stage,' she added quickly. '*Stage* charisma. You're going to be snapped up. You actually remind me of a sort of unproduced Robbie – if you can imagine that.' She smirked. A little joke. '. . . A sort of . . . *raw* Robbie.'

'Robbie?' He looked blank. 'Oh! Robbie Williams! Crikey! Is that a compliment? What's a *raw* Robbie Williams like, then. When he's at home?'

'Well,' she said patiently, 'I mean Robbie before he was *Robbie*. The real Robbie. Robbie, the troublemaker, the gorgeous unknown guy on the street with packets and packets of undiscovered talent.'

'Hm,' said Charlie seriously. 'So you think I'm a gorgeous guy on the street?'

'I'm just *saying*,' said Jo, more irritably than was probably necessary, 'you should think about getting an agent. That's all. You've got an amazing voice and I think you could go a long way with it.'

'*I* think,' said Charlie, who wanted to lighten things up, possibly even wanted to rile her a little bit, 'you're a gorgeous *bird*. Right here in a *winebar*.'

'Bird?' she said in amazement. '*Bird?*' She was offended. She tried to show it, but, oh, the shame of it! Something about the way he looked back, the lazy, easy humour in his face, made her break into a smile. A beautiful smile, or so Charlie thought; warm, self-deprecating, completely surprising. It was the smile which brought Jo to Charlie's full attention for the first time.

'Nobody says bird,' she muttered lamely. 'Anyway, it's not the point. I was trying to help you. Wouldn't you prefer to sing to a more discerning audience than this?'

He looked around the room. 'They're all right,' he said mildly. 'But it doesn't matter any more because I'm stopping. Got to find a real job . . . Can't go on behaving like a kid for ever.'

'I don't see why not,' she said. 'I certainly intend to!'

'Really?' He was unconvinced. She was beautiful all right, but she was about as *kid*-like as the old General. And she was obviously quite self-conscious about it, he thought. Or she wouldn't keep going on. 'What about you, then,' he asked. 'You don't look like a local girl. What brings you to Fulham?'

'Ya-hoo!' shouted Jessie.

Jo had forgotten all about her. She turned around with some annoyance (just when the conversation was getting interesting) to see Jessie waddling and waving her way towards them, closely followed by a bashful, dreary looking boy in a grey suit.

'I've found a fan for you Charlie. He says he thinks he might want you to play at his sister's wedding. But he says he wonders if you've got a sort of *tape* he can take back to his father.'

Charlie's expression, though polite, was hardly a picture of enthusiasm. Jo sniggered. 'Bloody hell,' she said quietly. 'Trust me, Charlie. You're much too talented to have to deal with this!'

NEW YOU RULE NUMBER TWO: Have you got it yet? Your new friends are b-b-busy with a capital B! Want to be a part of the dialogue? Then answer the fucking phone! Pretty soon 'leaving messages' is gonna be a thing of the past! That's right! These people like answers and they like them YESTERDAY! We're talking automatic call diversion 24/7; one number, one hundred per cent accessibility! We're talking picking up that mobile before it rings twice! Remember, every call you miss is a call someone else is gonna be getting! You need a State-of-the-art Communications System and it's gonna cost you! So get shoppin' around!

Jo woke up the following morning feeling a bit of a fool. She and Charlie had gone back to Jessie's house and stayed up drinking Gerald's whisky long after Jessie had waddled (still winking and chortling) to her bed. They discussed business, Jo remembered. She told him about Top Spin, and the incredible power of good PR. He told her about his twin – Charlie could never talk to anyone for long without mentioning Georgie.

Jo listened sympathetically. She was a good listener. So he told her about his father and the career crisis. She said, 'I can understand how your father feels. He must feel terrible. But Charlie, you can't lead your father's life for him. He has to get a life of his own –'

'He's too old,' said Charlie. 'And he's sick. He's already had one heart attack.'

'You're *never* too old,' she said severely. It was one of her convictions.

He felt a flicker of irritation. After all, what did she know? But then he looked at her; leaning forward, head cocked to one side, so earnest, so pretty. Pretty mouth, pretty breasts, pretty eyes . . . She was trying to be kind. And there was something touching about her dogged show of self-assurance. The last thing he wanted to do was to make her feel uncomfortable. He nodded politely and said nothing.

'Charlie,' she went on, taking his silence for encouragement and feeling, at that instant, utterly, one hundred per cent committed to the words hot-puffing from her mouth, 'you are a – very – talented – performer. You've got to forget what your Dad wants for once. You've got to follow your dreams!'

'But I haven't *got* any dreams!' he said. 'I just want an OK job so I can . . . marry a beautiful girl and have some nice children . . . And my father can . . . have something decent happen to him before he dies . . .' He laughed. 'Sounds pathetic, I know, but –'

'It does,' she interrupted. 'Charlie, forgive me. But it sounds to me like you're *giving up.*'

They glugged a bit more whisky in silence and then, quite suddenly, Jo leapt towards her purse. 'I've just remembered,' she said, fumbling around in it. 'Yes!' She produced a tiny envelope, the size of a thumbnail. 'How about it? If my memory is correct I've got at least enough for two lines in here.'

'What is it?' said Charlie. 'Is it cocaine?'

She thought he was joking, so she laughed. But he wasn't. He said he'd never had it before and after the disbelief had subsided she felt faintly revolted. She became suddenly aware of the Mont Blanc T-shirt again, and the cowboy boots, and the fact that she had to be at work tomorrow. She thought of cool, clever, successful Ed.

'I should go,' she said abruptly, shoving the envelope back in her purse. 'Sorry. I'm being stupid . . .' She tried to laugh. 'Too much whisky, I think.'

For Charlie too, the spell was broken. He had sensed her

revulsion. They stood up at the same time, almost bumping into each other as they did so. The room felt suddenly very oppressive. And then Jo, in her desperation to avoid bodily contact, lost her balance and stumbled back towards the sofa. He caught her by the elbows.

'Oh! Thanks!' she said. But the moment was brief. It was hard to tell whether he let go or she snatched her arms away first.

'Are you all right?' he asked.

'Of course.'

'How are you going to get home?'

'I'll find a cab down on Fulham Broadway,' she said. 'The walk'll probably do me good.'

'I don't think it will,' he said. 'You might get murdered.'

'Don't be silly.'

'I mean it's late, Jo. Why don't I drive you?'

His gentle concern was unfashionable and yet unaccountably attractive to her. So much so that his lack of cocaine experience was momentarily if not forgiven, then forgotten. 'Don't go pretending to *me*, Charlie . . .' It had sounded faintly familiar when she first heard his surname. Now it was completely gone. '. . . that you're not feeling a *little bit* pissed yourself!'

He shrugged and reached for his car keys. 'C'mon,' he said. 'I've got to drive anyway. So there's no point not driving you home as well.'

It was cranky logic and even in her whisky haze Jo could work that out. She disapproved of 'DUI', as she called it, almost as much as she disapproved of pregnant smokers, but – she liked him. Simply put, she wasn't ready to take leave of him just yet.

*   *   *

44

So. Nothing had happened. She'd given him her number, or rather her business card. She'd told him if he ever wanted any help with the music then to give her a call. She knew people, she said.

And she woke up feeling a fool. Not only had she spent the evening flirting with a man she might easily not want to acknowledge, under certain circumstances, if she were to meet him in the street. She had also been complicit in what was, in a small way, a truly reprehensible crime. It was typical behaviour of an ex-public schoolboy called *Charlie*, she told herself as she massaged her early morning face with rejuvenating essential oils. But she should have known better. What had she been thinking of?

She arrived in her office a few minutes before ten and immediately called Ed's mobile. She remembered to disguise her number before she dialled because she knew that otherwise he wouldn't pick up. Not because he didn't love her. Obviously. There were times when she was too busy to take his call too.

This morning, however, her desire to speak to him was work-related. She needed to discuss the Meals For The Homeless project – and with some urgency. Last night Penny, the founder of Top Spin Public Relations, had been pushing Jo to organise a meeting with him. But Jo, sensibly, was holding out until she and Ed had had a chance to talk about it, alone. Partly because she didn't trust Penny not to hijack the project for herself. Partly because she needed to cover herself for the one or two inaccuracies that had seeped into her presentation of the situation when describing it to them earlier. Ed hadn't yet obtained the written commission from Channel Foremost; a minor detail, of course, but one which she had omitted to mention either to her clients at Meals or to her bosses at Top Spin.

'Ed,' she said. 'Jo here.'

'Oh, hi baby. Howzitgoing?' he said pleasantly. 'Thought it was you! Nobody else calls me before ten o'clock.'

'Yeah, I know. It's just I need to talk to you about –'

'Jo, can I call you back? You've caught me in Starbucks and the guy's – Hang on. Excuse me – yeah. I said *tall*. No. Skinny. Please ... Yeah. And a bran and banana muffin. That one. Great ... Listen love. Can you give me ten?'

But he always said that. She ignored it. 'Penny wants to meet up with you but I'm holding out because I think we need to chat first. Are you doing anything tonight?'

'Absolutely no chance, sweetheart. Sorry. I'll be editing until at least two. Didn't go too well last night ... How about you? What did you get up to in the end?'

'Oh. Nothing much. Met up with Jessie.'

'Jessie?'

'You've met her at least three times Ed,' she said mildly. 'I went to school with her. Look what about lunch, then? A super-quick bite? We really do need to talk. Have you got the commission letter yet?'

Ed would have put her off indefinitely. There were various things he didn't much want to discuss with her at that moment, chief among them the Meals For The Homeless project. But he also wanted to unwrap his bran and banana muffin and he couldn't do that until he'd put the telephone down. So, somewhat snappishly and with every intention of cancelling half an hour later, he agreed to meet her for a *very* quick lunch.

She said she'd come to the edit suites at one. 'And don't

call up in half an hour to cancel because I won't get the message, OK?'

He chuckled. He quite liked it sometimes when she read his mind. It was kind of clever and flirtatious, he thought. It made him feel cared for.

'Yeah, yeah. See you in a bit.'

'Love you,' she said. And hung up.

They had lunch at Soho House, a fashionable members-only drinking club to be found, if you knew where to look, in a tall, thin maisonette overlooking Old Compton Street. It meant surreptitiously switching their mobiles to 'vibrate' since, like at the Groucho, people weren't officially allowed to receive calls there. The lovers were both hungover, though neither was likely to admit it, and they ordered a couple of Virgin Marys.

The emergence of Grey McShane on Ed's professional landscape would have a knock-on effect in most areas of his somewhat limited life. First and foremost, on his relationship with Jo, which at that moment was highly dependent on his relationship with their shared project; a behind the scenes documentary about the putting together of a Meals For The Homeless concert which promised to be as culturally significant to the new millennium blah blah blah. His position was slightly complicated, in that he didn't want to chuck the Meals project entirely, just in case the McShane project didn't come off. On the other hand, nor did he want to waste too much time on it in the short term in case the McShane project did come off, in which case the timing of the two stories meant he would have to drop Meals altogether. He didn't want to hassle Geoff about it yet, because he didn't want to find himself in a position later on whereby he himself would have to back out, which would mean setting himself in a bad light with Channel Foremost. And lastly, of course, he didn't much relish the prospect of letting down Jo, though he could hardly be expected to take responsibility for every one of her career setbacks. They were a part of life. Jo was an adult. Her career choices, like Ed's, were hers and hers alone.

A further complication, of course, was busty Mel. Who'd last night had to be subtly bribed by Ed to keep the whole Grey McShane possibility to herself.

'Of course I've got to tell Jo!' Mel had said. 'She'll be so excited for you. And she'll be so pleased with me!'

In between writing second-rate 'lifestyle' articles for any wretched features editor who asked her, Mel had been trying, without success, to get into television presenting. She had her own TV agent, whose chief occupation, it seemed, was to send her invitations to streams of irrelevant press launches – and she had been attending half-baked auditions intermittently for years. Ed said the McShane project had to be kept TOP SECRET until things looked a lot firmer. But there was a possibility that Mel might be able to get involved. They would need a sympathetic interviewer, he said. And it was obvious that she and Grey got along.

So, it was a difficult lunch. They perched opposite each other in the low armchairs, Ed with a copy of the *Guardian* and a tiny laptop laid casually at his feet, both with their work books and their personal organisers in front of them. Jo ordered some salad which did nothing for her hangover, and failed to get a single honest answer out of Ed about anything, except how he wanted his hamburger cooked.

'Frankly,' he said, 'the way things are looking for me at the moment, I don't see us hooking up with Top Spin for at least another week.'

Jo said her clients needed paperwork. When would Ed be able to get anything out of Channel Foremost?

'Next week,' he said. 'Definitely by the end of next week.'

'We're going to need it before that.'

'Well look I'll try. I'll definitely try. But you know what they're like. As soon as they sniff desperation – *snap*!' He clicked his long thin fingers, 'they stop returning your calls. Trust me. I know what I'm doing.'

Neither got around to mentioning what they'd been up to the previous night. Ed said he'd call her later. Perhaps, if she was still awake when he'd finished working he might spend the night at her place.

'I'd love that,' she said. 'I don't think we see enough of each other Ed.'

'True . . .' He smiled at her, even lent across the table and stroked her cheek. 'Maybe we can go away together for a weekend sometime . . .' He frowned. He realised that the suggestion evoked images of rustic bedtimes not with Jo but with busty Mel and her naked breasts. It annoyed him.

'I'd *love* that. I could do with a break.' And suddenly, quite inexplicably, she felt she was going to cry. She needed Ed. She needed him to love her. Or someone to say something tender every now and then. She blinked away the sting of tears and simultaneously picked up her vibrating telephone. Mel's number flashed up on the little screen. She switched it to divert. 'Got to go,' she said, picking up the bill. She would pay on the way out. 'Work's bloody hectic at the moment . . .'

They pecked each other on the cheek and Jo left on her own, feeling unusually fragile and let down and lonely. It was the hangover of course.

Mel had been invited to a film premiere whose PR was being handled by Top Spin. She needed an extra ticket so she could take her new friend Grey McShane. There was no question that Grey would be welcome. But Mel calculated, quite rightly, that she'd be doing Jo a favour if she approached her about it first. That way it would look like Grey was actually a friend of Jo's and everybody at Top Spin would be pleased and impressed. She was slightly offended to have had her call put on divert so she disguised her number and tried again.

'Jo here,' said Jo above the roar of Old Compton Street traffic.

'You stupid cow,' said Mel. 'I knew you were there.'

'Oh. Sorry darling. I was in the middle of a meeting. Finished now. So what's up?'

'I was only trying to do you a favour –'

Jo sounded grateful when she heard, though not as grateful as Mel thought she ought to have sounded and not as grateful as she actually felt. In fact she would be delighted to drop Grey's name at the office. But her pleasure was outweighed by her irritation that the opportunity had been presented to her by Mel.

'You'll never guess what, though.' Mel couldn't keep the jubilation from her voice. 'I *fucked* him last night!'

It was the last thing Jo needed to hear right then. '*Mel!*' she said, putting her mouth into a shape so she would sound as though she was smiling. 'I didn't know you even knew him!'

'Well I don't. Not really. But I swear, Jo. You've got to meet him. His dick is honestly about the size ...' She paused to think of something to compare it with, just as Jo's telephone emitted a small electronic bleep, indicating a new message on her voicemail. '... of a genetically modified – what's the name of that vegetable that looks like a cucumber only it's much bigger? Begins with an m –'

Jo couldn't remember. Anyway she had to go. She said she would probably be going to the premiere herself, work allowing. If she didn't bring the ticket in person then Grey's name would definitely be on the guest list, 'and whatever happens,' she said, 'I'll meet you at the after party.'

It wasn't exactly what Mel would have chosen. Jo was not the ideal accompaniment to a second date, due to the number of men who found her attractive. Still, she made herself sound properly enthusiastic and left Jo to pick up her voicemail.

'Jo. Penny here. Look, I've got Meals on the line. Could you get back to me ASAP. Many thanks.'

Shit. What the hell was she going to say? Then the mobile rang again. She didn't recognise the number.

'Yes. Jo Smiley here.'

'Hi Jo.'

Her stomach lurched, though whether in delight or horror, or a mixture of both, she was too disturbed to wonder. Above all she wished she hadn't answered the telephone.

'... Jo?'

'Ya. Hi! God, how are you?'

'It's Charlie.'

'What? I know it's Charlie! ... How are you anyway?

51

Don't know *what* we thought we were doing, driving home like that. I feel very ashamed of myself.'

He laughed. 'I couldn't leave the car at Jessie's. It would have been clamped.'

There was an awkward pause. Jo was trying to cross over Oxford Circus, which was distracting enough. The sound of the traffic was deafening – and then, just as he began to speak, that little voicemail beep went off in her ear again.

'I was just ringing to say hi . . . Check you hadn't died of alcohol poisoning. But you sound very busy.'

'Ya. Yeah. No I didn't. In fact. But actually I am a bit busy . . . Can I call you back?'

'Don't suppose you'd want another drink with me tonight?'

'Erm . . .' But it was out of the question. He wouldn't fit in. He would be a total embarrassment. He'd probably arrive in a pinstripe suit. He'd probably – ah! – ask the actors for their autographs! Mel would never let her forget – It was unthinkable. An image of his face, his shoulders, his chest; the memory of his rich warm voice, his rich warm honest eyes, made her hesitate. But only for an instant.

'I don't think I can,' she said. 'Not tonight. Can I call you back? I mean . . . It'd be great, maybe, some other time.'

They chatted politely until Jo's beep went off again. 'I've got to go,' she said. 'I'll call you.' But Charlie didn't imagine that she would. She hadn't asked for his telephone number. And, he was forced to acknowledge, she had made it clear on various occasions the previous evening that she didn't consider Charlie quite equal to her own group. He assumed it was because of the job situation. But he was going to remedy that. Anyway, whatever the problem was, he was keen to overcome it. There was something about Jo Smiley, quite apart from her lovely looks, which made Charlie determined to see her again.

Jo arrived in excellent time, not just for the film and the 'after party' but for the pre-film drinks. She looked radiant of course, in a knee length lilac dress with velvet trimmings which hinted, with the utmost delicacy, at the well-toned perfection beneath. Though the occasion was not one for which she was directly responsible and she was officially off duty, Jo was well aware that her colleagues might need her at any time. Her priority that night (every night, Jo was never really off duty) was to ensure the comfort of all potentially useful VIPs.

She spotted Grey and Mel immediately. Grey was bellowing at one of her junior colleagues, easily loud enough to frighten the pigeons.

'It's McSHANE,' he was yelling.

'I'm sorry, Sir. I'm going to have to ask you to stand aside –'

'M-C-S-H-A-N-E, you snotty-nosed cow. Look again. But Jesus, you're like a fuckin' machine!'

Mel stood impatiently beside him, scouring the crowd – for Jo, Jo presumed, or for celebrity friends. She wore seven-inch Gucci heels and another of her tight, cleavage-revealing dresses. Her dark hair had been tied into pigtails and adorned with several glittery clips. She looked very much a woman of her time; dedicated to hard work, serious issues, riotous sex and fun, fun, fun.

'Having a bit of trouble?' said Jo with an ironic lift of the eyebrow. 'It's all right Kit-Kat,' she turned to her

53

beleaguered colleague. 'This is Grey McShane. I'm sure you recognise him –'

'Well of course I do,' said Kit-Kat, her bland face transforming itself with a broad smile. 'Only I couldn't find his name on the list and Penny said –'

'Yeah. Not to worry, Kit-Kat. All under control!' With a small nod she motioned for Mel and Grey to go through.

'You're a darlin',' he muttered. 'And I love your little frock.'

Moments later he had produced a Barbie Doll autograph book from his pocket. He spent the entire event barging up to anybody whose face looked faintly familiar or otherwise attractive, and demanding they sign their name. Luckily, everyone thought it was hilarious.

'*I'm* not the celebrity,' Jo had laughed when he barged up to her. 'You need to talk to Hugh here.' She smiled sweetly at her companion (a television cook). 'Now *his* would be an autograph worth taking!'

'Aye and yours too,' said Grey, gazing at her intently. 'Mel's told me all about you. She says you've got a very uptight boyfriend –'

'She does?'

'Probably because she fancies him.'

'Mel?' Jo laughed. 'Fancy *Ed*? I don't think so!'

'No?' he looked purposefully unconvinced. 'However . . . I've been ordered not to talk about him tonight so I shan't say another word.'

'What d'you mean, ordered not to talk about him. You don't know him.'

'Ha-*ha!*' He zipped up his big mouth facetiously. 'But my lips are sealed. Now then. Are you going to sign my book or aren't you?' He turned to her companion. 'I'm sorry, Mike.

Nick. Darlin'. I'll be coming to you in a moment. I just need Jo here to explain to me who you are.'

Jo smiled charmingly but she felt uncomfortable. It went without saying that she could see the funny side of his behaviour and it was clear that some pretty big names could see it too, but it was she who had invited him, and she who would be held responsible if he took the joke too far. He was already drunk, the single uncontrollable element to what was otherwise a very controlled affair. She expressed her concern to Mel just before the film was due to begin.

'He's being ironic,' Mel explained. 'He's an artist, and a lot of these people can recognise a fellow artist, you see.' Especially, she might have added, if his handsome artistic face had been plastered all over the newspapers less than a fortnight ago. 'Grey's a natural performer, so he can get away with these things. Don't worry about it. You worry too much. Try to relax, OK?'

All the same, Jo suggested that she, Mel and Grey give the later party a miss. 'We could grab a bite somewhere nice,' she said. 'I don't know about you but I'm starving . . . And anyway, Mel, I want to get to know your gorgeous new boyfriend.'

'He's not a *boyfriend*,' snapped Mel. 'You sound like my bloody mother. He's a *mate* who I happen to be shagging. But he is gorgeous though, isn't he?'

'Amazing,' said Jo, smoothly. 'By the way what's all this about you forbidding him to mention Ed?'

'Mm? God knows. Grey's always talking rubbish . . . Ed's not here, I presume?'

'Holed up in the edit room with Geoff, poor guy.'

'Oh yeah?' said Mel.

'Probably won't finish until two again tonight.'

'Well forget him, useless sod. Grey and I are hooking up with *Sean*'s party after the film. You should come along.'

'You mean *Sean*, Sean? But you can't!' Sean, playing the film's lead, was a nerdy little actor over whom (thanks to Top Spin) the English press had recently whipped up a large puff of undeserved enthusiasm. The least he could do in return was to show up at their official post show party.

'Oh come on, Jo. For God's sake look impressed.'

'I'm trying to,' she said distractedly but she wasn't concentrating any more. All she cared about at that instant was preventing the star's escape. 'Look . . . we'll catch up later. The film's about to start. I think we're all meant to be going in.'

But afterwards Jo couldn't find them anywhere. She searched in the lavatories, the empty auditorium, the bar on the top floor. She waited for twenty minutes in the deserted foyer, and finally made the short walk to the party on her own. They were not at the party either. She checked her mobile. No messages. She called Mel's mobile. It was on voicemail.

'Melanie, Jo here,' she said, sounding much calmer than she felt. 'Just wondering where you guys have *got* to! Give me a call, will you? I'm on the mobile.'

Half an hour later she had still heard nothing. Her hurt feelings prevented her from contributing usefully to the party and she felt uncharacteristically bored by the important company. She decided to head home. It was stupid, she told herself, to take Mel's behaviour so personally, since Mel always had and always would do exactly what she liked at the instant that she liked it. (After all, it was one of the qualities that had initially attracted her. They believed so adamantly in the same things – freedom, independence, minimal home decor, going for it and so on.) But nobody likes to be forgotten, even – or possibly especially – thrusting young achievers at the top of their important careers. Of course the fact that Mel had a swanky new boyfriend who actually appeared to want to spend time with her only made matters worse. Poor Jo. As she tramped towards Piccadilly Circus in search of a cab, she couldn't help feeling dowdy and unloved.

Her mobile didn't ring until she was three-quarters of the way home.

'Jo! Where ARE you?' Mel shouted over pulsing music. 'We've been looking *everywhere*!'

'Where are *you*? God! You disappeared right after the film. I thought you'd gone. Don't tell me you're still at the party!' She felt relief flood through her. So she did exist.

'We sort of left before the rush. Sean had seen it so many times before, hadn't you Sean? I mean he was brilliant. Bloody outstanding. It's just a shame he's got to be wasted on this kind of useless material.'

'Where are you exactly?' Jo said carefully.

'At Chinawhite. Come and join us! Only hurry. It's *kicking* down here! I don't know how much longer they'll go on letting people in.'

Jo's taxi was just then turning into her street. She looked up at her dark flat, and across the road at the usual gaggle of spliff smokers and thought – she was just in time to watch *ER* on the telly. Ed would be coming round in a couple of hours. And Chinawhite sounded very noisy.

'Piss off, Mel,' she said, and hung up. She hadn't been so frank in decades. For an instant it made her feel quite cheerful.

But not for long. The flat was always so unwelcoming.

The wooden floor, white walls, stainless steel breakfast bar island and three exciting pieces of primary-coloured furniture which made up the entrance hall-cum-sitting room-cum-kitchen looked spectacular when the place was filled with the right people. But at the end of an evening when your best friend has given you the slip, and there's only '1 message' blinking on the answer machine, it was a lonely place to call home.

The message was from Ed. He could have called on the mobile but he'd obviously preferred not to talk to her. It was eleven o'clock, he said. A stupid lie since it wasn't even 10.45 when Jo got in. He'd finished earlier than he thought he would but had decided, due to his high exhaustion level, that he'd head back to his own place and 'concentrate on getting a good night's sleep'. He asked her not to call in case she woke him up.

In Parsons Green, Charlie Maxwell McDonald was spending a similarly rare evening in. Laid out before him were the *Daily Telegraph* Appointments pages and his twin sister's old electric typewriter. He'd been gazing at the newspaper for twenty minutes, and was still only fractionally less bewildered than when he began.

Would he make a good Technical Services Manager, he wondered. Or a better WAP Consultant? Should he jump at the opportunity to Optimise his Career in World Class Manufacturing? Or if not then how about E-tail finance?

Dear Sir/Madam, he wrote.

It had taken a while to make the paper sit straight in the typewriter, and his 'keyboard skills' were far from polished. The following letter took him more than an hour to type:

*I would like to apply for the job advertised on page A22
in the Appointments insert of today's* Daily Telegraph. *I
feel I would make an excellent School Administrator due
to my experience with children while teaching them how
to ski during the winter months. I am also an excellent
administrator.*

*I am available for interview, either over the telephone
or in person, at any time. Also, I could start immediately.
I look forward to hearing from you.*

Yours faithfully,

CHARLES MAXWELL MCDONALD

He was considering sending an enigmatic response to
a minuscule advertisement for 'professionals in all disci-
plines to work with SMEs as part of a support network'
which, due to its size and total incomprehensibility, would
be unlikely to attract many other applicants, when the
telephone rang,

It was Jo.

'Jo!'

'Don't sound so surprised,' she said, irritably. It only
reminded her of what a surprise the call was to herself.
When she said goodbye to him that afternoon it hadn't
occurred to her that they would talk again. And if Ed hadn't
cancelled and then told her not to call, if Grey hadn't said
that funny thing about being forbidden to mention him,
if *ER* had been on when she thought it was, if Channel
Foremost had biked over its written confirmation, if her
flat wasn't so uncomfortable, if Mel wasn't such a bitch,
if she hadn't been feeling so sorry for herself, she might
not have remembered what a warm and attractive proposal

Charlie Maxwell McDonald was, in comparison to the rest of her life.

'But I am surprised. Happily surprised, obviously. You didn't take my number.'

'It was on the mobile.'

'Oh – of course. So what time is it? The pubs are closed but I'll come round if you're still up for that drink. In fact, wait there. I wanted to ask your advice.' There came the sound of shuffling paper followed by a loud rip, and Charlie muttering, 'Fuck!' He picked up the receiver again. 'Sorry,' he said.

Jo laughed. 'What have you got there?'

'Job application.'

'Oh yes,' said Jo, adopting an encouraging tone. 'What for?'

'A school administrator. Don't laugh.' (She hadn't. Or not so that he could have heard.) 'It's the only advert in the whole bloody paper I can understand. Listen. Listen to this . . . Anyway I've ripped it. I'm going to have to start again. So, I mean any corrections, now's the time to say . . . *Dear Sir/Madam,*' he began and immediately interrupted himself. 'D'you mind me doing this?'

'Of course not! I'm interested. Go on.'

'I mean, did you ring to say something in particular? Because I'm banging on . . . haven't given you a chance. Shall we meet up or shall we have a drink over the blower?'

'I've already got one.'

'What is it?'

'Mint tea.'

'Oh.' He sounded unimpressed.

'I'm still hungover from yesterday.'

'Mint tea's not going to help.'

'It's delicious. Very good for you. You should try it.'

'I'm going to get a beer. Wait a sec. Then we can pretend we're meeting for a drink, without the inconvenience of actually having to find our keys, etcetera.' He came back chuckling to himself. 'Right then, are you ready?'

'What are you laughing at?'

'Nothing.'

'Oh come on. Nobody laughs at nothing. What's the joke?'

'Nothing. I'm being a jerk . . . I was just thinking . . . something stupid. I'll tell you when I know you a bit better.'

When she thought, with a wave of something alarmingly close to pleasure. 'Then I imagine,' she said coolly, 'it's something along the lines of "We're having a 'phone drink', tee hee. Which sounds a bit like phone sex, tee *hee* hee"?' She took a slurp of her tea and in the astonished silence which followed wondered if she'd made a mistake. The guy had never taken cocaine. He'd probably never even heard of phone sex. And if he had, he certainly hadn't been thinking about it in the context of the two of them . . .

'How did you work that out?' he said in undisguised awe.

Her relief, though enormous, was imperceptible. 'It was obvious.'

'I was only joking.'

'I hope you were.'

'You're a mind reader. You're a bloody genius!'

She smiled, quite collected again. 'Are you ever going to read this letter to me?'

So he began – and almost immediately wished he hadn't. By the time he'd reached the end he didn't need Jo's

tactful silence to inform him of its outstanding feeble-
ness.

'Hm,' she said eventually. 'I'm not sure . . . I think . . .
What do I think? I think it's *great* but I think it needs a little
bit of work. What about the résumé? Any – administration
– work mentioned in that?'

'Er, not that I can think of . . . No.'

There was a pause while Jo rummaged to find a positive
spin on this added setback. Suddenly Charlie giggled. 'All
right, it's crap. Which is *good*. In a way. Saves me typing it
up again.'

'The thing to do . . .' Jo faltered. Never having encoun-
tered such a career illiterate before she didn't quite know
where to start. 'The thing to do . . . is to concentrate on your
strengths.'

'Yes,' he said seriously. 'I think that's where the problem
is.'

'I don't really understand why you thought school
administrating was your thing.'

'Ah,' said Charlie. When she put it like that, neither did
he. But then what the hell was? Christ, he thought. This
was a can of worms. He should never have begun. 'I think
I can hear the old drawing-board beckoning. Anyway.
Anyway, anyway, anyway that's more than enough about
me. What about you, Jo? What are you up to? Why are you
telephoning me? Have you finished your mint tea?'

'I can help you, Charlie,' Jo said forcefully. 'Tell me what
you want to do and I bet I'll be able to help you. Whatever
you want – it's *out there*. You've just got to go and get it!'

Charlie felt embarrassed. For all her apparent sophistica-
tion she was capable of sounding very adolescent. He could
think of nothing to say.

'Everything,' she continued blithely, 'or not everything. But I mean . . . so much of everything is about *presentation*. You've just got to know how to sell yourself. And Charlie, without wishing to blow my own trumpet, I think I told you the other night, I am – I mean packaging, *presentation* is my thing.'

'Is there something wrong with my packaging?' Charlie asked mildly. He wasn't quite clear what she was getting at. 'Actually, I'm not sure I want you to answer that. I was much happier when we were talking about tea.'

'*No!* I mean Yes!' But she was not to be distracted. She loved nothing better than a cause. And helping Charlie was much less humiliating than fancying him. 'I mean, it depends what you want to be. There's a lot wrong with your packaging if you want to –' She stopped. She could have said 'join my group' since that was what she meant though, to be fair, she probably hadn't realised that yet. She could have said 'reach the top' but already she knew him well enough to know it would be misunderstood. (He would need to be eased towards the realisation that he was as ambitious as everyone else. It was only his sense of failure, she believed, which prevented him from already appreciating the fact. And she was determined to rectify that.) 'For example if you wanted to work in the music industry.'

'But I don't. I told you. I want a job with a desk!'

'Yes, so you say. Well there are lots of desk jobs in the music industry, or TV or film or journalism or . . .' Her imagination ran dry. 'Whatever you want. Only the people who've got them don't *package* themselves like you! D'you get?'

'I think I package myself perfectly all right,' he said bolshily.

'I'm not saying you don't. I'm just saying the people in the sort of jobs you probably want package themselves differently.'

'How do school administrators package themselves?'

'But you don't want to be a school administrator, do you?'

'Not particularly.' He thought for a moment. 'Probably get quite long holidays, though.'

'Yeah, but what I'm trying to say to you is –' Oops. He'd stumbled upon another conviction. 'If you love your job enough then you don't even care about holidays! Because every day is a holiday in a way.'

Charlie chuckled. 'When did you last take a holiday?'

It was a sore point. Jo hadn't taken a decent holiday for over two years – ever since she'd been going out with Ed, in fact. The three they had planned had each had to be cancelled due to pressure of work (twice Ed's; once her own). Then last winter she'd made a vague arrangement with Mel to spend Christmas on a Yoga Retreat in the Himalayas but Mel had got involved with some man who'd flown her off to the Bahamas instead, so that too had been forgotten. She'd spent a long weekend in Venice with an ex-boyfriend almost exactly two years ago, before she and Ed had really got into the groove. And that was it. Holidays were not her field of expertise. Packaging was.

'I'm too busy to take holidays,' she said. 'I'm just trying to say –'

'I know what you're trying to say and you're being very – kind. Very helpful. My packaging is all over the place. But I don't really think,' he laughed, 'that my *hair-do* or the cut of my jeans is seriously going to affect my job prospects, especially, come to think of it, as I'm applying by letter.'

'It does,' she said stubbornly. 'They can tell.'

He laughed. 'You sound like the General.'

That stung. The General, for Christ's sake. Of all the people in the world to compare her to . . . It was one slight too many for a single woman in a single evening. She felt an overwhelming urge to strike back. 'It's not just the bloody clothes. It's the voice. It's the things you say. It's the – everything about the way you present yourself. When I first saw you on that stage, Charlie, I thought you looked like a . . . prat. A typical pea-brained public schoolboy living off Daddy's trust fund, too bloody thick to notice that the world's moved on and left you behind.'

'Well . . . That's cleared that up, then,' he said coolly. 'You were about right, except for the bit about not noticing . . . Is this what you called me to say?'

'No. God. I'm being a bitch. I'm sorry. I don't know what came over me.'

'It's all right. You made it pretty clear what you thought of me last night. Serves me right for leaving my number on your mobile.' He paused. 'Probably needed saying though, before we could be friends. I suppose. A sort of hurdle we had to get over. I actually have a few comments to make about your . . .' He stopped. He was a kind man. And anyway he wanted to see her again. 'But I think, overall, we seem to be getting along famously. When shall we meet up for our drink?'

She laughed. 'Will you let me help you?'

'If you can. I'd be very grateful. But let's agree now that if at any point it begins to resemble a sort of New Age Class War, then we'll revert *immediately* to more conventional flirting techniques.'

She laughed again. 'You've got to lose the accent. It's too posh.'

'When shall we do it?'

'What?'

'Have our first elocution lesson. What time is it? . . . Midnight. I'm free now.'

'Well I'm not,' she said automatically. 'I've got work in the morning. And even if I hadn't,' she said as an after-thought – it had never occurred to her before – 'I'd pretend I had. Only losers and students meet up after midnight on a weekday, OK? Unless, er. You know, obviously. Unless they're spending the night together.'

'Well –'

'That was lesson number one.' She smiled. 'We're not at war yet. So, according to your terms, Hooray flirting techniques are still forbidden.'

'Fine,' he said. 'I'm going to bed.'

'Same here.'

'I'll call you tomorrow.'

'Yeah, OK.' She hesitated fractionally. She needed to get this right. 'That'll be cool.'

NEW yOu RULE NUMBER THREE: Nobody starts out looking this casual, believe me! It takes work and – yes – you guessed it! It takes one hell of a shed load of money. Because there's one thing these guys can sniff a mile off, and that's a Marks & Spencer lambswool and a cheap suit!! You'll find a list of useful shops on page 179, but beware! This one's a minefield. Boys, we want to see loose fits, subdued shades, super-subtle coordination. We want it finished off with that essential hint of 'individuality'; a splash of unusual colour, a conversation-piece accessory! As for you girls . . . that's right, it's the same old wicked world it's always been! We can't even START with you until you've checked into that gym! I want to see SWEAT on your forehead! I want to see SKIN AND BONES on your arse! And when you're a size eight, get back to me; we can start talking sh-sh-sh-SHOPS!!! Are you ready? So whaderya waiting for?

A SMART UNIFORM

Ed needed to talk to Geoff's boss about the football anyway. Ed's production company was putting together a team for the TV and Media Soccer Challenge Special, which was allowed to take place at Stamford Bridge each year because it raised money for – children. Ed could never remember which ones, exactly, but they were definitely unfortunate.

The TV and Media Soccer Challenge Special offered an excellent opportunity for Ed to indulge in some good, clean fun with some very useful people. Geoff's boss was not a great footballer, but it was well known that he loved to play. Ed was by no means the first independent producer to offer him a position on his team. He was, however, the captain of the team that won last year. (He'd been making a documentary called *Footballers & The Ladies Who Lunch 'Em* at the time and had managed to rope two premier league boyfriends onto his team. Not only that, he'd done it in such a charming and jocular way that only a few people of any significance bothered to complain.)

Ed had no premier league players on his team this year and he was actually quite a weak player himself but Geoff's boss didn't know it. He had been holding out for the Ed call-up for several weeks. So when his pretty and clever assistant Anna told him which of the innumerable independent documentary makers was on the line for him that morning, he broke every convention in the book – and took the call.

Clever Ed. What he needed from Geoff's boss was a green light for the Grey McShane project and he needed it, or rather he wanted it, by the end of the day. He couldn't afford to waste time going through Geoff because each moment that he failed to get the thing tied up was a moment when Grey might change his mind. Grey was totally unreliable, that much was obvious. Ed would need every millimetre of his ingenuity, determination and downbeat jocular charm to pull him in.

Geoff's boss was slightly confused. The idea was excellent, without a doubt. And Ed would unquestionably be the ideal person to do it and yet, he couldn't put his finger on it. Something about the project was strangely familiar. While he attempted to work out why, Ed suddenly said, 'Oh, by the way, Tom. I suppose you've already been bagged for the Stamford Bridge football shindy? We've got a pretty strong team but we're still in need of a good left back. I think Geoff mentioned that was your er –' Ed sounded delicately ironic. After all, it was only a bit of fun, '– *preferred position* . . . Was he right?'

'Good for Geoff!' said Geoff's boss. 'I didn't know he cared! I think I'd love to. Remind me. When is it again?'

'It's the – er.' (They both knew perfectly well when it was.) 'I think it's the third weekend of September. About four weeks away.'

'Fine. Sounds absolutely fine. Excellent. I shall look forward to that. And as far as this Mr McShane character is concerned I think I can provisionally say "go". Yeah. Get something in writing would you, *soon as*. And talk to

Anna about arranging lunch. In the meantime I'll try and dig out the old football clobber! Let me know in advance when you're having a practice, won't you?'

'Certainly will.'

'Who else have you got playing on the team?' Tom said slyly. 'Anyone I should know?'

On quick and careful consideration Ed decided to ignore the question. 'Wait a bit. Here we are. Yeah. It's actually on Sunday 27th. Nine-thirty start. Stamford Bridge . . . Entrance on Fulham Road . . . Sound OK?'

There would be a budget for the Grey McShane documentary on Tom's desk by the end of the day, he said. The sooner the finance was in place the sooner he could get the thing rolling. Grey McShane, Ed warned, was 'arguably the most fascinating man to come out of Britain for fifty years. And you know how it is with these guys. You've got to tie them down.' Tom did know. He transferred the call so the pretty and clever assistant Anna could firm up the details, and sat back to fantasise about David Beckham gasping at the artlessness of one of his match-winning diving headers.

The idea of a documentary about Grey McShane sounded familiar to Tom because it was. That very morning he had signed four rejection letters to independent producers whose football teams were not so good as Ed's. Each had suggested the same documentary. Each had promised they had Grey McShane's personal commitment to the project.

> *I have read your proposal with great interest,* one of his minions had explained in one of the letters Tom had forgotten he'd signed. *However, I feel that*

Grey McShane, although undoubtedly a remarkable and
talented man, as a poet *might prove something of a turn-*
off for our audience. Also the 'literary' subject matter is
at odds with our current Autumn/Winter schedule, with
its emphasis on new technology and women.

I am sorry to disappoint you on this occasion, however . . .
do continue . . . with many thanks . . . and so on. Yours
entirely sincerely, Tom Faulkner, Head of Documentaries
and Current Affairs, Channel Foremost

Clever Ed.

He immediately put in a call to Grey's agent, who referred
him to someone called Jerry at Phonix, who referred him
back to Grey. If Ed had been a fraction less focused on his
goal he might have noticed the resignation in both their
voices. He might have been forewarned.

'If Grey wants to do it – then *great*.' said Jerry at Phonix.
'But I have to warn you, he's fallen out with a couple of
producers already. He can be a bit . . . moody.'

'I noticed,' said Ed. 'It's cool. If he wasn't so difficult I
wouldn't be so interested. This – What I'm after, Jerry, is a
study of modern genius, if you like.'

'I *do* like! I like very much. Of course I do . . . Look. Why
don't you talk to Grey and get back to me. Obviously if
you guys *can* get along, we're gonna want to offer all the
assistance we can.'

'That's what I thought.'

'Well – best of British!' said Jerry, dryly.

Ed laughed. 'Yeah, thanks,' he said, without an inkling of
how much he'd need it.

* * *

Jo was feeling terrible. She'd been feeling increasingly terrible since the moment last night when she and Charlie had hung up. Fortunately for her, some sort of shame-shielding mechanism in her brain meant she could no longer remember her exact words, but she knew they had been horrible; unkind, strident and stupid. And he'd been so – *gentlemanly* about it, refusing to retaliate, somehow managing to turn the whole thing into a joke.

She hadn't fallen asleep until 5 a.m. Then she'd slept through her alarm, all the way through the *Today* programme and not woken until ten o'clock. She'd had to skip the early morning facial, and the shower, so her hair felt dirty. Worse still, as she determinedly wormed her way towards the only empty seat on the London Underground, she noticed that her expensive T-shirt had an oil stain on top of the left nipple.

When she arrived at work, a full hour late, there was a hostile Post-it message in the middle of her desk.

'*We need to talk,*' it said. '*Penny.*'

She knew what that was about. Feeling slightly panicked she decided to take the law into her own hands and was just dialling Geoff's number when she saw Penny marching across the open-plan office towards her. 'Two minutes,' Jo mouthed at her and turned slightly away. But Penny continued her approach, came to a halt beside her and waited with quiet aggression until Jo hung up. Jo hung up.

'Good morning, Penny,' said Jo, with a bright smile. 'I'm right on my way over to talk to you. If you could give me half a minute. I need to make a quick call –'

'Jo, what the hell is going on? We simply can't wait any longer! Where's Ed Bailey? Where – the *fuck* – is the letter

72

from Channel Foremost? I've had the people from Meals breathing down my neck three times already today, and now you decide this is the morning to go AWOL. I've been trying to reach you on the mobile for half an hour –'

'I was on the tube.'

'We're going to lose this account. Get me Ed Bailey. On the telephone. Now.'

Jo didn't appreciate being spoken to like a secretary. 'He's on voicemail,' she said coolly. 'I've just tried him. Penny, I did explain yesterday, he's on a very tight deadline and he will be until the end of the week.' She smiled patiently. 'Trust me. I'm on the case. He'll be in here the first moment he can. And in the meantime pass the Meals calls over to me. I can deal with them. Really. There's nothing to worry about.'

'I hope not,' said Penny, retreating slightly, feeling irritably reassured. 'I just don't understand. Why are you finding this so difficult? I thought he was your boyfriend.'

'So he is.' She forced herself to smile. 'He's also a very busy man.'

'Whatever. Frankly I don't care. But I must insist that you get me Ed Bailey before the end of today. And keep me posted.' With a businesslike nod, she strode off to spread her well-valued sense of urgency elsewhere.

Jo spent a couple of valiant hours on the telephone. Meals, after all, was only one of her clients. She had the amazing new Members Only drinking bar called Sip Code due for its official opening in three weeks. She had recently been handed the account for *Mostly Motoring*, an amazing consumer show on Sky, whose viewing figures had recently been dwindling. Also, an amazing new bottled water, due to be launched in October, which was especially amazing because of the amazingly environmentally friendly way it was pumped out of the Swedish mountainside. She had two amazingly talented actors on her books and an amazing new interactive doll which called for *Daddy*, when it needed its nappy changed. Poor Jo. It all seemed amazingly unamazing to her that morning. For the first time in her working life she found she just couldn't muster the belief. It was horrible. She wondered if she was falling ill.

With the threat of Penny discovering the truth temporarily subsided, she decided against trying Geoff's number again. Ed was right. It was something unpleasant about most people, not just the people at Foremost, that any hint of desperation tended to make them less, rather than more, inclined to help. If she told Geoff she urgently needed confirmation in writing about the wretched Meals documentary, she would probably jeopardise the entire project. Best to be patient. Keep cool. Keep smiling. Sit it out.

She was doodling on Penny's Post-it message, wrestling determinedly with the urge to daydream about Charlie, once again, when her mobile rang. This time she recognised the number. With a discreet smile and a heart full of relief she leant into the receiver, 'Hello, hello!' she said warmly. 'I didn't expect to hear from you again. After last night.'

'Oh.' He sounded taken aback. 'I thought we'd left it that I'd call – But perhaps – God. I'm an idiot. I never can take a bloody hint. I thought –'

'*No!* I mean *yes*. You did. We did. It's great to hear from you. Only *I* thought, after all the – You know. After me being such a –' She cast around for the right word but nothing seemed appropriate.

'I thought you were going to help me remodel myself.

74

Or did I dream the whole thing? We did *talk* last night, didn't we?'

'I'm so sorry,' she said. 'I think it's very – forgiving – of you to want to speak to me at all. I can't believe what an idiot I was.' Immediately she regretted it. It was too straight. Too humble. Any minute now, she thought, he was going to start sounding conceited.

'Oh God, forget it!' he said. '*I* have . . . More or less. I was wondering, what are you up to for lunch?'

'Nothing.' But it wasn't what she meant. She meant nothing *with him*. Nothing at such short notice. Nothing – with dirty hair and an oil blob on her nipple. Charlie and Top Spin were never meant to mix.

'Excellent. Because I'm –'

'No! I meant nothing except work. I'm *working*! I've got so much *work* to do. I'm frantic!'

'Ha!' he said triumphantly. 'Jo, you can't teach a person a trick one minute and then expect him to fall for it the next!'

'What?'

'I may be stupid but I'm not a total spastic!'

'For God's sake, Charlie, nobody says spastic . . . What are you talking about?'

'OK,' he said. 'I know you're busy. And I know you're not a loser, so you don't have to pretend. You obviously aren't having lunch with anyone else, because it's half past one already. You might as well have lunch with *someone*. So. I was just thinking – how about me?'

'I honestly do not know what you're getting at,' she said feebly. 'Firstly I can't have lunch with you because I'm in my office. And secondly I am *not* pretending I'm busy so you don't think I'm a loser, I actually –'

75

'Just a little bit?'

'No!' she snapped indignantly. 'Not even a bloody –'

'All right. Sorry. I've no idea what people get up to in offices. I know if you go and visit them it always takes them ten minutes to come and get you. But what are you all actually *doing*? Like now, for example. Describe what you're doing right now, apart from talking to me. What were you doing the instant before I called?'

'I was –' She stopped. *Thinking about you. At a loose end.* 'I was er –' She shuffled a few papers on her desk. 'I was thinking about the, er, opening of a bar – It doesn't matter. You wouldn't be interested. The point is, although I'm really pleased you called and I'm really, truly sorry about yesterday, I cannot make lunch.' Thank God, she thought, he couldn't see her now. Until something made her look up.

There was a thud as she dropped her mobile, followed quickly by a faint but embarrassing scream as she leapt in horror from her perspex swivel chair. Standing for all to observe at the glass double doors a couple of metres from her desk was a tall, languid figure in a stupid cowboy hat. He still had his telephone pressed to his ear.

'Jo?' said one of her thin PR neighbours. 'Are you OK?'

She fumbled under the desk for her mobile, grabbed her wallet and keys. 'Fine. I'm fine. Absolutely fine. Got to go out. Could you, er –' But she was gone before she'd finished the sentence.

Ed had been sitting at the table, making little balls out of organic sundried tomato bread, writing notes and fingering his silent telephone for well over three-quarters of an hour.

The restaurant wanted its table back and staff were becoming increasingly ruthless in their attempts to achieve it. In the last five minutes, the same waitress had asked six times whether he was ready to order. But Ed remained unbroken. The place was extremely expensive and it was he who would be paying for lunch today – if his companion ever showed up. He nursed the lukewarm dregs of his single mineral water with the same determination he did everything – and waited. It seemed to him that he had no other choice.

Finally Grey McShane shuffled in, looking dishevelled and triumphantly unapologetic. Clamped to his waist, and tripping slightly in her efforts to keep up with him, was Mel. Ed had purposely not invited her – partly, he explained to himself, because he 'didn't want to have to pay to watch her fat arse getting any fatter', and partly, of course, because now he had Grey, he no longer needed her. He never had the slightest intention of involving her in the final project. He thought. But as she settled herself defiantly on the chair beside him it occurred to him that he had underestimated her.

'Hi Mel!' he said, leaning over for a kiss. 'What a lovely surprise! Jo said you were out of town! On some freebie in the South of France. Otherwise I would have invited you along.'

'Not to worry.' Mel gave a pert smile. 'I came anyway.'

'Excellent. *Excellent* . . . And good to see you Grey, mate. I was worried you wouldn't turn up!'

'Aye.' Grey caught the eye of a waitress who happened to be ogling him (a common occurrence in Grey's new life). She scuttled at once to hear his bidding. 'I'll have a large gin,' he said. 'With ice. And, Melanie, what's that stuff they put in last night? Makes it go purple? I want some o' that.'

'Angostura,' said Mel. 'Angostura Bitters. Delicious, isn't it?'

'I'll have some of that. But don't you put it in, mind. Bring me the little bottle.' He turned to glance at Ed for the first time. 'It's fantastic,' he said. 'You've got to watch it dropping in. It's fuckin' beautiful, isn't it Mel?'

'Oh. God. Yeah,' said Mel. 'It's like – when you cut yourself shaving in the bath –'

'It's like blood,' Grey said. 'Spurting blood.'

'How wonderful,' said Ed brightly. 'So. I talked to Jerry at Phonix. He was very keen.'

'Aye.'

'And as you know I've liaised with my people at Foremost, who are *over the – fucking – moon*. Really –' Ed's laugh sounded unnaturally gruff, *'ridiculously* excited.'

'If you think it's ridiculous to be excited,' Grey cracked back, 'then I'm wondering why you're interested in doing it yourself.'

With a dry smile and without missing a beat, Ed said, 'I, on the other hand am sensibly excited. Overwhelmingly excited, but *sensibly* excited, none the less.'

'Good,' said Grey. 'And I don't want you doing any poking around behind my back. Understand? If I catch you talking to anyone –' He glared at Ed. *'Anyone* without my knowledge you will be . . .' Grey hadn't raised his voice, hadn't needed to move a muscle, but his manner was chillingly, unmistakably threatening '. . . extremely sorry. D'you understand?'

'I might have to –'

'Do you understand?'

'Yes. Yes, Grey. Of course.'

'And I want Mel to do the interviewing.'

'Absolutely . . . Of course . . . Isn't that what we already agreed?'

Grey turned to gaze on Mel's minuscule T-shirt. He casually flicked one of her nipples (for an instant she actually looked put out) before offering it a slow, private smile; 'I want to take her home to interview my Mammy. I'd like to see how the two of them get along.'

'Tremendous!' said Ed. 'Sounds *tremendous*!'

'But – sorry, Grey, darling,' said Mel. 'Sorry to be rude. I thought you said she was dead.'

'Aye,' said Grey. 'And so she is. In a way. So she is . . . Now *that*'s a very nice pullover you've got on there, Ed.'

It was going to be a difficult lunch.

After she'd overcome the terror that somebody in the office might suspect he was a friend, Jo began to realise how happy she was that Charlie had come to call. He'd laughed so hard as he watched her stumbling from her desk, and then laughed even harder as she bundled him across the reception hall, frantically lurching at him to remove the hat. It was a rare laugh, an uninhibited, unpretentious rumble that came from deep within his chest. It would have been impossible, in the face of it, for her to remain angry for long. She couldn't even feel tense. By the time the two of them had walked a couple of yards down the street she found she was laughing too.

'You can't!' she said, failing to sound as severe as she wished she felt. 'You *can't* come into my office. Just *come into my office* – and just – stand there. In that *hat*!'

'I'm sorry,' he said. 'I had no idea. I had no idea a hat could have such an effect.'

She hesitated. 'It's just – *not* on.'

'But I've taken it off!'

'I mean you can't just come into my office in a hat.'

And then she realised how absurd it sounded. They both started laughing again. Poor Jo. She was so shaken – by the hat, by her loss of cool, by the general effect of his easy presence, and she was so unaccustomed to her own laughter she realised she was in danger of becoming hysterical. She was teetering on the edge. It could have gone either way, until she became aware of an observer. Standing before her, a vast, aggressive grin encasing her expensively whitened teeth, was Penny. Jo snapped to attention.

'Well *Goodness!*' said Penny. 'You two look like you're having fun!'

'Hello, Penny. We were just, em. This is my friend . . .' In desperation Jo turned towards Charlie. 'I mean this is Penny. The founder of Top Spin. You've probably heard of her. One of the, er, smartest PRs in Soho. In the business, actually . . .' But she knew she couldn't go on for ever. At some point she was going to have to explain who Charlie was. And why she knew anybody who – Christ! She hadn't noticed until now – was still wearing a T-shirt celebrating a Michael Jackson tour.

'And you,' Penny's tense, jolly grin looked absurd on her well-toned face, 'must be the eternally elusive, notoriously talented Edward Bailey. Am I right? You look – *younger* than I imagined.' She put out her hand. Charlie put out his, but before the hands could meet, or Charlie could say a word, Jo had leapt in between them.

'No!' she said. 'The thing is we're running horribly late. Got a meeting to get to. Very important. And we really ought to be there *now*. Penny, sorry to dash off like this but we've got to get on.' She gave Charlie a nudge and the two of them started moving away. 'I'll be back in the office later,' Jo shouted over her shoulder. 'I'll let you know how it goes . . . Sorry!' Penny was left standing by the Top Spin swivel door, the remnants of a grin still clinging to her face, too astonished, yet, to be angry. A millisecond later her mobile rang.

'What was all that about?' said Charlie.

'Quick!' said Jo. 'Don't look back. She thought you were Ed.'

'Who's Ed?'

'Ed?' They turned a corner and she stopped to look at him. God. He didn't know about Ed. Should she tell him? She didn't want to, though she was unwilling to acknowledge why. 'Ed – is a producer. Amazingly talented documentary maker. We're working on something together . . . Penny's been driving me mad all week because he's too busy to come in and talk to her. She's holding me responsible.'

'Why? Seems a bit unfair.'

'Because –' She hesitated. 'Because she's a silly cow. Or no. Not really. Because I'm the connection. I introduced him to the project. It's sort of my responsibility. Anyway, it's not interesting. Let's talk about something else. God knows what I'm going to say when I go back in.' She laughed. For a moment, she didn't even care. This good-looking man who gazed down at her with such easy confidence, with so much intelligent attention, made her feel like nothing mattered any more. Not Penny, not Channel Foremost, not Ed's elusiveness or his coldness, nor Mel's irrepressible career, not even the oil stain above her left nipple. 'Let's go and get drunk!' she heard herself say.

And they did. They took a cab to an old-fashioned oyster bar in St James's, far enough from Soho for Jo to feel reasonably safe. The place was virtually empty. A handful of old men in pinstripe suits were dotted around the small marble tables, all of them defying modern convention, glugging peacefully at midday bottles of wine.

'It's my father's favourite place,' said Charlie. 'Or it used to be. He used to bring Georgie and me here for a treat sometimes, before putting us on our trains back to school.'

In truth, though she hid it well, Jo felt embarrassed whenever Charlie mentioned his sister. Until she met Charlie she had never had any great difficulty in dealing smoothly with other people's grief. Her lack of experience (or heartfelt interest) lent her a fearlessness which actually helped her to say the right things. But Charlie's suffering unsettled her – because it was always there, so much a part of him, she couldn't be untouched by it, and it made her feel helpless. For the first time in her life – and it came as a shock – she found herself regretting the limits of her understanding.

However, she was not such a highly paid Professional Pleaser for nothing. She had learnt in her years in public relations that the best way to camouflage any moment of inadequacy was to inject it with a gentle stream of meaningless agreement.

'It must bring back a lot of happy memories,' she said.

'Actually it usually ended up with Dad squeezing in a final lecture about my report and then poor old Georgie bursting into tears because he was being horrible to me again.'

'She must have been such a wonderful sister.'

'Yup.' He turned away. It had been a mistake to come, he

realised. He hadn't been here since he left school and he'd thought it would have been OK – a funny little detour into his past. But Jo's gentle, well-intentioned nothingnesses, her sombre delivery, were making things worse. Suddenly the smell, the leather seating, the wooden panelling around the walls, the quiet shuffling sound of old men going about their business, reminded Charlie of the undertaker's waiting room.

'You know what?' he said. 'Let's get out of here. I think we should go somewhere really *jolly*.'

'Of course,' she said. 'Of course.'

They climbed back into a taxi and immediately started squabbling about where to go next. Jo didn't want to go back to Soho but nor did she want to go too far from work. Charlie argued that as the intention was to get pissed, it wouldn't matter how far from work she went since she presumably wasn't planning on returning.

'Oh God,' said Jo, suddenly feeling a wave of her old self overcome her, 'I can't get pissed. What am I going to say to Penny when I go back?'

'She's a horrible woman!' said Charlie. 'I wouldn't tell her anything.'

'But she's my boss!'

'I've never seen such a creepy smile.'

Jo chuckled. 'She was trying to be engaging. Count yourself lucky. She doesn't normally smile at all.' Just then Jo's mobile started ringing. A glance at its miniature display screen quickly wiped the smile off her face. 'Oh my God. It's *her*. What am I going to do?'

'Switch it off.'

She looked at him in astonishment.

'Switch it off. You only saw her twenty minutes ago. I

don't suppose she's got anything new to say. Anyway, she thinks you're in a meeting.'

'But she'll want to know –'

'She's bullying you,' said Charlie. 'She's a bully. I could see it in her scary grin. Go on –' He leant towards her and snatched the phone.

'No!'

He held it up towards her, giving her a final chance to grab it back. She chose not to take it, and he switched it off.

'Well then!' she laughed shakily. 'That decides *that*, doesn't it? Fuck it! I think we should head *West*.'

'Excellent!'

'There's a fantastic place just behind Notting Hill Gate . . .'

Towards the end of the second bottle of wine Jo said, somewhat tentatively, 'Now Charlie. About this remodelling work.'

'Ah yes.'

'I think . . . we need to have a think . . . About the T-shirts.'

'Oh!' He looked down in surprise at the one he had on. 'It's no good then? I thought it was rather . . . I always thought the collar was quite nice and . . . thin. It's very comfortable.'

'It's terrible. I'll tell you – Shall I tell you what it says to me?'

'Pea-brained public schoolboy who's too bloody thick to realise –'

'N-no!'

He laughed. 'It's too late to start lying to me now.'

'I'm just saying, it doesn't give off a very – contemporary

– feel. The point is T-shirts with pop concerts – any pop concerts, let alone ones that are ten years old – just –' She grimaced. 'Trust me. Just don't work.'

'Hm,' he said mildly. 'But I'd never wear this to an interview.'

'Yeah, but that's the whole thing. You've got to realise, you're always on interview.' She looked around the airy dining room, charmingly chock-a-block, as usual, with appropriately presented Career Opps. 'I mean you're always on show. Someone could come up to us now, someone who might turn out to be – someone helpful. It could happen anywhere, at any time. London is such a *tiny* city. And if a potential contact approached us now, they'd look at your T-shirt and they'd think . . . Well, to be honest, because you're with me they might just think you were being ironic. Otherwise they're going to look at you and think –'

'Something rude about my schooling, I imagine.'

She nodded ruefully. 'I'm afraid so.'

'Let's have another bottle of wine.'

'Definitely. And after that, I think we should go shopping . . . Because,' she examined him through fuzzy, inebriated, half-closed eyes, 'if you could be bothered you could look so amazing. I know guys who'd kill for a figure like yours.'

'*Really?*' said Charlie.

'Totally,' said Jo seriously.

'What funny guys you know.'

Except for the skirmish over who should pay the restaurant bill, and although there were instances when both felt they were talking to a Martian, it was generally a confused but very happy lunch.

The argument about the bill began as soon as it was put on the table. Charlie was adamant that he should pay, since it was he who had made the original invitation. Jo said she 'wouldn't be comfortable with that. It may come as a surprise to you Charlie, but these days women do tend to pay their own way.' Anyway, she reminded him, she could always get it back on expenses.

'Which means that creepy woman with the teeth would be paying for it?'

'Exactly.' At which point Jo, assuming the matter was properly settled, leant forward to take the bill.

'But why should she pay for it?'

'What?' Jo was confused.

'This has nothing to do with your work.'

'So?' Jo was completely confused.

'Well, it's stealing.'

She didn't know whether to laugh. Was he joking? Or retreat. She was embarrassed. After all, it was she who was meant to be teaching him about the right way of doing things. She was the one with the highly developed New Moral Code, the one who cared about irresponsibility of the press, unfair distribution of opportunity, cruelty-free beauty products, AIDS in Africa, computers in schools, air pollution in Bangkok, fossil fuel consumption in Silicon Valley . . . Her hand hovered uncertainly. She decided that the only way to survive this – ludicrous little blip – was to brazen it out.

'Don't be absurd,' she said. 'Everything has a little bit to do with work. How do you know this isn't a job interview anyway?'

'Because I'm wearing the wrong T-shirt.'

She laughed.

But he didn't. 'I'm not – Jo I'm sorry, I don't know how to say this without sounding pompous, and you can call me pea-brained as much as you like. But I'm not really joking. I mean, the idea that we would *steal* from that maniac, it's, for me, anyway, it's – I just can't.'

He took the bill and paid it quickly. Jo could only look on, dumbstruck. There were a few minutes of unhappy silence while they waited for his credit card to return, and then they both started apologising at the same time, and then they laughed, and the mood seemed to lighten again.

It was four o'clock before they finally left the table. Jo dared not even glance at her mobile for fear of the messages piling up. 'Come on,' she said. 'I know a brilliant place for you, just around the corner from here.' And together they staggered out of Kensington Church Street towards Westbourne Grove. It was her and Ed's favourite shopping street; one of the few places worth the pilgrimage from North London, and one of the most expensive oases of excellent taste in the whole of the developed world.

It was while they were in the men's department of agnès b, and just as they'd staggered to the cash till, carrying a pile of clothes the size of which could only be accounted for by their drunkenness, that Jo's boyfriend walked in. Ed, looking like a bad tempered Roman slave and loaded down with his master's shopping bags, was trailing several yards behind his new lord, Grey McShane. (Mel, unfortunately, had had to leave immediately after lunch, to write a piece about celebrity summer footwear for the *Express*.) So it was Grey who saw them first.

'Well bugger me!' he bellowed across the elegant wooden

floor. 'Eddie my boy. It's your fancy lady, if I'm not mistaken. And with a *very* fancy looking man. Don't you people ever do any work?'

'. . . Ed!'

'. . . Jo!'

'Good God!' chuckled Grey, 'you don't look very pleased to see each other!'

It was Ed who recovered first. 'What a lovely surprise,' he said. 'Why aren't you in the office?'

'I – er. Well, I am, sort of. This is –' She pointed to Charlie, who had turned to look at them and was leaning against the counter, his back to the sales assistant as she began the laborious process of toting up his final bill. 'This is Charlie. He's actually an amazingly talented musician. We're just in here, as you can see – sort of. Doing a bit of remodelling.' She wobbled slightly, although it was already obvious that she was drunk. If she hadn't been, she might have stopped right there. Instead, conscious of the wobble and keen to recover the damage, she dug herself a little deeper. 'Remember him,' she said, with a feeble smile. 'Remember the name. Because if Top Spin has anything to do with it you're going to be seeing a *hell* of a lot more of him soon!'

Grey burst out laughing. 'Well Ed,' he said. 'Do you believe her? Cos I bloody don't. But then *I* don't know when you last fucked her. And these sort of things tend to turn, in my experience, on a ve-ry fine fulcrum. Fuckrum –' he snorted at his own wit. 'A very fine fuckrum indeed.'

'Shut up,' said Jo.

'Strikes me it might have been a wee while ago. If you don't mind my saying so, darlin'. In which case, Eddie . . .' He shrugged.

'Piss off,' said Jo.

Grey chuckled comfortably. Still, Ed said nothing.

'And who is this?' Charlie said coolly.

'That's Grey.'

'I meant the other one.'

'This is Ed,' said Jo and fell silent.

'The amazingly talented documentary maker?'

'Mm,' she said.

'So,' said Grey. 'What happens now? Do we have a fight? Or do we just get on with our shopping, or what?'

Suddenly Jo came to her senses. 'What are you two doing in here anyway? I didn't even know you knew each other.'

'Bloody hell!' said Grey. He turned to Charlie. 'Can you believe this couple? How'd'yedo, by the way. I'm Grey McShane. The poet.'

'Charlie Maxwell McDonald,' he said, to whom Grey's name clearly meant nothing. 'The amazingly talented musician.'

'Ha!' said Grey. 'You're a posh wanker. But I like you.'

'Och, well that's a relief,' said Charlie good-naturedly, and in a fair imitation of Grey's accent. 'I have to tell you tho', I fuckin' ha' the Scots.'

'You do?' said Grey, his face alight with pleasure. 'And why's that, you fuckin' posh wanker?'

'I dunno,' said Charlie, using his normal voice again. 'Probably because they hate the English so much. Trying to redress the balance. Seems only fair.'

'Oh yes. Very fair.' Ed Bailey had found his reedy, reasonable voice at last. 'Except of course the Scottish actually have good reason to hate the English. The English have been stealing their land and exploiting their resources for more centuries than I would like to count.'

'How many centuries is that, then?' said Grey.

Ed ignored him. He had no idea of course, and nor did he care. The aim of the speech had been threefold: to divert Jo's attention from her original question, to make Jo's posh wanker companion look ignorant, heartless and generally inferior, and finally, and most importantly, to inform Grey of his own profoundly sympathetic line on Scotland's pain.

It failed on all counts.

'I don't know who exploits who,' said Grey mildly. 'But I know the English give us a fair number of subsidies. And all the Scots ever do is complain.'

'And they're smug bastards,' said Charlie, 'especially the newscasters.'

'Stupid, whingeing, vindictive buggers,' said Grey.

Charlie chortled drunkenly. 'And it's bloody cold up there, too.'

Jo and Ed looked from one to the other in dismal confusion.

'Edward,' said Grey. 'We're drifting. You were about to explain to your beautiful girlfriend here what you and me are doing in this shop together this afternoon. And I think she deserves an explanation, don't you?'

Ed glanced murderously at his master. 'Jo,' he said. 'Let's talk. We need to talk. I've been trying to call you all afternoon –'

'Bollocks!' shouted Grey.

Ed ignored him. 'Please, Jo.'

They eyed each other nervously as she weaved across the floor towards him. He put the shopping bags on the floor and beckoned her to a far corner of the room.

'What's going on?' she said.

'Nothing. *Nothing.* Look – there's something else I've got to tell you first.' His face was filled with gentle concern. 'It's not good news, I'm afraid. I've tried to reason with him. But he won't budge. He's fucked us around big time.'

'Who?'

'*Who?* . . . Geoff, of course.'

She looked completely blank. 'Geoff who?'

'Jesus, Jo,' Ed snapped. 'What's the matter with you? *Geoff,* Geoff. At Channel Foremost. They're dropping Meals. They've lost interest. You know what they're like. I'm sorry.'

It was as if she'd been dropped into a cold bath. 'What? *Why?* They can't do that! What am I going to tell Penny?'

'I'm sorry, love. Truly I am. There's absolutely nothing I can do.'

'But can't you – We can take the project somewhere else. Carlton might want it. Loads of people probably want it. We've just got to –'

'Jo. Listen.' He sounded so calm, so measured. It was impossible for Jo not to believe he was on her side. 'They've offered me something else – And I just daren't turn it down. It's a *challenge,* yeah? And that's so important for me.'

'But what am I going to say to Penny?' she repeated. 'We're going to lose the account! They only came because I told them we'd got a terrestrial. I *promised* them . . . I'm going to lose my job!'

'No you won't. You said they were about to make you a partner.'

'Not now. Of course not! I told you. It was conditional on the – Oh, forget it!'

'Jo.' He rested a light hand on her shoulder. 'Believe me, I'm sorry. If there's anything I can do . . . *Anything* . . .'

'Oh . . .' With a great force of will she pulled herself together. 'I'm sorry, Ed. I know it's not your fault . . .' She tried to smile. 'So what's the big opportunity then? You didn't tell me.'

'Oh God,' Ed rolled his blue eyes to heaven. 'Can't you guess? What the hell else would I be doing in this shop at this time in the afternoon? . . . He's the hottest story of the year, and probably the most difficult individual I have ever met!'

'You poor thing,' said Jo. 'What a nightmare.'

'It's not easy.'

'But it'll be worth it. I know you'll do it brilliantly.'

Ed laughed, feeling much more comfortable with the tone the conversation had taken. 'Not if *he* can help it! You know who he's insisting on doing the presenting?'

'Tell me.'

'Your friend Mel.'

'Mel . . . And Foremost is OK with that?'

'Of course!'

She nodded, inhaled deeply and turned away.

'Jo?' Ed laughed. He was genuinely bewildered. 'What's up?'

'I'm very happy for her.' It came out as a monotone. 'As you know I love her to bits. But now I must get back to Charlie . . . See you later perhaps.'

'Yeah . . .' He watched her with something loosely resembling concern as she weaved back towards the counter, tripping slightly on the back of one of her own boots. 'Get yourself some black coffee,' he said. 'And I'll call you. Tonight.' He couldn't prevent himself from glancing nervously at Charlie's back. 'We need to talk.' But she didn't respond.

She walked on past Charlie who called out to her, but again she didn't respond. She walked past the counter and right out of the shop.

'There we are!' said the assistant cheerfully as she laid Charlie's final, tissue-wrapped extravagance into the carrier bag. 'And that's two thousand, eight hundred and ninety pounds and forty-one pence, please.'

Grey, his elbows resting casually on the counter beside Charlie, let out a long, lazy whistle. 'They charge stupid prices in these places. You'll never guess how much I paid for a fuckin' overcoat last week! It's lucky I'm so rich or God knows . . .' He paused to think what God knew on the subject that he might not. But he was drunk, and not very interested in the answer. 'God knows, eh?'

'Did she say what I think she said?' said Charlie.

'What did you say again, darlin'?' said Grey.

'Two thousand, eight hundred and ninety pounds and forty-one pence.' She grimaced daintily. 'It's terrible how it tends to add up, isn't it?'

Charlie laughed. In his vagueness, post-lunch drunkenness, and his complete lack of familiarity with the shopping process he had failed to look at a single price-tag. He had been imagining a bill (and was feeling quite uncomfortable about it) in the region of maybe two hundred pounds. 'This is silly,' said Charlie. 'I mean, really. I'm sorry. I obviously should have looked at the prices. I had no idea. But I mean – this is silly. I'm very sorry, but – This is *silly*. We're going to have to put it all back.'

'*Charlie Maxton-Flipmeover-Andoitagain!*' Grey cried in delight. 'What are you thinking of? You can't do that! The poor lady's wrapped it all in tissue paper.'

'I'm sorry,' said Charlie again. 'Really, I am. But I don't

think I want any of it.' He was backing towards the door. 'I've got to go and see what's happened to Jo. She was looking pretty unhappy.'

'Oh sod it,' said Grey. 'It's all so nicely packed up now. It'll save me looking through the shelves.' He tossed his credit card onto the counter, turned to Charlie and winked. 'They all looked nice enough. Give them to me!'

Charlie grinned. 'They're not even your size!'

Och. What does that matter? With clothes of this quality I'm sure size is the last thing that matters. Isn't that right, Missie?' The assistant looked nonplussed. 'Besides – I'm only doing it to show off.'

Charlie bellowed with laughter. 'Who to? Me? Or Ed over there? Or – or the shop assistant?'

'You, you posh wanker.'

'Ha! Well – I think it worked. Nice meeting you anyway,' he said. 'Enjoy my clothes.'

Ed waited for the door to bang shut before he approached Grey at the counter. 'Bloody hell, mate,' he said in a jovial voice which reflected nothing of his general tetchiness. 'Tell me you're not really going to buy all that!'

'Of course not,' said Grey, leaning across the counter and retrieving his credit card from the girl's manicured paw before she'd had time to do anything with it. 'Just didn't want the guy to feel badly about changing his mind. He looked very embarrassed . . . It's all right darlin',' he said to the assistant. 'Show's over. You can put it all back now.'

NEW YOU RULE NUMBER FOUR: Here at New You Central Office we don't know if it was Bob Dylan or JFK, but one of 'em was bang on when he said 'every time a mate succeeds a little bit of me dies'! It's tough, but you're gonna have to GET USED to 'dying', yeah? And look HAPPY about it, too! Because your new mates are ALWAYS 'succeeding'! And if they weren't 'succeeding' what WOULDN'T they be? . . . You got it! Believe it or not, success IS contagious! If you swim with the sharks long enough you're gonna start looking like one, too! AND they'll let you share their scraps, if you're lucky. But remember, your new MATES are running the same race as you, and there isn't an UNLIMITED number of prizes out there! It means your greatest mates double up as your greatest ENEMIES, too. Confused? You may be! EITHER way, keep smiling! Whether they're 'mates' or 'enemies', they're CONTACTS, OK? You're gonna NEED them!

SOME GREAT MATES

Half an hour and two shops later Grey decided he was bored. He slipped away while Ed was examining his reflection in a flattering £536 donkey jacket, and headed instinctively for the nearest pub. He'd ordered a quadruple gin and was trying to remember the name for Angostura when he caught sight of Charlie and Jo for the second time that afternoon. They were at the opposite end of the bar, huddled together at a corner table kissing, like a couple of teenagers. At Grey's ear-shattering howl of delight, they leapt guiltily apart. But it was too late.

'You dirty bastards!' Grey bellowed ecstatically. Jo hid her head in her hands. Charlie sighed and watched helplessly as Grey picked up his tumbler and strode across the room towards them. 'You dirty, dirty bastards! What am I gonna tell your fella, Jo? Can I join you?' He'd plonked himself down before they had time to reply. 'So –' he said.

'Get lost, Grey,' said Charlie good-naturedly. 'As you can see we're pretty busy –'

'Ha! I most certainly can! Eh, Jo? Am I going to get a hello from you, or what? I left Ed poncing about in a shop called Time Zone. He's trying on a jacket for five hundred-odd pounds, and he's thinking to himself, "*It's pricey,*" he's thinkin'. "*But is it going ta make me stand head and shoulders above the other lads? Is it going to make my little lady a-beg me for a proddin' this happy Friday night?*" . . . Or what, eh Jo?' He leant back in his chair. 'You might at least go and tell him to save his money.'

'Leave her alone,' said Charlie. 'It's not funny.'

'Och, yes it is,' Grey said impatiently. 'Don't be so bloody soppy.' Grey tilted his enormous shoulders towards the table and attempted to peer into Jo's still hidden face. 'Bloody hell!' he said in astonishment. 'Charlie! The poor lass has been crying! What's been going on around here?'

'I'm not sure,' mumbled Charlie. 'Work stuff, I think. And her boyfriend's being a bit of a jerk.'

'Aye,' said Grey, taking a giant gulp from his gin. 'I can believe that. You should watch him, lassie. I'd say he's got a soft spot for young Melanie. Which is a cheek, really. Considerin' it's me who's s'posed to be satisfying her at the moment.' He paused to reflect, nodded to himself and chuckled. 'Aye. And I think I'm doing that OK. Anyone for another drink?' In a single mouthful, he drained the rest of his glass.

'Actually I think –' said Charlie.

'Oh come on!'

'I've got to go,' said Jo.

'Of course you haven't,' said Grey. 'What's the matter with you girl? You've got a gorgeous fellow beside you who obviously cares for you very much. There's ladies I know who'd offer up their teeth to be sitting where you are now. Come on! For God's sake! I'm offering to buy you a drink!'

'It's you who's causing the problem.'

'Och, she shouldn't mind me!'

'Please. Would you two stop talking about me as if I wasn't here? I said I've got to go. Because I've got to. Charlie, thank you for a lovely day. But I must. Really.' She smiled. 'If I don't get home, have a cold shower and hit the phone I'm not going to have a job to go to in the morning.'

'So what?' shouted Grey. 'This man looks like he can take care of you. If you ask him nicely.'

'You may find it difficult to believe, Grey, but I happen to enjoy my work. And I'm more than capable of looking after myself. Thank you very much.'

'I'll just bet you are,' muttered Grey. 'Excuse me for breathin'.'

Charlie stood up. 'Grey – no offence, but I think I'll pass on that drink too.'

'No,' said Jo. 'Please. Stay here. I'd much prefer it if you stayed here.'

He looked at her thoughtfully. 'OK,' he said slowly. 'If you're sure . . . I'm working tonight, but I'll call you later. I'll call you in the break.' He lent across to kiss her cheek but she quickly turned away.

'Oops,' said Grey McShane.

Charlie ignored him. He watched Jo as she made her way out of the pub and sat down again. 'You should take care with girls like that,' Grey said seriously.

'I'll have a pint of Pride then. If you're offering.'

'Aye.' He shambled off towards the bar and returned soon afterwards with a six-measure of gin and not one, but two pints of bitter. 'It's very rare that I buy anyone a drink,' he said. 'Except myself. So I thought I'd push the boat out.'

Charlie didn't laugh. He took the closest pint and gulped from it mechanically.

'I can't see what you see in her myself,' said Grey. 'I mean she's pretty, OK. A bit scrawny but then they all are. Nice smile. Nice, pert little titties . . .'

'For God's sake.'

'Don't tell me you haven't noticed.'

'It's none of your business. It's beside the bloody point.'

'Oh, she's got to you, hasn't she?' said Grey with a chuckle.

'I like her.'

'You fuckin' *love* her, you poor sod!'

'I hardly know her.'

'That's right.' To Charlie's alarm, Grey suddenly thrust an emphatic finger towards his face. 'And I'm trying to tell you Charlie, you're never going to. I see girls like that everywhere, where I go now. Scrawny and beautiful and fuckin' charmin' and full of fuckin' charmin' concern . . . Worrying so much about this, caring so fuckin' much about that. Talk, talk, talk, fuckin' chatter, chatter, chatter. With their great big bloody eyes . . . and Charlie, I'm telling you – listen to me – fuckin' *ice cold. Ice cold* little hearts, they've got.' He shivered. 'I swear, someone in the factory switched their blood for antifreeze . . .'

Charlie laughed. 'What, *all* of them?'

'Every last one. The men too.'

'So why do you spend so much time with them?'

Grey double took. Such a simple question and he didn't have an answer to it – or not an answer that he liked. He shrugged and his handsome face looked suddenly very bleak. 'They keep inviting me places,' he said.

'I don't suppose,' said Charlie, after a gloomy silence, 'this girl you're satisfying's any better than the rest?'

'Oh no she's awful. Truly *awful*.' Grey laughed. 'You know – if the newspapers and all that suddenly decided I was crap (which I've no doubt they will) I think the silly bitch wouldn't even remember my name.' He smiled at the thought. 'But who cares, eh? If her breasts were half a size smaller I don't suppose I'd remember hers.'

'Jo said you'd been in prison.'

'Aye. They like all that.'

'What was it for?'

'Robbery,' Grey lied in a dreary monotone. 'Attempted armed robbery of the Britannia Building Society in Bonnyrigg. Bonnyrigg's in Scotland.'

'I know.'

'. . . Is that all you've got to say?'

Charlie shrugged. 'What did you do that for?'

Grey looked faintly surprised. 'You ask a lot of questions,' he said mildly. '. . . It was a *girl*. That's what it was.' The look of desolation returned to him, this time with double the force. He took a gulp of his gin and very slowly placed the glass back onto the table. 'She was young and I was fuckin' stupid.'

A little later, because he wanted to leave the pub himself and didn't have the heart to leave Grey on his own while he was looking so depressed, Charlie invited him back to his flat for something to eat, probably baked beans, and afterwards to the winebar where Charlie would be playing. 'It's nothing great. Old hits, mostly. But it might cheer us up.'

'Ha!' said Grey, bounding to his feet like a child, in an instant his sprightly self once again. 'I haven't been invited back for anything but a fuck for as long as I've been in bloody England!'

'Yeah, well. If you play your cards right . . .'

Grey laughed.

'Incidentally, what happened to all my clothes?'

Jo was so desperate to feel in control again that as soon as she get back to the safety of North London and her echoey, minimalist flat, she did the first thing that came into her head. And her head, after all the wine, the disappointment, the kiss, the panic at being caught, the kiss, the wine, the damn kiss – was in a terrible state of confusion.

She called Geoff. Before she'd even put down her bag. Before the bath, before the coffee, before checking her answer machine. But he didn't pick up. Instead she left a garbled, alcohol-drenched message on his voicemail, exaggerating the extent of their friendship (they had met three times) and describing at some length her sense of personal sadness at his sudden decision to withdraw from the project. A project (she continued) which in spite of overwhelming pressure, Top Spin had been offering exclusively to him. She told Geoff that unless she heard from him first thing tomorrow morning she would feel forced to take his silence as final.

Jo conducted most business conversations with a mixture of flattery, enthusiasm and self-righteous indignation but she was usually neither drunk nor frightened. This had been a terrible performance, a caricature of her normal professional self; aggressive, transparently dishonest, and, worst of all, utterly charmless. She regretted the message the instant she put the telephone down. With a cold sweat of shame breaking out on her forehead and the beginnings of what promised to be a vicious headache, she took a couple of aspirin and headed for the bath. Seconds after getting into it, she had fallen asleep.

She was woken some time later by a gentle hand on her shoulder and somebody calling out her name.

'Charlie?' she said.

But it was Ed.

'Ed!' she leapt up, panicked but still half-asleep, splashing water onto Ed's new jacket and all over the floor. 'What are you doing? That's a nice jacket. How did you get in here? What's going on?'

He dangled a set of keys between finger and thumb. 'You weren't answering the telephone,' he said. 'I was worried.'

'What time is it?' She took the towel he offered and climbed, shivering, out of the bath. The water was cold.

'Half past nine.'

'Christ! I must have been asleep for hours!'

'I was sitting on your doorstep for most of them. Getting some *very* funny looks from your friendly minicab drivers –'

Jo smiled half-heartedly. She assumed he was lying. Sitting on doorsteps – especially hers – wasn't Ed Bailey's style.

'And then I remembered you'd lent me some keys. Ages ago. When my computer broke. So I went back to my flat and picked them up. Jo are you OK?'

Jo smiled half-heartedly once again. She realised that, for reasons she had yet to understand, they would not be

102

mentioning the fact that she'd woken up shouting another man's name. 'I'm fine,' she muttered. 'Heavy lunch. Bad day at work. But you know about that.'

She was being unusually distant towards him. Ed found he rather liked it. As he watched her drying off her perfect body with the usual brisk efficiency, slapping the fifty-pounds-a-bottle circulation enhancing, cellulite inhibiting essential oils onto the back of the thighs, he felt a desire he hadn't felt for Jo in a long time.

He was a pragmatic man who had never, in an unbroken, eighteen-year history of having enviable girlfriends, been the one to be dumped. He had no intention of changing that now. He first sensed danger several hours ago, when Charlie had followed Jo out of the shop and, Ed being Ed, he had wasted very little time. Soon after buying the donkey jacket, he made a couple of calls, and set into motion the wheels of his re-seduction.

'By the way I think we can salvage the Meals situation,' he said. 'I've just got off the phone to a couple of guys from RBC – I think they could be very useful to you. Anyway, I sold the idea to them brilliantly, if I say so myself. They're gagging to meet up.'

'Really?' She was instantly alert. 'Where are they? Are they in town?' RBC (Reality Broadcasting) was an enormous and highly successful American cable channel specialising in all programmes involving celebs. Media-savvy sophisticates in Britain liked to comment on RBC's professionalism, and laugh ironically at the high watchability factor of so much of what it produced.

'They're staying at the Rookery. I said we might hook up for a drink in the bar around half ten. Want to come? They actually sound pretty keen to get the whole thing sewn up. You know what Americans are like. If they think something's hot –' he snapped those long thin fingers, 'they want it yesterday. Not like us. They don't enjoy wasting time.'

Jo and Ed smiled warmly at one another. In the background, the telephone had started to ring. She hardly registered it. 'Ed,' she said. 'You know it's times like this, I remember why I love you. You're a magician. I think you may have saved my life.'

He took the cue, stood up from his seat on the edge of the bath, crossed over to hers, on top of the lavatory, and kissed her slowly on the lips. As she lifted her face to meet his Jo imagined the scene in her office tomorrow; *Penny charging up to her desk, Penny ranting and screaming and then Jo calmly, unresentfully waiting to explain . . .* She found she was kissing him back.

Ed unhooked the bath towel. In the sitting room, her answer machine clicked in.

She would hand Penny a sheet of A4 (An RBC headed sheet of A4) confirming their commitment to screen a behind-the-scenes-documentary-as-culturally-significiant-to-the-millennium . . .

Ed's tongue was working with lizard-like efficiency on her pretty little nipples and she was moaning politely, imagining Penny's face . . .

'Oh hi Jo,' Charlie's upper-class voice echoed noisily across the sitting room and through the open bathroom door. Ed's lizard tongue halted, but only for a fraction of a second. The message played on . . .

'. . . Just – er – checking in. Hope you're OK. I'm about to go on, so I'll call you again in the break . . .'

And on . . .

'. . . Thanks for a lovely day . . . I think – Really, I don't

104

think I've ever had such a fantastic day. Not in a long time . . .'

Ed's tongue continued its work. Jo, in an attempt to distract him, increased the volume of her appreciation twofold, threefold, then four . . .

'. . . I hope I'm not completely off course here. Did you have a good time? Slightly? You seemed to. I think you did. Anyway I'm really only calling to say I think you're wonderful. In spite of everything . . .'

Desperately she pushed Ed back on to the bathroom floor, undid his trousers, straddled him; her moans turned into yells. But the message played on.

'. . . The first song's for you. So think of me. OK? Talk later – Oh –' he chuckled. 'By the way. Grey's blowing you a kiss. He says sorry.'

Afterwards she and Ed told each other they loved each other. Jo reapplied her oils and they headed to the bedroom so she could pick out a pretty dress to wear.

'I should be keeping more of an eye on you, I think,' Ed said casually as he watched her dab highlighter onto her collar bones and pluck a single hair from the perfect arch of her right eyebrow. 'Sounds to me like that boy Charlie's got a bit of a thing for you.' He snorted, as though his next observation was a new one and an unimportant one, which he knew it wasn't. 'What an unusual voice he has. Where on earth did you discover him?'

'Oh God!' she said, laughing awkwardly. 'Isn't it outrageous?'

'Where did you say you met him?' Ed asked again.

'Friend of a friend. You don't know her. She asked me to come and watch him play. He's actually bloody talented. But his sense of career management is a joke.

She thought I might be able to do something for him. Maybe help him out a bit.'

'Not too much, I hope.' He kissed the back of her neck.

'Don't be so silly,' she said. She felt terrible; disloyal, guilty, slightly sickened by their hurried, dishonest sex. But there were the men from RBC waiting. 'I'm not interested in guys like Charlie. Honestly Ed! I'd have thought you knew me better than that!'

The meeting, in the peaceful courtyard behind the hotel conservatory, went well and ended early. The Americans had been charmed, especially by Ed – to a point which might have been embarrassing if he hadn't been delicately enjoying it so much. Ed just couldn't help selling himself, even when he didn't need to. In fact, he'd had to redirect their attention back towards Jo more than once.

But they were tired. They were still on LA time, they said and Jo, though they would never have guessed it from her own charming performance, was suffering from the hangover from hell. They did not hand her a sheet of headed A4, guaranteeing their interest in her wretched project, but they promised to courier one to her office by noon the following day, immediately before getting on the flight back to California.

Afterwards, her gratitude, as she and Ed ambled along Cowcross Street on that sultry August night, had Ed feeling uncharacteristically attentive towards her. Her gratitude and his own pleasure at a job well done, as well as the fact that he was due to leave for Scotland on Monday to start work on the McShane documentary, led Ed to take the unusual step of suggesting that they spend the whole night together, something for various reasons (Ed's 'deadlines') they hadn't done for some time. It was something Jo had long been secretly yearning for, and if his offer happened to have come too late Jo was still unwilling to admit it, even to herself. Ed was perfect for her. She knew it. Her friends knew it. Everybody knew it. Now he was apparently willing to accept it himself. She would have been a fool, she thought, not to accept the invitation.

In the morning they kissed each other goodbye and agreed to meet up again that evening. Ed was behaving as Jo had always dreamed he would, as she had always known he could. With every ounce of her formidable will, Jo suppressed almost all memories of Charlie's delicious, tender embrace and left for work convinced that she was ready to take on anyone, including Penny.

Penny's Post-its were becoming more frenzied every day. The one on Jo's desk that Friday morning read:

WHERE THE FUCK ARE YOU?
P.

She was on the telephone when Jo presented herself. She indicated for Jo to sit and continued to talk for another ten minutes. There was a problem with the Serbian cleaner, apparently, who couldn't read the instructions on the washing machine.

Jo waited patiently. If Penny could be persuaded to talk about her delicates until noon, Jo would even be able to provide her with paper-headed proof of her achievements. It was not to be. Penny slammed down her telephone eighty-five minutes too early. She glared at Jo.

'What happened to you yesterday afternoon? I must have called you thirty times.'

'I'm sorry. We had a problem with Meals. Channel Foremost withdrew their interest at the last minute –'

'I know we had a problem. Never mind Foremost.'

'And I didn't want to talk to you until I'd sorted it. Which I now have.'

Penny wasn't impressed. She tapped her simply accessorised fingers on the stainless steel cover of her Top Spin work book and looked at Jo consideringly. 'Point Number One,' she began. 'If you ever go walkabout for a whole afternoon without calling in again you can forget about having a job to come back to. Is that clear?'

'Of course. But –'

'Good. Point Number Two. As from –' she looked at her watch, 'about five to nine this morning, the Meals concert is dead. Dumped. Non-existent.'

'No!'

'The sponsors pulled the plug when Martine McClutchen said she wasn't available. They realised they just weren't going to get the artists.' She chuckled to herself. 'Everyone was saying no. Quite wisely, in my opinion, when you remember the cock-up they made of Inter-Aid.'

'But I've got RBC!'

'Not interested. You could have the Queen of Sheba for all I care. Now. We need to talk about Sip Code. Entertainment. I'm thinking something *very* new. Something crazy. It's got to make people sit up. Any ideas?'

Jo took only a moment to conceal her disappointment. Such is life in the happy-go-lucky world she moved in;

a promise today is only warm, stale air tomorrow. She would have to call the guys from RBC of course. Drum up some sort of explanation for them. Or perhaps she wouldn't bother. Perhaps they wouldn't send the confirmation letter anyway. What did it matter? They were very irrelevant now. Moving on. Pushing on. Bashing on . . .

'There's quite a buzz about magicians at the moment,' said Jo. 'I was actually thinking *naked* magicians. Apparently you can get these incredibly erotic magic shows. It could be very funny.'

'Gay or straight?'

'Well – I think you can get both.'

Penny shook her head. 'Don't like it. What else?'

'Or I thought we could get one of those Jamaican steel bands –'

'No.'

'No. Too ethnic. I'm now veering back towards some sort of performance artists. Maybe a poet. Grey Mc—'

'Poetry's boring.'

'Not Grey McShane. He's fabulous! Really sexy! He's the new –'

'People don't go to parties to listen to other people talking. Poetry is boring. What else have you got?'

'Loads,' said Jo smoothly. 'Millions of ideas. Let me just go and get my notes.'

A couple of hours later Jo was back at her desk, trying very hard not to let her mind wander back towards – Charlie's kiss; trying and failing to concentrate on her search for a band of club friendly all-female knife throwers, when Penny shuffled up. She was looking uncharacteristically sheepish.

'What was that you were saying about RBC?' she said.

'RBC?' Jo looked blank. Their letter, which had, aston-
ishingly, been delivered as promised, lay open to view
beside her. But since it was no longer relevant she hadn't
bothered to read it yet.

'Because it's on again. If you can believe it. New venue
– in *Northampton*.' She pulled a face. 'New sponsor –
fizzy health drink, also new, apparently. Fz^z. Heard of it?
We should pitch for them. Anyway, massive downsizing
operation going on but the Meals guys have got the bit
between their teeth and who am I to argue?'

'Quite right!'

'They've got no bloody artists to speak of. I mean
we're talking Latvian flautists if we're lucky on this sort
of timescale. However –'

'Absolutely!'

'They've got a whole load of money they don't know
what to do with. And you and I, Jo dear, are here
to help them spend it. Yes? So I mentioned we were
considering switching to RBC – Ah, here we are,' she
reached for the letter, 'and they're very interested. They
want to go ahead . . .' She started reading. 'So we need
to talk to Ed.'

'Ed? What's Ed got to do with it?' Penny looked at her
in amazement, until Jo remembered, quickly, that Penny
was still not quite *au courant* with the current situation.
'I mean Ed's busy.'

'Busy? He didn't look very busy yesterday. At least not
until I turned up.' A faintly lustful look passed across her
face. She smiled. 'Quite the opposite, in fact . . .'

'But that wasn't –' She stopped. Did Penny need to
know the truth? She'd lied once already. Or at any rate,
not *not* lied. She'd rushed off pretending she and 'Ed' were

late for a meeting and amazingly, so far, had managed to get away with it. Since the real Ed was now off the project, and likely to spend the next month safely hidden away in Scotland, there was no reason why Penny and he should ever meet. At which point why, she thought (and oh, how she would come to regret it) why rock the boat?

'That wasn't what?'

'Today. That was yesterday. He's busy again today.'

'And he obviously wasn't too busy to meet these guys,' she indicated the RBC letter. 'I don't know why he's always too busy to meet me. I'm beginning to wonder if I shouldn't take it personally.'

Jo laughed obligingly. 'Don't be absurd!'

'I'm joking,' said Penny. 'Of course.' She tossed the letter back onto Jo's desk. 'Can you arrange a meeting. SA, Jo?' She grinned – her creepy grin – suddenly lent over and kissed Jo on the cheek. 'You and Ed are quite some double act, aren't you?'

'Not really, no –'

'You're a star.'

'Penny –' She knew she should explain that Ed was no longer involved, that it didn't matter because RBC didn't mind, but Penny had looked so pleased with her; her unexpected kiss had brought immediate resuscitation to Jo's dream of a Top Spin partnership. Why spoil things now? Ed was a mere detail, after all. She would tell Penny about his absence as soon as she had thought of a suitable substitute. With a faint sigh, Jo finally picked up the unread letter. And realised at once that the situation was more complicated than she thought.

A misunderstanding. The idiots at RBC had clearly not been listening. The number of times they mentioned Ed

Bailey in their letter, anyone would have thought they'd fallen in love with him. Whichever way she read it, and however many times, it was obvious that their confirmation was conditional on his agreeing to be involved. *But why?* Hadn't she made herself clear? And hadn't they actually admitted they'd never seen anything he'd done? With an almighty sigh Jo chucked the letter onto her URGENT pile and stared gloomily into space. Back to square one, then. How bloody *boring*. She felt a wave of fear, followed by a wave of total inertia. Highly unusual.

Now what was she meant to do?

She had been sitting there for some time, quite unproductive, trying – still trying – in spite of all her new trouble, not to think about that kiss. She'd been flicking through the tabloids, in fact, briefly and happily diverted by a story about a teenage acquaintance of Prince William who'd tried to sell a picture of him on the lavatory, when Charlie's call came through. She recognised the number and forced herself to switch it to voicemail.

The message (which she played back at once, and then found herself storing for indefinite reference) informed her that Charlie was going to the country, and that he probably wouldn't be back for the rest of the week. His father was sick and the farm needed his attention. He left a number and apologised for disappearing so abruptly. He asked her to call.

She needed to ring him anyway, she told herself. To apologise for dumping him with Grey last night, and for telling so many lies in agnès b. She needed to ring him just to say she hoped his father was all right. She wanted

112

to ring him. But she couldn't. She didn't trust herself. She and Ed were back. The formidable double act. The ideal couple, with just a couple of business problems to sort out. Charlie had to be forgotten.

In her hurry to be reassured that he was indeed her perfect partner she had forgotten to disguise her telephone number, so when she called Ed's mobile it was switched to divert. She left him a message, full of ironic humour, telling him how their efforts with the RBC men were in danger of backfiring, thanks to Ed's charm. 'But not to worry,' she told him. 'I know you can't do it. I'll sort it out. I swear, though, those guys have *fallen in love* with you! Not-that-there's-anything-wrong-with-that . . . Oh. Which reminds me. Bit of a confession to make. I think I may have left a slightly pissed message on Geoff's answer machine last night. I hope I haven't mucked things up for you too much.'

He called back at once, sounding very tense. 'What did you say to him?'

'Oh God. I can't remember. But you saw the state I was in. I think I may have been a bit rude.'

'Have you spoken to him this morning?'

'No!'

'Well don't. I'll call him myself, yeah? And next time,' she heard him talking through his teeth, so he must have been smiling, 'you might find it advisable to wait until you're sober before making business calls. Especially when they're to *my* friends!'

She laughed, doggedly upbeat. 'By the way,' she said, 'are you still on for this evening? I thought I might get a few people round for dinner. Give you a send-off for Monday.'

'Yeah?' He sounded unenthusiastic. 'Who were you thinking of?'

'Well – Mel. To congratulate her on being in your documentary. I haven't seen her for ages. And I'd really like to ask Jenny and Geoff, to apologise to Geoff, really.'

'I can tell you straight away. Geoff's completely whacked. He won't want to come.'

'But I'd like to ask them, at least. I feel so bad about that stupid message.'

'Just let me talk to him first.'

'Of course, Ed. If that's what you want . . . And then I thought we could try Sasha and Tracy. They're in town at the moment, I know, because I saw Tracy in South Molton Street a couple of days ago. Loaded down with shopping.'

Ed smiled. Tracy, a former make-up artist, was the dimwitted wife of the third most exciting film producer in Britain. She'd hooked up with him soon after his first film had been a hit, squeezed out a couple of children, and spent the following two-and-a-half years killing time and growing sour in increasingly expensive clothes shops. She had snubbed both Jo and Ed on separate occasions and neither of them – in fact nobody – held her in very high esteem. However, for the time being she was Sasha's wife, and for the time being Sasha was the kind of guy ideal couples like Jo and Ed bent over backwards to have to dinner.

'Well,' said Ed. 'If *they're* around.'

Sasha was free. So the party went ahead. Jo called up her favourite restaurant and, having reeled off the guest list, negotiated herself a token discount, which made her feel important. An amazingly simple dinner involving mint-marinated Asian beef salad, zucchini flowers and mini mango galettes, would be delivered to her flat by seven-thirty that evening. Guests would be offered Angostura vodkas to ease the wheels of their clever conversation and at some point during the evening, between elegant name-drops and barely discernible put-downs, they would touch on all matters relevant to the day. The overprivileged teenager with the lavatory picture would be condemned, and then someone would pretend not to know what Prince William's brother was called and then someone, or two, would slip off for a line or two of cocaine . . .

Except for the fact that Mel had turned up with an uninvited Grey in tow (making the hostess understandably tense) it was all going remarkably well. Supper was delicious and more or less finished. Tracy and Mel were in the lavatory with Mel's wallet, and Sasha, in his flat South London accent, was delighting the table with a pointless anecdote about domestic life *chez* Guy and Madonna Ritchie.

But then Grey, who'd been strangely well-behaved until that moment, decided he'd had enough. 'I'm sorry not to see Charlie with us tonight, Jo,' he bellowed, winking flamboyantly first at her and then at Ed.

'So, go on,' Jo carefully ignored him. 'Did Madonna find it amusing?'

'Well,' said Sasha, 'she looked at me like I was bonkers! But you know, Madge is a bright girl. She knew what I was saying.'

'These guys have so many people telling them they're fabulous,' said Geoff's girlfriend Jenny, who advised on policy for the Labour Party and was apparently trying to get pregnant. 'I'm sure she appreciated some straight talking for once.'

'That's not what was important to me,' Sasha said. 'The point is – isn't it bizarre how emotional people get about their bloody cars?'

Ha ha ha! went the successful guests.

Except Grey. 'Jo, darlin'. I don't understand what you're doing with all these ponces when you've got a lovely fellow like Charlie wantin' to be your friend.'

'Would anyone like some coffee?' said Jo.

'Don't tell me you've gone and *dumped* him, you stupid cow?'

She cast around for a distraction but everyone had fallen silent. They were waiting for her reply. 'He's in the country, I think,' she said lamely. 'His dad's sick.'

'So, you've spoken to him?'

'Yes. No – Bloody hell.' She pretended to laugh. 'Grey. It's none of your business.'

'But you like him, don't you?' Jo didn't respond. She looked extremely uncomfortable. Grey smiled wickedly. 'Go on, darlin'. Tell me you like him! I *know* you do! You *know* I know you do!'

'Not, I think,' Ed said smoothly, casually lighting himself a cigarette, 'as much as she appears to like me.'

'Meanwhile I'm agog,' said Sasha. 'Who *is* this nice man who's so amazingly much nicer than the rest of us?'

'Charlie *Max-well Mc-Donald*,' said Ed, his clever voice indicating light disdain for the length of surname, among many other things, 'is a little bloke who went to *Eton*, Grey tells me, who my girlfriend seems convinced is destined to be the next Robbie Williams!'

Sasha looked a bit shifty.

'Not *the* Charlie Maxwell McDonald!' said his wife, tripping in from the lavatory at that moment, with much renewed vigour. 'The guy we saw singing in that pub?'

'What pub?' mumbled Sasha.

'He was gorgeous! He came rushing over to Sasha after I'd been ogling him all night. D'you remember Sasha? Evidently they were at *school* together!' She rolled back on her heels, laughing. 'Sasha was *very* unfriendly. Weren't you Sasha?'

'No more unfriendly than I have to be, these days . . .' Sasha said stiffly. 'And actually I hardly knew him. In fact.'

Tracy snorted.

Geoff said 'actually' in a posh voice and sniggered. Sasha glared at them both.

'That guy wasn't after anything,' said Tracy. 'Don't give me that old crap! He was giving the game away. Sasha doesn't like to admit he's really a posh boy, do you, darling? Plus he was so bloody gorgeous – I bet all the girls always fancied him more than you! And that sort of thing's very hard to get over . . .'

'Did you really go to Eton, Sasha?' said Mel, tottering in behind Tracy, pausing at the door for a final nose-wipe before rejoining the party. 'That's amazing! I never realised you were posh! What's it actually like then?'

'I hardly see how that's relevant,' snapped Sasha.

Things were going wrong. 'Now then,' said Jo. 'Coffee!'

But Grey had only just begun. 'So, Jo,' he said, 'Geoff's been telling me about your little concert. It sounds like a very worthy cause if I may say so.'

'Thank you, Grey . . . Actually,' she couldn't help adding, 'I'm surprised Geoff was remotely interested.'

'But he would have been, darling',' said Grey, 'if only he'd known. He wasn't given a chance.'

'Grey, my old mate,' Ed laughed unnaturally loudly. 'What mischief are you trying to cause now?'

'Fuck off, Bailey. I'm not your old mate and don't fuckin' interrupt me.'

'Not that it matters, Grey,' said Jo, smiling, conscious that there was unpleasantness afoot and trying desperately to keep her tone light, 'but I think you're a teeny bit drunk.'

'Of course I'm fuckin' drunk. I'm just telling you, for your own sake – Geoff, tell Jo what you just told me about her stupid bloody concert. Go on! Hurry up! She wants to know.'

'Well . . .' said Geoff, looking very sheepish.

'He's trying to tell you he knows fuckin' fuck all about it. Because until yesterday he'd never even heard of it!'

'I must admit. Your message did – confuse me.'

Ed laughed uneasily. 'Geoff's obviously got a very short memory.'

'Oh bollocks!' snapped Grey. 'Why can't you tell the truth for once in your pathetic life?'

'Sorry mate,' mumbled Geoff, 'but on this occasion I'm gonna actually have to second that.'

'Ed?'

'What does it matter?' Ed snapped defensively. 'I got you the RBC guys didn't I? What's the fuss about?'

'But that was a fluke!' said Jo.

'Of course it wasn't! Nothing is a fluke in this business. And I mean that. No such thing as fluke.'

'Of course it was! For God's sake they barely knew you.'

An idea occurred to her. 'And you probably wouldn't even have bothered if you hadn't seen me with Charlie!'

To Jo, it was the ultimate treachery. Ed, the clever, reformed Ed, who'd kissed her so affectionately this morning, and again so affectionately tonight, whose babies she had been attempting to imagine all afternoon, had never cared about her career at all! He'd been doing what he always did and what she'd always admired him for doing so well; sniffing around for the best story, lying to anyone who bothered to listen, keeping his options open. Why had she been so vain as to imagine that her own precious little project might have been treated as an exception?

Ed looked at her, saw that she was about to cry in front of the third most exciting film producer in Great Britain, and felt a wave of irritation. 'For Christ's sake, Jo. You should know by now not to put all your eggs in one basket . . .'

'But we're – I'm your –'

'I begin to think,' said Sasha, leaping at the chance to remove himself from a place where he'd been made to feel less than marvellous, 'that we're surplus to requirements. Trace are you about ready? Jo, thank you for a *truly fantastic* evening . . .'

After Sasha left, of course, Jo's party lost all its edge. Mel's suggestion that they should move on to the Medicine Bar was greeted with enthusiasm by everyone except Jo, who said she wanted to go to bed.

'Come on, Jo,' said Mel, pulling her aside. 'Why are you so *boring* these days? I don't get it.'

'I'm not boring, I'm tired.'

'Is it – the Ed thing? Because if it is the Ed thing, then I have to say, Jo, I do think you're overreacting. Like Ed said. We *all* know what it's like out there. You can't expect people to sacrifice their own careers, you know? Even if they're –'

'Lovers.'

'Exactly,' said Mel, missing the intended irony completely and happy, now that she had fulfilled her official role as Jo's friend, to edge back towards the group. 'So, come on. Come out with us.'

'I'm tired, Mel. I want to go to bed.'

A few minutes later they headed off, one jabbering mass, to open negotiations with the cab drivers opposite. Ed lingered behind.

'I hate to leave you with all this clearing up.'

'I'll be fine,' Jo said coldly. 'I thought you hated the Medicine Bar.'

'Not always.'

'Not when the alternative is talking to me.'

He smiled. 'Don't be silly,' he said, and leant forward to kiss her.

'Fuck off, Ed.'

He recoiled. She never spoke to him like that. 'D'you know I'm actually wondering,' he said coldly, 'if this relationship doesn't need a bit of a rethink.'

She was about to argue, her instinct to make things pleasant kicking in even then. But he'd already left the room. On Monday Ed would be off to Scotland. It was unlikely, she realised, that he would take her call before then.

NEW YOU RULE NUMBER FIVE: Remember guys, those all-important doors of opportunity are gonna stay locked tight if you don't ACT NICE!! But the good news is NICE doesn't cost a dime! It's a no-time, no-money, do-nothin' 'activity'! It's a win-win-win conversational thing! Remember: organic veg prices are OBSCENE. Property prices are OBSCENE. The *Daily Mail*, Railtrack safety measures, hunting with hounds, paparazzi photographers, anyone richer than you are . . . they're ALL OBSCENE, OK? But so's 'BEING JUDGMENTAL', yeah? So take care! There's a fab list identifying WHICH is WHICH on page 345. Look at it CAREFULLY before shooting your mouth off! . . . And don't panic! Basically guys, this is the EASIEST rule of them all! We need to SEE you FEEL. Yeah? Cos when it comes to hearts 'Actual Size' DOESN'T matter! It's the ACCESSORIES we're all gonna be looking at!

A BIG, BIG HEART

The morning was a long time in coming, but when it did Joanna Smiley (forever the fighter) had devised what she called a P of A, the first and final stages of which involved welding on her most cheerful demeanour, telephoning Charlie and politely but determinedly inviting herself to stay. It hadn't even occurred to her to wonder, as she'd lain awake, dry eyed and miserable, counting the minutes before she could speak to him, whether Charlie's own 'P of A' (plan of action to the non-Yous) might possibly be inconvenienced by her own. All she knew was that she missed him. She wanted to get out of London. And she desperately needed time to think.

But when she suggested coming down to stay even she, so wrapped in misery and so focused on her goal, couldn't fail to notice his lack of heartfelt enthusiasm. 'Trouble is,' he said, 'you might find my father a bit difficult.'

'Oh God. I'm sorry. I should have asked. How is he? Is he any better?'

'He's fine. Much better. I'm just saying . . . he's quite particular about things.'

'I can handle that!'

'I won't be able to look after you much. Our farm

manager's on holiday. Plus Dad needs a lot of attention. The horses haven't been exercised – Do you ride?'

She laughed. 'God, no.'

'Shame. We could have taken them out cubbing. There's a meet tomorrow.'

'What's cubbing?'

'It's – sort of early season hunting. But now I come to think of it you probably wouldn't approve.'

'I certainly would not!'

'An-y-way,' he said warily; uncharacteristically warily. She should have listened. 'So, I'm going to be pretty busy. And my dad can be terrible. He's very opinionated ... I tend to ignore it, but I've got a feeling you might find it more difficult.'

'Oh! I *love* a good argument!'

'Yes but he doesn't.'

'I'm good with old men.'

'Maybe not this one.'

That was when it finally came to her, through the fog of her own upbeat determination, that he was trying to say no. He didn't want her to come – and she couldn't bear it. Her jovial shield evaporated and with it all pretence that she could possibly survive if he refused. To her great shame, she burst into tears.

Charlie came to fetch her at Tiverton station that afternoon, wearing green wellington boots, a filthy Barbour jacket and a ludicrous Farmer Higgins hat. He was leaning casually against a row of suitcase trolleys reading a copy of the *Sun*; hardly the image of Jo's perfect knight, but she was shocked by the effect he had on her. She was about to bound up to him, but at the last minute she lost her nerve. She felt quite shy all of a sudden.

He must have noticed her out of the corner of his eye because he glanced up to see her standing there, looking unusually hesitant . . . and beautiful and hopeful and full of life . . . But she hadn't even explained the cause of her tears over the telephone. All he knew was that she was coming to see him because something in her other life had gone wrong. She wanted comfort, he suspected, and an ego boosting shag on the side. Now, Charlie was an easy-going man, rarely troubled by personal vanity, and under normal circumstances he would have been happy to oblige. But there was something about Jo (and Grey was wrong, it wasn't her coldness) which made him hesitate. He knew, because he'd watched her, how adept she was at appearing to give, while actually giving nothing at all. And, of course, he would have been a fool not to notice she was spoilt. But these things didn't matter to him. They were unimportant when compared to everything else, and Charlie thought Jo was amazing. He didn't want to be just a recuperative fling, someone she would be embarrassed about later. He wanted more. And he had decided he would make no move on her (nor respond to any of hers) until he knew – if he ever did – that his feelings for her were at least partially reciprocated.

So. Their greeting was filled with unspoken tension. Jo offered him her moisturised lips and he ignored them; didn't, in fact, attempt to kiss her at all. He put an arm around her shoulders, gave her a friendly squeeze, took her case and led her to the car. Or to a dirty Land Rover, to be more precise.

*　　*　　*

'What did you get up to the other night then?' Charlie asked Jo. 'I pictured you, drinking mint tea and doing 2,500 sit-ups as penitence for our lovely lunch. But I called you a couple of times. You can't have been in . . .'

'I don't seem to be able to get the seat-belt to work,' she said evasively.

So, Charlie told Jo about the evening he'd spent with Grey instead. It was in gratitude for the baked beans that Grey had set himself up as chief cheerleader during the first half of Charlie's act. During the second half, he'd grown so overexcited he'd had to be thrown out. Afterwards, Charlie found him lying on a bench outside, too drunk to speak. He'd taken him home and given him coffee and Grey had wound up spending the night on Charlie's sofa.

'He told me last night you were much nicer than all my other friends.'

'Did he!' chuckled Charlie. (So she hadn't been alone with Ed, then.) 'Poor old sod. I actually feel a bit sorry for him.'

'Grey McShane?'

'Something's making him miserable.'

'He's a poet,' said Jo complacently. 'Poets are always miserable.'

'Well, perhaps he should think about a change of profession.'

Forty-five minutes later they drew up outside a small cottage. Charlie had to drop something off, he said. He would only be a minute. But then an old man appeared, leaned an arm against the frame of his front door and immediately launched into a lengthy description of the pike in the General's river. The pike had eaten all the trout, he said. Nobody had caught a trout all summer and sales of fishing permits had plummeted. After a few minutes (they looked so picturesque, she thought; the younger man and the old, chewing the cud, discussing nature), Jo decided to join them.

'Ha!' said the old man, 'we've got a spare pair of hands now. Shall we do it?'

'Absolutely!' said Jo, unconsciously adopting the matey enthusiasm she always used when communicating with those who were fractionally less equal than others. 'How can I help?'

'Actually, Jo, I don't think,' Charlie grinned, 'you're going to want to get very involved in this.'

The old man chuckled maliciously. 'Ladies don't tend to enjoy this sort of thing.'

'Ah, but not all "ladies" are the same, you know!'

'Honestly, Jo . . .' But she looked very determined. 'Well – please yourself.' With a shrug, he ambled to the back of the Land Rover and opened the doors. On the floor, lying on newspaper and, if not covered, then certainly peppered with flies, lay the skinned but unbutchered carcasses of two dead sheep, heads still attached and empty eye sockets staring blindly towards the fields that had once been their home.

Poor Jo, who'd grown up in Fulham. It wasn't in the least what she'd expected.

'You take the head then, Madam,' said the old man in delight.

'I, er –' She took a couple of steps backwards.

'Ha Ha Ha! These modern girls! Think everything comes ready wrapped in cellophane, don't they? Come on then, Charles. I'll take the top one, and you follow me in . . . I think,' he shouted as he disappeared through the front door, 'I'll just leave them in the back room for tonight.'

Charlie chuckled quietly. 'I should have warned you,' he whispered. 'His wife eloped with a school dinner lady and he's been a bit peculiar ever since. I sort of hoped you'd stay in the car.'

Charlie's father's house was grander than she had expected. It was very handsome; a redbrick Queen Anne manor house, covered in old wisteria and set in a large landscaped park. It must have had at least fifteen windows at the front. Jo didn't like to count. Not, she reminded herself, that there was any reason why such a large house should have intimidated her. Except it did. As the car swept up the long drive she couldn't help wishing she was back in London, on her own territory, somewhere smarter but less threatening, like Soho House.

To make matters worse, a slight chill had settled between Jo and her host. Jo had been made to feel a fool about the sheep's heads. She was bewildered by Charlie's lack of ardour, and in the face of it, all the more ashamed of having begged to come and stay with him. She'd felt an urge to redress the balance, to try and reestablish herself as a serious, responsible human being. 'Those carcasses,' she had said, as the old car rumbled through sun dappled lanes that might, if only she'd remembered to look, have helped her to feel more peaceful, 'are exactly the sort of thing that give British farming a bad name. They're a walking death sentence for anyone stupid enough to eat them.'

'They're hardly walking,' Charlie had said mildly.

'It's no wonder we get things like foot and mouth.'

'Jo. Come on. You don't know anything about it.'

'Yes I do! Don't be so bloody patronising.'

He hadn't bothered to reply until the car came to a halt in front of the house. But then he'd glanced across at her, noticed the uncertainty in her face and immediately felt sorry. 'Don't worry,' he said. 'There's no lamb on the menu tonight, I promise. It's Friday, so the General has to have fish.'

'Thank God,' she said.

'And you're quite right, they looked completely disgusting.'

She smiled. 'I suppose dead sheep normally do.'

Charlie switched off the engine and a wonderful peace descended on them. He looked out at the imposing house and the acres of well-tended gardens and tried to imagine how they might appear to someone for the first time. It occurred to him how little she knew about his life down here and simultaneously how very much he wanted to tell her about it. 'The old man's called Mr Gunner,' he said. 'He does something repulsive with the heads, I've never dared to ask what exactly, but they end up in glass cases all over his house. So it's become a sort of tradition. He gets a cottage and a regular supply of illegal heads, with sheep bodies attached, which I presume he eats, and we get regular bulletins on why he's completely failed to look after our trout.'

'Do trout need much looking after?' she said vaguely. The answer couldn't have interested her but it was so lovely in this quiet car, just the two of them, friends again, with the early evening sun, the distant sound of lowing cows and the cooling engine clicking gently. She would have discussed trout care for hours if it could delay the moment of moving.

He was describing the trout hatcheries that he'd built in the East Wood a couple of years ago and was about to move on to discuss problems with the hatchery water filters, when he noticed the glaze setting over her eyes. He chuckled. 'Am I boring you?'

'A bit.' She laughed. 'But it doesn't matter. It's so lovely here . . . By the way I've got something for you.' She reached for her suitcase. 'To say thank you for letting me invite myself to stay. And for buying me lunch on Thursday. And for not blowing my cover when I was telling all those lies about you to Ed. And . . . I don't know . . .' She watched him tearing back the agnès b paper and suddenly wished she'd brought him something less extravagant. He would think she was showing off.

'Ha!' he said, pulling out two shirts and some elegant, mustard coloured trousers. 'I thought I'd seen the last of these!'

'I couldn't really get everything.' Jo smiled.

'I hope not!'

'So. You still like them?'

'What? Of *course*! Jo I love them! Thank you!' She'd thought they might kiss at that point. She leant across the handbrake in anticipation but Charlie didn't seem to notice. Instead he shook off his jacket, pulled his T-shirt over his head and revealed, without the slightest warning, a torso of breathtaking, movie star perfection.

'I'll wear this for dinner,' he said, undoing the buttons of his new black shirt. 'D'you think I can wear it with these jeans? . . . Jo?'

But she wasn't listening. The sight of his sunburned chest had, once again, sent all her careful urban training to the dogs.

'Jo?' he said looking at her, smiling. Because it was pretty obvious what she was thinking.

'Mmm?'

He pulled on the shirt. 'Like this? Or shall I wear the new trousers?'

'With the – er. Like that. Definitely,' she said desperately. 'Looks brilliant. Amazing.'

He made a polite attempt to examine himself in the rear-view mirror. 'It's great,' he said. 'Thank you, Jo. I look so employable now, my poor father won't even recognise me.' Again, she leant forward to be kissed and again he disappointed her. 'Come on. I'll show you round before it gets dark. Dad can wait another half-hour for dinner.'

He showed her the park, and the two beloved old Highland cows that he and his father kept as pets – yet another extravagance, he said, which they couldn't afford. Charlie, with the help of Mr Tarr, the farm manager, had taken over the running of the estate soon after Georgie died and had been surprised to discover that it was heavily in debt. He'd sold off several pieces of land to pay the bulk of the bills but he hadn't the heart to demand that his father, at such a late and lonely stage in his life, substantially alter his style of living. He would continue selling, he told Jo, until his father's death. After that there would have to be big changes.

'But it's your inheritance!' said Jo. 'You've no idea how long he'll go on living!'

Charlie shrugged. 'It's his estate.'

'But why don't you just explain to him?'

'I can't,' said Charlie. 'I don't want to. I don't see any point.'

He led her through the rose garden, and the herb garden,

past the kitchen garden to the stable yard. The old loose boxes, with only two horses in them, were emptier now than they had been in years. Charlie patted both horses affectionately. He would take them both out first thing in the morning. 'Before you're up,' he said to Jo. 'Don't worry. I promise I won't leave you alone with my father.'

'He can't be that bad. Old men never scare me.'

Charlie considered whether he could avoid what he was about to say. But it was not a coincidence that he never brought anyone home any more and it would have been unfair, he thought, not to warn her of what lay ahead. It was why he hadn't wanted her to come down in the first place. 'I've told him you're coming and I know he wants to try,' he said slowly. 'But I'm afraid it's girls of Georgie's age he's particularly bad about.' Charlie's attempt at a reassuring smile only emphasised his lack of hope in the situation. 'I'm just saying, try not to take it personally. It's not you, it's . . .'

'Poor guy,' said Jo. 'Poor old guy.' In a flash of spontaneity she put her arms around his neck and kissed him.

Again, and with great will power, he managed not to respond. He gave her another friendly squeeze and quickly disentangled himself. 'Grey McShane,' he observed mildly, 'says girls like you had their blood replaced with antifreeze in the factory.'

'I hope he's not comparing me to that silly bitch he's shagging.'

'I thought she was your best friend.'

'And I thought he was her lover.' (He laughed.) 'Bloody hell, what am I saying? I adore Mel. This country air is making me too honest.'

'It wouldn't be such a bad thing,' he muttered.

They had come to a halt on a grassy slope beside the General's troutless river. It was such a beautiful evening. They sat down and immediately fell silent, listening to the water and to each other's breathing. For a moment Jo forgot to worry about why she was there, why Charlie didn't seem to want her, why she so badly wanted him, and for a moment Charlie stopped reminding himself she was only after a diverting fling, and they were happy together.

'I saw Ed last night.'

'Oh. I wondered . . . Did he ask about me?'

'Yes he did.'

'And what did you say?'

'I – um.' It was because of the way he looked at her, with so little judgment. Or perhaps it was in the air. But she found herself saying more than she would have liked. 'I just went on lying, Charlie. And then so did he . . . And now I don't think either of us wants to keep lying any more.'

'Oh.' He thought about it for a moment. 'You can't be a bit more specific?'

She smiled. She thought she'd never been more specific in her life. 'I mean . . . what I mean is . . . I don't . . .' God, this was difficult. Her defences were so sophisticated and so firmly in place that any attempt to rummage beyond them to her heart caused, among other symptoms, an uncomfortable gagging sensation at the back of the throat. She struggled to overcome it and to find the right words, and finally came up with a compromise. 'I don't *love* him.'

'Well that's good,' said Charlie. 'I didn't much like the look of him myself.'

'And I . . . And I . . . Charlie . . .' She looked at him in desperation but he offered nothing to help. 'The point is . . .' He waited. 'The point is . . .' She was never going to get to it, and the realisation suddenly made him laugh. His will power was evaporating with every second she hesitated. He leant forward to kiss her, but she leapt back.

It was the laugh, at such a crucial moment, which ruined it. For him to have laughed just then, when she was feeling so vulnerable, seemed to her incomprehensibly cruel. Her fragile pride was wounded. She felt humiliated.

'What?' she snapped. 'What's so funny? Why are you laughing at me? I wasn't saying anything funny.'

'I wasn't laughing!' he laughed again. 'I was just – happy – you had a point.'

'It wasn't meant to be a *funny* point,' she said. She could feel tears stinging at the back of her eyes. 'Why are you always mocking me? Why does everyone think I'm such a bloody joke?'

'I don't!'

'I was trying to be serious.'

Just then the sound of the dinner gong echoed across the park, and the moment was wasted. They headed back towards the house, both feeling sad and lonely and faintly foolish.

Any residue of summer light had been blocked out by heavy velvet curtains in the General's gloomy dining room. It was lit by a mixture of candles and ugly strip lights, positioned to highlight the portraits on the walls. Charlie, it appeared, was the unlikely product of a long line of lugubrious looking military gentlemen. The General, who would no doubt be the last to excel in the tradition, sat beneath a portrait of himself, at the head of a large mahogany table, glowering at his plate.

'You're late,' he said. 'And Mrs Webber's gone gaga. She's forgotten it's Friday.' He nodded at the lamb chops in front of him. 'Unless *I'm* mad. Does that look like salmon to you?'

'Looks more like a lamb chop,' said Charlie. 'How peculiar. I hope she's all right.'

'Poor woman. This may be the final siren. Perhaps we should persuade her to see someone.'

'Dad, this is Jo Smiley.'

'How d'you do?' He offered her a hand, but he didn't stand up.

'I mentioned she was coming down.'

'Yes, yes. Of course you did. Help yourself to some lamb, if you'd like it.' And then to Charlie, 'Unless she's a vegetarian.'

'Not at all!' said Jo, bravely. 'Nothing I like more than a bit of home-grown lamb.' She exchanged glances with Charlie and made her way to the side table, where the chops and an array of dreary looking vegetables were laid out on silver dishes.

'That shirt makes you look like a wop, Charles. Is it new?'

'Does it?' said Charlie mildly. 'It's supposed to make me look like a highly desirable potential employee. It comes from one of the most expensive shops I've ever been into. Jo gave it to me.'

'Very kind of her. But I don't care what shop it came from. People in black shirts look like poofters or fascist wops ... which I suppose,' he added, after a moment's

134

confused reflection, 'is all anyone wants to employ these days. God knows why.'

'Hard-ly!' Jo said brightly, sitting herself neatly beside him. 'I think you'll find "wops" of any political – or sexual – persuasion still find it very hard to get work in Britain, even today. Sadly, people's attitudes haven't changed that much. Not when you scratch the surface.'

He asked her to pass the mint sauce.

'Jo works for a public relations company in London,' said Charlie. 'She's been giving me a lot of *career* advice. Which is very helpful.'

'We're trying,' said Jo, aware of the General's obsession with his son's professional life, thinking it was something they had in common, and keen to impress upon him her intelligence and usefulness, 'to approach things a lot more strategically. I suggested he needed to make his overall *image* a little more employer-friendly.'

The General grunted. He thought it sounded ghastly, but he didn't like to offend. The girl obviously meant well – if what she said meant anything at all. Which he doubted.

'Whole lot of journalists camped outside the Whalley-Bakers this evening,' he said suddenly. 'The idiot boy's in hiding up there. Nobody wants a picture of the Prince on the crapper, I'm pleased to say. But they do want a picture of the Whalley-Baker boy. And now they've all turned on him, silly ass. Annabel can't get out to feed the horses. So I sent Sam up. Absolute bloody mayhem up there, apparently.'

'D'you mean you know him?' said Jo.

'You work in this wicked business,' said the General, oblivious to the distaste on her face. 'Couldn't you help him out?'

'I'm not sure he deserves it.'

'I didn't say he did,' said the General. 'But we all make mistakes, don't we? They're under siege up there. The boy's sitting in his room in tears.'

'They're bullies,' Charlie said with sudden bitterness. He was thinking of the small handful of journalists who had parked outside his own front door nine months earlier. They hadn't even been particularly abusive, but their dimwitted, insistent presence had still revolted him. 'Someone should open a hostel so the people the press are tormenting that week can hide away until it's over. Everyone would know where they were and nobody would be able to get at them. It would be the perfect revenge.'

'You'd get a very funny mixture of inmates,' said Jo, 'lots of poofters, probably. And unemployable wops. Don't know how your father would deal with them.'

The General chuckled. 'But we'd have right of veto. We could turn most of them away.'

'Everyone except the ones who went to public school, I suppose?'

'Absolutely! Quite right!'

'He's being funny,' said Charlie wearily. 'Aren't you Dad? He's trying to get a rise.'

'Well he's succeeding,' said Jo dryly. She had come to the table full of pity for the old man, with every intention of causing him nothing but pleasure. But his opinions were too offensive. Ed would have taken him to task by now. So would Melanie. Her own failure to do it was beginning to make her feel inadequate. 'I don't actually think he's very funny.'

Infuriatingly, the General chuckled again. He was beginning to take quite a shine to the little impostor. She spoke up for herself. She was pretty. And she rose to the bait so well. It had been a long while since he'd spent time with an attractive woman and he'd forgotten what a pleasure it could be. He looked across at her warmly, but she didn't notice. All she'd heard was that chuckle. She was trying not to lose her temper.

But perhaps, thought the General, noticing how unhappy she looked, he was being too hard on her. She was only a girl, after all, and the first girl Charlie had brought home in months. He had an urge to make her feel more welcome. 'Does your friend hunt, by any chance?' he asked Charlie. 'There's a meet tomorrow at the Friendship. You could both go out. Might be a good day.'

As a reflection of the General's misjudgment of his pretty guest, it was quite remarkable. But there was another problem. Charlie had never got around to telling Jo the details of his sister's death; they had been quite well publicised at the time, and he hadn't wanted to hear Jo's opinions any more than he had wanted to hear those of the *Daily Telegraph*, nine months earlier. Opinions, in his opinion, achieved very little. They certainly didn't ease the loss.

Jo didn't know that Georgie had been out hunting the day she was killed. Charlie had only ever told her it was a riding accident. But it hadn't been an accident, not really. As she and her father had approached that fence an anti-bloodsports campaigner had leapt up and smashed a giant cymbal in her horse's face. The horse had shied, and the rest is history. Nobody ever discovered who was responsible. The General had been convinced it was a youngish woman, about Georgie's age, somebody fairly ignorant of how things worked. After all, if the horse had shied to the right, she could well have been killed herself.

Afterwards, some of the campaigners sent a wreath to the funeral, and the majority stayed away from that hunt for the rest of the season. But whatever they thought of the tragedy amongst themselves, they were unwilling to send one of their own to jail for it, and nobody was ever prosecuted. The General still received gloating hate mail through the post.

Jo knew none of this. She only knew that she'd let the General off too lightly with the poofters comment. And the wops comment. And the mocking laugh. And the fact that he was trying to bait her.

'To be frank with you, General,' she said, 'hunting isn't my big thing. It may strike you as peculiar but we simple townsfolk don't *tend* to find killing fun.'

'Good God!' said the General. 'I was only offering –'

'Jo!' said Charlie. 'Shut up. Please. You don't know what you're talking about.'

'That's the second time you've said that to me, Charlie. You've no idea if I know what I'm talking about!'

'Believe me. You don't. So just shut up. For once.'

'Why? Because I happen to prefer it if animals are treated humanely? It's obviously the difference between us, Charlie. Call me an idiot, but I don't happen to be in favour of spending my leisure-time indulging in sadism and murder!'

Charlie laughed. Not because it was funny. Because he could see his father's face had changed colour and because Jo's sudden, noisy moral outrage seemed vaguely manu-factured and completely incongruous in the dreary dining room. 'Jo,' he said. 'Of course I don't think you're an idiot.'

But all she heard was that laugh. Again. 'Don't – Charlie – *don't* patronise me!'

'Charles,' and now the General was laughing, too. 'Is she being awfully rude? Or am I being old-fashioned?'

'She's being rude,' said Charlie.

'*Me* rude?' she said angrily. 'You two sit here complacently in your enormous mansion, making judgments about "poofters" and "wops" and *I'm* the rude one?' She slapped down her knife and fork. 'I can't even believe I'm eating with a guy who thinks I – *I* – might actually *want* to go hunting – It makes me so ashamed. And you know why?'

'Just shut up, Jo!' said Charlie. 'You've said enough.'

'Because I despise hunting. If I went out with you people tomorrow, I'd be the one holding the banner!'

'Jo, *shut up.*'

'Doing my level best to frighten the bloody life out of your horses.'

'Dad, I'm so sorry –'

'Because I *hate* people who go hunting. I *hate* them! And I *rejoice* every time I read about one of them getting hurt. It gives them a taste of their own snotty-nosed medicine . . .'

She stopped. Slowly, terribly, she began to absorb the effect of what she'd said. She began to put it all together . . . the name, Charlie's stupid double-barreled name, which had always sounded so familiar, the girl with the catering company, something about a cymbal . . . She'd read about it, vaguely, months ago. Of course.

She looked from Charlie to the General back to Charlie again. The General's head was bent down towards the table, his shoulders hunched. He was covering his ears, trying to block out the noise – though the room was silent. She watched, wordlessly, as her world moved into slow motion. Charlie was trying to pull his father to his feet. But the old man was shaking. His whole body was shaking. Jo didn't know if he was crying, or choking or –

'Sorry,' she whispered.

'Call an ambulance,' Charlie said.

'I'm so sorry . . .'

'Call a fucking ambulance. And then get out of here. Please. You can call a taxi at the same time.'

'Of course. Of course . . .' She stumbled out into the vast, dark hall. 'Where is it? Charlie, where is it?' Her voice echoed off the ceiling. 'Charlie? Where's the telephone?' But from behind her all she could hear was the sound of the desperate old man, gasping for breath.

NEW YOU RULE NUMBER SIX: We all need DOWN-TIME to recharge our batteries, OK? So CREATE a WINDOW! Factor it in! This one's about TIME MANAGEMENT and if you want to keep up with your new mates, you need to GET ORGANISED mega-style! Write a list! And STICK TO IT! Be tough but be realistic, yeah? Calculate the time you're gonna need for personal grooming, people-greeting, information downloading. DELEGATE where you can, and don't fanny around! You gotta be GOAL oriented, 24/7! Cos nobody ever got rich sitting on their arse all day! If you've got a hole in your schedule, don't just 'relax'! Make it positive! Get a massage, and make it ME-TIME. Go to the gym, make it WORKOUT TIME! 'cause face it boys and girls, if you're really doing 'nothing' it means you're DOING SOMETHING WRONG!

An Amazingly Packed Agenda

She found the telephone but then discovered she was unable to offer up an address. 'It's a mansion,' she was saying, 'a great big *red* mansion. Near Tiverton. Or quite a long way from Tiverton. There's a church . . . For God's sake, help! I think he's dying!' Charlie came up from behind and lifted the receiver out of her hand. She stood uselessly beside him, listening as he gave instructions and trying desperately to catch his eye. But he wouldn't look at her, even after he'd hung up.

'Is he – Is he all right?'

'Jo, I'm sorry. I shouldn't have spoken to you like that.'

'Yes you should. God, *I'm* so sorry. Is there anything I can do?'

'You could give the guy a cuddle,' he said dryly.

'Really? Would he like that?' She was already halfway across the hall.

'Bloody hell, Jo, I was joking!'

'Oh.'

'But he'll be fine, I think. He's as strong as a horse, so don't panic. It's not your fault. I mean you were pretty unpleasant. But you didn't know.'

'Charlie, I'm so, so sorry.' She was on the verge of crying, and he knew she was sorry, and he even felt sorry for her. But he still wanted her out of the house.

'It doesn't matter,' he said. 'Jo. Calm down. It doesn't *matter*. What you said doesn't matter.'

'Yes it does!'

He shook his head. 'Listen, I'm going to call you a cab, OK? I'm going to go with Dad to the hospital, and I think it would be better if –'

'Yes. Yes. Absolutely.'

'The trains leave quite late. You'll be fine.'

'Please, Charlie. Don't worry about me.'

He ordered the taxi and she went upstairs to fetch her things. When she came down again he had gone. She dithered in the hall for a while. Should she wait for the cab outside? Should she go to the General to see if there was anything she could do? She tiptoed towards the half-open dining-room door and peered furtively inside; he was lying on the floor with his eyes open, and Charlie was crouched beside him, a hand on his father's shoulder, a mixture of anxiety and incredible tenderness on his face.

'I'm feeling a bit funny myself,' she heard Charlie say impassively. 'D'you think Mrs Webber's been poisoning us?'

She could see the General looking gratefully up at his son and trying to laugh.

'She was acting pretty shifty this morning,' Charlie went on. 'Perhaps I should call the police.'

They smiled at each other and Jo felt a surge of jealousy. Would Charlie ever look at her like that? Not now, he wouldn't. Would anyone ever look at her like that? She tiptoed away.

The taxi arrived before the ambulance did and she climbed into it without troubling her hosts again. When her driver came to a halt outside the station she looked up numbly and said, 'Oh God, I can't face it. Do you mind driving me all the way?' She sat back and spent the next three hours staring blindly out of the window. But however hard she tried (and she tried, and she would continue to try) she could not yet escape the fact that she was ashamed of herself.

Charlie had switched off his mobile when she called him that night, and there was no answer at the house. She tried again in the morning with the same result, and by lunch time on Saturday she was desperate. She circled her telephone, every now and then checking that it still had a dialling tone. But it didn't ring. In a way she was relieved because, as much as she longed to hear that the General was alive, she dreaded to hear Charlie's new coldness. She dreaded to discover that their friendship was over.

All in all it was not a happy weekend. She had made no back-up social arrangements on this occasion, and her parents, the only people she wasn't too proud to call at such a late stage, weren't answering the telephone either. When their machine picked up for the third time she remembered with irritation that they were in Tanzania, embracing their twilight years, (as Jo had earlier noted so approvingly) by carrying a tent to the summit of Mount Kilimanjaro.

She spent the rest of Saturday and most of Sunday in the gym trying to exercise her way towards a more positive frame of mind. By Sunday afternoon she'd burned well over 2,000 calories and at least partially persuaded herself that her outburst had been justified. Homophobia was wrong. Racism was wrong. Large houses were obviously wrong. In any case, she told herself repetitively, as she pounded the treadmill in time to the beat on MTV, how the hell was she to have known about Georgie? She'd never been told. She'd *still* never been told. And the fact remained that the General's opinions were an abomination. She had been horrible, but he was a horrible old man.

She would send them a large bunch of flowers first thing tomorrow morning and she would apologise for the trouble she'd caused. And she and Charlie would be friends again. And the General would be well. Most importantly she refused to be worried. Because she knew, in the way only people who've led calamity-free lives dare to, she just *knew* that the General would be all right.

She arrived at work that Monday morning looking even leaner and cleaner than she usually did, having spent her quiet Sunday night in an orgy of self-beautification. The first thing she did was to call the florist where Top Spin spent almost £5,000 a month, and confuse them by insisting on paying for the Fiddleford-bound eighty-five-pound order with her own credit card. The flowers were to be delivered by lunch time, she said, with the simple message attached:

Apologies.

They would know who it was from.

It was a nice gesture, she thought, as she ticked her first task off the day's to-do list; warm, conciliatory (but not grovelling) and stylish. Jo and her colleagues believed that flowers, especially when wrapped in brown paper and

145

clustered jauntily with thistles or bits of stick, generally spoke more effectively than words. She would not allow herself to ring the house again until the end of the day, by which time the flowers should have gone a little way towards repairing the damage.

In the meantime there was the other problem. Judging by the show of Post-its already littering Jo's desk Penny must have spent at least part of her weekend in the office. Her notes were beginning to get on Jo's nerves. Some of them –

SUN. 14.35
RE: KNIFE THROWERS: girls too big

– made no sense at all. Others were illegible. A couple made Jo wonder if Penny wasn't going slightly mad. She was certainly making no attempt to conceal her fancy for Charlie, otherwise known as Ed. There were at least ten separate messages concerning him. Most of them, while hinting noisily at an unbalanced passion, ostensibly dealt with the role he should play in the forthcoming documentary.

RE: ED: WE NEED HIM ON SCREEN NOT BEHIND CAMERA/NUMBERCRUNCHING. Organise facilitator/in-house prod. We have budget. Yes?

RE: ED: I know he's busy (!!) but will he do States?? We need a pre-show big name intro. Either NYC or LA. What think?? I should go with - Or you!!

RE:ED: <u>WEEKEND</u> I'm IN TOWN!! Why
didn't we arrange a meeting? JO , THINK!!

Think what? Bloody hell. Now that she had succeeded
in alienating both Eds she did need to think – fast. And
by the look of things Penny wasn't even going to give her
the time to do that. 10.11 a.m. Monday morning and the
old bitch was already making a beeline for Jo's desk.

'Good morning, Jo,' she beamed. 'Nice weekend?'

'Lovely thanks,' Jo said automatically. She pulled a wry
face at the wad of Post-its. 'Looks like you've been busy.'

'Have you checked your e-mail?' she said tartly. Penny
didn't like the implication that she'd had nothing better
to do with her own weekend. She glanced significantly at
Jo's computer. It hadn't been switched on. 'Could you do
that? You've got a lot of CCs on there from a new guy at
Meals called Des. *Very* keen. Lots of ideas. Some of them
interesting, some of them . . . well. You'll see for yourself.
Have you met him yet?'

'. . . Diz?' she said blankly. She was having difficulty
concentrating. Memories of the weekend were not proving
as easy to banish as she'd hoped, and her mind had already
wandered back to beautiful Fiddleford, to the look on
Charlie's face when they had been lolling together by the
water, before everything had gone so wrong . . .

'*Des*. Come on, Jo. Get with the programme! Read your
e-mail, yeah? And then come and talk to me about Ed.'
She smirked. 'He's not busy *today*, I presume?'

Christ, thought Jo. 'Er. No.'

'Good. We can have lunch. Book somewhere decent,
will you?'

'No. I mean, *no*. He's busy. Penny I told you. He's busy until at least the end of the week.'

'That was last week.'

'No! It . . . absolutely wasn't.'

Penny left a moment's power-filled silence before releasing her long, controlled sigh. 'This simply isn't good enough.'

'I'm sorry –'

'I really don't have time for this. I'm giving you ten minutes. And then I want to see you in front of my desk telling me all about the fabulous restaurant where you, me and your bloody boyfriend will be eating lunch. Today. At one o'clock. *Capisci?*'

'Well –'

'OK?'

'Penny –'

'Excellent.' She spun away. 'And check your e-mail.'

There were at least twenty messages from des@homeless to be waded through, most of them enthusiastic but unhelpful. Des, a former management consultant and new to the Homeless team, had been invited aboard only recently, and at great expense, to ensure, among other things, that the Top Spin budget didn't spiral out of control. It was appallingly obvious to Jo that he knew nothing about dealing with celebrities (a Top Spin speciality, after all, and one for which the homeless would ultimately be paying heavily).

'I suggest we approach inner city schools and colleges,' he had written, (and 'CC'd', apparently, to the majority of computers in central London and Northampton) *'and maybe run a competition (TV tie-in?) for fledgling make-up artists/stylists. This would cut the cost of artist entourages while offering a*

fabulous opportunity for youngsters and an excellent publicity stunt for us!'

Ten-and-a-quarter minutes later Penny buzzed Jo's extension. 'Well?'

'Des is going to be a problem.'

Penny didn't reply. It wasn't Des she was calling about.

'Look, Penny, I've called Ed. He's actually on a train to Newcastle at the moment.'

'Why? What the bloody hell's he doing in Newcastle?'

'He says the best he can manage is –' she had to say something, so why not – 'Thursday.'

'Thursday?'

'We can set up a conference call from his hotel,' she went on quickly. 'He's going to be running around a bit so he doesn't know exactly where he'll be. He says he's definitely going to keep us abreast. So that's OK. In fact, I actually suggest we book a time with RBC and Meals – Ha! And let's hope Des doesn't insist on getting involved – [Penny didn't laugh] – and, er, press on from there. So to speak. It's all looking very good. Very very good indeed . . .' She ground to a halt. Long silence. It was making her head spin. She took the telephone away from her ear and glanced across the room, but Penny was still there, still listening, head thrown back, thirty-six-year-old throat exposed, scrawny but well depilated legs resting flamboyantly on the desk in front of her. She looked ridiculous, Jo realised. Like someone from an advertisement for Häagen Dazs. '. . . Hello Penny?'

'Fine.' Her voice was cold and businesslike. Jo was right to feel terrified. 'You explain that to Des and the people at RBC. And get back to me.' She hung up.

149

Which meant Jo had until Thursday to work out what she was going to do next.

Seven o'clock and still no news from Fiddleford Manor. Jo was due to meet up with Mel, who'd called up at lunch time and almost vindicated herself by spending twenty minutes simultaneously flattering Jo, and being very rude about Ed. 'The funny thing is I think he really loves you,' she'd said. 'But he's so busy tossing off over his own navel he forgets to let himself really express it. I mean I just *know* he adores you. You should see the way he looks at you sometimes. It's so obvious it's actually sick!'

It wasn't remotely obvious. But that wasn't the point. Mel knew that Jo was annoyed with her and she didn't like unnecessary animosity. It made things complicated for her. Plus she happened to be working on an article that Jo could probably help her with, and she'd just been rudely blown out by Grey. Which meant she wasn't doing anything else tonight. The conditions were perfect. And she and Jo hadn't been out together for weeks.

Mel had already started on a bottle of champagne by the time Jo joined her. 'Don't worry,' she said casually, after delirious greetings had been exchanged. 'It's on expenses. I'm doing a piece on the irresistibility of ex-Etonians. It's called the "Post Wills Factor". Do you know about it? It's very interesting. I'm actually going to go back quite a lot, too. Nelson and people. And Lord Lucan. Apparently Disraeli was really sexy. Did he go to Eton? Anyway I thought I could pick your brain.' Mel had identified the PWF herself, shortly after dinner at Jo's, when Tracy had said this guy Charlie/Hugo, whatever, was so attractive.

'It got me thinking,' she'd explained breathlessly to one of her friendly editors the following morning, 'because obviously everybody fancies Prince William. So it's a thing, isn't it? It's a definite *thing.*' The commissioning editor was impressed. But Jo wasn't.

'Piss off, Mel. You're not being funny.'

'What? I'm serious.'

'Ex-Etonians are *not* irresistible, as you know perfectly well. Anyway, I don't know any. And if you put my name in your article I'll sue you. I swear.'

'You know Sasha Joshlin.'

'It's beside the point. I don't want to discuss it. And if you're going to spend the whole evening trying to annoy me then you can fuck off –' She stopped. She sounded ridiculous, she realised. They both started to laugh.

'So. What's new?' Mel poured Jo a large glass of champagne. 'Apart from this guy Charlie/Rupert, whatever he calls himself, who apparently you don't know. So I won't ask about him. Although I'm very, very curious. Have you patched it up with Ed yet?'

'Oh . . . No.' Jo sounded very weary.

'But I told you to call him! You want to keep someone like Ed on side, Jo. Even if it doesn't work out for you as a couple. He's always going to be useful. He'll probably end up running Channel Foremost.'

'I've been busy.' In fact, apart from when Mel had been talking about him at lunch time that day, she'd hardly given a thought to their relationship since he'd threatened to finish it the other night. 'And you know what? Right now I don't think I'd mind much if he dropped dead.'

'Wow!' said Mel happily. 'That doesn't sound like you! Has he done something else I don't know about?'

'It would get me out of a load of trouble at work. You've no idea what a bloody mess I've got myself in.'

There was something about Mel which made people confide in her, often – as was about to be the case – when it was exactly what they had promised themselves they would not do. Because when she chose to be, Mel was quite an irresistible force. She could zoom in on someone, ask them two questions, laugh hard at one of their jokes, spend the rest of the evening talking about herself and still leave them glowing with the knowledge they were the most interesting person in the room.

That night Jo was tired and feeling unusually susceptible. She held out for all of fifty seconds before launching into a detailed description of the crisis that had developed at Top Spin.

'But Ed's going to be out of town for at least four weeks!' said Mel.

'I know that.'

'So what's the problem?'

'That's the bloody problem! Have you been listening to a word I've said?'

'But Ed was never going to do it anyway!'

'So?'

'So, Penny thinks Charlie's Ed, and she loves him and she wants to have sex with him.'

'Don't exaggerate, Mel. I didn't say that.'

'What's Charlie doing at the moment?'

'Ha! That's another story.'

'I mean apart from being the new Robbie Williams? Or is he such a posh boy that he doesn't actually do anything at all? And seriously Jo, I'm not being funny. Can I get his number? I've desperately got to interview him. Is he a Post

Wills Factor? I don't know. Because unlike you, darling, I genuinely don't know any Etonians.'

It was always the same. She'd draw out the confidences, and straight away start using them as ammunition. Jo regretted having spoken. As usual.

'Forget it, Mel. Forget I said anything. I don't want to think about work anyway. It's boring . . . By the way have you got any C? I feel like a perk up.'

'Don't be silly. You always want to think about work. All I'm saying is, if the silly cow thinks he's Ed anyway, and Ed's not around to tell her any different, and your commissioning editor is in fucking *Los Angeles*, and your person at Meals is a moron called Diz, and Charlie isn't doing anything else anyway, then what's stopping you? Tell RBC that if they want Ed to direct they've got to provide a separate producer. Hire in a decent cameraman who knows what he's doing. Jo, it's easy. It's bloody brilliant! You've just got to get Charlie to pretend he's Ed. And anybody can direct. It's a piece of piss, we all know that. Doesn't even matter if he's never watched telly in his life before. In conclusion, Jo, I think you owe me a drink.'

Jo's brain was racing. She pretended to laugh. 'Ha! Mel, you're ridiculous. What kind of a cowboy outfit do you think I'm running here?' But the way Mel put it did make it seem terribly easy. Top Spin would keep the account. She would keep her job. Ed – need never know anything about it, or not until it was too late. And Charlie would get the career break he longed for. There were just two problems. Firstly that Charlie would probably refuse to lie . . .

'It's not ridiculous,' said Mel. 'It's bloody *great*! In fact, I think it calls for another bottle of champagne.'

153

Secondly, Charlie hated her now.

'It's completely ridiculous,' Jo said. 'Apart from anything else Charlie and I have temporarily fallen out.'

'Already? Shit! Who the hell am I going to interview, then?' She laughed. 'I don't suppose Sasha'll want to talk to me, do you?'

'Sasha's a busy guy, Mel,' Jo said unhelpfully, knowing exactly what was coming next.

'You couldn't give me his number? Just in case? He's such a lovely person. I'd like to get to know him better anyway.'

Jo said she didn't have his number on her, which was a lie, and then, because it was all that was really on her mind she found herself telling Mel about her brief and disastrous stay in the South West.

'. . . And then when he asked me if I wanted to go hunting,' Jo said, 'I sort of woke up, you know? Hunting! Me! I thought, *What the hell am I doing in here?*'

Mel nodded enthusiastically.

'So I started telling him what I thought, because, Mel, you should have heard the way he was talking.'

'Too right!'

'I just saw red.'

'You *go* girl!' exclaimed Mel, using an American accent and punching the air self-consciously.

'Actually, no,' she said suddenly. 'Actually it was awful. I said something about being happy every time there was a hunting accident. But I didn't – I mean, *of course* I didn't mean it . . .'

'Yes you did!'

'No. I didn't.'

'Of course you did!'

'Mel. D'you remember that story about a year ago?

Some girl was killed when an anti-bloodsports campaigner banged a drum or something and made the horse jump? D'you remember it? She broke her neck.'

'No.' Mel's face looked like thunder. 'No of course I bloody don't. For Christ's sake, what are you getting at? Why would I remember it?'

'It was Charlie's twin.'

For once Mel had nothing to say. After a moment's silence she picked up her champagne glass. But it was empty. She lit a cigarette, inhaled deeply. 'Just because the stupid bitch had a twin who you happen to want to shag this week, doesn't mean she had any more right to be hunting than anyone else does. Does it? Don't be so fucking inconsistent.'

'Mel!'

'And just because *you*, for some inexplicable reason, suddenly want to hang out with the chinless Hooray brigade, doesn't mean the rules have to change for everyone else. Torturing defenceless animals isn't suddenly OK, all right?'

'What? I didn't say it was. I just said –'

'Yes you did.'

'I didn't. What are you getting so uptight about? I had no idea you felt so strongly.'

'Yeah. Well, I do. OK?'

After that the evening never quite recovered. They gulped down the rest of the champagne, and Jo listened politely while Mel described the plot of the screenplay she hadn't started writing yet.

'I'm actually so excited about it,' said Mel. 'That's why I can't bring myself to begin! Because at the moment it's *cooking*. I'm just – letting it simmer and mature, letting the

155

essence really come out. And I'm obsessed! My trouble is I don't want to inhibit things by creating sort of false, manufactured barriers. That's why I'm actually *forbidding* myself from putting anything down on paper right now. Does that make sense to you?'

'Sounds like an excuse to me,' Jo heard herself saying.

Mel looked at her in wounded, wordless amazement. When people waxed lyrical about their creative juices other people stayed quiet and nodded encouragingly. Mel knew that. Everyone knew that. It was a – well, for heaven's sake, it was almost a *rule* (if such a thing existed in Mel's world, which of course she knew it didn't).

'Sorry!' Jo said quickly, as appalled as Mel by her own coarseness. 'Why did I say that? I mean, you've got so much on at the moment it's a wonder you can even *think* about it! You're amazing. I actually have a lot of admiration for you.'

They pretended to patch things up but it was too late. A few minutes later, just as the waiter was on his way over to take their order, they both announced they were exhausted. The champagne had robbed them completely of their appetites, they said. It had been a wonderful evening, but why ruin it? They decided to go home.

The telephone was ringing as Jo came in through the front door. She rushed to answer it, but the machine got there first, and then the line went dead. She checked the number. Charlie's mobile. With a thudding heart she called him back.

'Charlie? . . . It's Jo.'

There was a pause which seemed to last minutes before he spoke. 'Ah,' he said slowly. 'Hello there, Mrs Angry. And before you begin, I should warn you, any more speeches, even a hint of a speech, if I hear you taking a deep breath, I'm hanging up.'

She felt faint with relief. 'Ha!' she said. It was slightly hysterical. 'Ha ha! You're there! Thank God! I'm so sorry. God, Charlie. I'm so sorry. How's your father? Is he all right? I've been trying to call you! Did you get the – How is he?'

'He's fine. Absolutely fine. It was a false alarm. It was, em. Actually it was the bloody lamb chop. A chunk got caught in his throat but he'd already coughed it out by the time the ambulance arrived. We felt a bit idiotic at the hospital.'

'Poor guy. Oh Charlie, I'm so sorry. I'm so, so sorry.'

'So you bloody should be! You can't invite yourself to stay with people and then start shouting at them because their houses are too big. Never *mind* the rest of it! Luckily, Dad saw the funny side.'

'He thinks it's *funny*?'

'Well – No. Not yet.'

'The thing about the hunting –'

'Forget it,' he said more sharply. 'I should have told you.'

'But I didn't mean it.'

'Of course you didn't.'

'No, but I really didn't. You do believe me, don't you?'

'Of course I do. Do you think we'd be talking now if I didn't? You just got carried away. Not for the first time either, come to think of it.'

'Well. Yes I did. But I mean –' *Was she being patronised? Was she letting herself down?* 'That's not to say I *approve* of blood sports –'

'Oh, shut up, Jo.'

'No, I'm just saying –'

'I'm not interested.'

'I just want to say –'

157

'I'm hanging up.'

'NO!'

Silence.

'OK,' he said. 'Still here.'

'Where?' And now she sounded, what? Too eager? Too conciliatory? This wasn't the Jo she knew and admired. She cleared her throat and started again. 'I mean, where are you? Are you in the country?'

'No I'm in London. In Fulham, actually. Where you came before. It's my half-time. I'm back on in five minutes.'

'Oh! Can I come down?'

Another long pause. *Fuck*. What was happening to her? She never laid herself open like this. She never admitted she was at a loose end. And now he was going to say no – or worse, try to say no and she would be too insensitive to realise. 'Oh well. Look,' she added quickly. 'On second thoughts, forget it.'

'You'll probably miss most of it,' he said. He sounded cautious.

'No. Never mind. Come to think of it I'm whacked anyway.'

'Really?'

'Yeah, really. Busy day tomorrow.'

'Well maybe another time.'

'OK,' said Jo. She realised she sounded crestfallen. 'I'd better go. I'm glad your dad's all right.'

'He's fine. Thank you, Jo.'

'Goodbye, Charlie.'

'Actually Jo . . .'

But she'd already hung up.

*   *   *

158

Charlie stared down at his telephone in unhappy confusion. Ten minutes earlier he'd been persuading himself
to take Grey's advice and forget about her. Not so much
because of the speech she made to his father but because of
the flowers. The flowers – and especially the brittle message
which accompanied them – had reminded him, more than
anything, of Grey's antifreeze theory. What the hell was
Charlie's father meant to do with a bunch of bloody thistle
flowers? Why should they want any more thistle flowers
than they already had? They were irritating, irrelevant and
pretentious. In fact they were the main reason he'd been
putting off calling her all weekend.

But he'd forgotten them as soon as he heard her voice.
She sounded so warm and concerned, and so happy to
hear from him. So why had he hesitated? He considered
calling her back, but there wasn't time. He returned to the
small stage feeling angry with himself and impatient for
the evening to be over.

He struck the opening chords of his next song without
the usual flirtation with his audience, but it didn't seem
to put them off. He'd seduced them already, and anyway,
they all recognised the tune. The sound of their boisterous
cheering eventually persuaded him to look up. He smiled
lazily at the audience. 'Hello,' he said.

'Oh no,' someone shouted. 'Not that soppy crap!'

Charlie didn't care. He sang it anyway, and within
minutes the audience was singing along.

Half an hour later, he looked across the blissful, frenzied
diners, most of whom were providing vigorous support to
Charlie's rendition of Captain Sensible's 'Wot', to see Jo,
shaking the late night rain off her shoulders, standing out
like a sore thumb, looking very awkward. He watched as

a waiter led her to a table in the far corner of the room:

I said Captain . . .
I said WOT?
I said Captain!
I said WOT D'YOU WANT?

and Charlie skipped to the final verse. He'd already announced that the song would be his finale so when he cut it short his adoring crowd was furious. 'All right, all right,' he shouted over their barracking. 'I'm going to do one more. And this one's for my beautiful friend who's only just walked in. And who's been kind enough to come all –' he strummed at his guitar absent-mindedly, 'the way,' he strummed again, playing for time, wondering what he would sing next, 'from London's-most-caring, London's-most-sharing – *Is-ling-ton!*'

The drunken crown booed good-naturedly, and Charlie looked across at Jo, who was possibly even blushing slightly . . . And for some reason his mind went blank. Suddenly, for the first time in his life, he couldn't think of a single song.

'Er – any suggestions?'

'*The lunatics have taken over the –*' came a deep, inebriated slur from the middle of the room.

'Um, no,' said Charlie. 'Thanks. It's not quite what I was looking for.'

'Yes it is!' the man shouted back. 'Fucking fabulous song!' He beat the table and started to sing. His neighbour joined in, and so, very quickly, did people on surrounding tables. Within seconds the room was reverberating to the same funereal beat, and a hundred voices were droning in exaggerated monotone, the only line to the song that anyone ever knew.

The lunatics have taken over the asylum – they sang louder,
The lunatics have taken over the asylum – and louder,
The lunatics have taken over the asylum –

Charlie looked across at Jo to see how she was taking it. To his surprise he discovered she was laughing, and the louder the drone, the harder she laughed, the harder everyone laughed until he started laughing himself. With a shrug and a wave that was meant to encompass the whole, uncooperative audience, he laid down the guitar and made his way over to Jo's table.

The lunatics have taken over the asylum –

There were tears of laughter on her cheeks, or so he thought. They might have been the rain. But it didn't matter anyway. He had never seen her look so lovely. Never. They must have gazed at each other for a moment too long or for a moment too obviously, because gradually, though the beat remained the same, the restaurant chant was changing.

The lunatics have SNOG! SNOG! *over the asylum*
SNOG! SNOG! *taken over the* SNOG! SNOG!
SNOG! SNOG! SNOG! SNOG! SNOG! SNOG! SNOG!
SNOG!

And for some strange reason, they obeyed. At which point the other diners went so wild that the restaurant manager had to stand on the stage and beg everyone to calm down. 'And guys, please,' he said to Charlie and Jo, 'break it up. If you have a heart. You're making the rest of us feel lonely.' To the sound of more good-natured general booing (though the audience didn't quite know who they were meant to be booing, or why) Charlie and Jo pulled apart, huddled into their corner and tried to disappear. By the time the crowd had settled down they were deep in conversation.

It took another half an hour before either of them thought of mentioning their work. Charlie said, 'How's it going at "Top Spin", then?' because the name Top Spin tickled him. He had no particular interest in the answer.

'Oh, hectic,' she said automatically. 'Penny's being a –' But then she remembered the real answer, and how Charlie might be able to help. Or how she might be able to help Charlie. And she couldn't stop herself. Her mind clicked instinctively into professional mode, and she started working.

'I think I've got something for you,' she said, eyeing him suddenly. 'But it's secret, OK? Top Secret. I mean it.'

Charlie nodded. 'Top Secret at Top Spin,' he said. 'Sounds like a – what?'

'Basically there's a job going,' she pressed on. 'A Very Big Job – and it needs someone who understands musicians. I mean *really* understands them. Someone who isn't going to be intimidated by stars, someone who's a natural performer themselves, who isn't afraid to ask questions or tell people what to do, someone who has a lot of personal charm, and a little bit of knowledge on the subject. And

I've thought about it and I just think – You're the man. You'd be perfect for it.'

He laughed. 'Well I'm certainly flattered,' he said. 'What is it?'

'Basically it's –' She hesitated. How was she going to do this? She hadn't decided. Five minutes ago she hadn't realised she was going to do it at all. '– an amazing opportunity for you. People can spend years – literally, decades, trying to get themselves considered for things like this.'

'OK,' said Charlie, 'so what is it?'

She told him about the Meals For The Homeless concert and about Top Spin's role in the proceedings. She told him about the amazing American television channel that wanted to commission a documentary about it. She told him Penny had taken a great shine to him when they'd met the other day (Charlie shivered). She told him Penny had mentioned how keen she was to get Charlie 'on screen'. Then, with the ground prepared, she told him the rest. It was just that somehow Ed Bailey's name didn't happen to come into it.

'A *director*? Are you mad? Why the hell would anyone want to offer me a job like that?'

Jo hesitated. She looked long into Charlie's warm brown eyes. 'Well . . .' And started lying. 'Because you'd be brilliant,' she said. 'I know you don't like her, but Penny's right. She's been in the business a long time. She knows what she's doing.'

'What business? She a works in PR,' said Charlie.

'No, but she was in television before that.' Once she'd begun, and there was a goal in sight, Jo could lie with as much fluency as anyone. She lied so automatically she didn't even notice she was doing it. Charlie didn't stand a chance. She was so persuasive and the opportunity seemed to be so exactly-not-dissimilar to what Charlie had been vaguely hoping for. What could he say? Eventually he said yes. Jo gave him an excitable squeeze and promised him he wouldn't regret it. 'We've got a conference call booked on Thursday with the guys from RBC and Meals –'

'Already? How did you know I'd agree?'

She looked momentarily nonplussed. 'What? – No. Well I didn't –' She shrugged. 'I didn't. I just – The conference call was already booked. Anyway, the point is you don't have to *be* there, obviously, but you do have to be on the phone. I'm going to coach you, OK? Because I must admit I have talked you up a bit to Penny. I don't want her getting the idea that you, you know, that you *really* don't know what you're about. Because you do,' she added quickly. 'You do. You know a lot about pop music. You know a lot about *people*. You've just got to learn to talk the talk. OK?'

'Talk the talk,' said Charlie slowly. 'I've just got to learn to "talk the talk". Between now and Thursday. How difficult is that?'

'Easy. What are you doing tomorrow? We need to spend a couple of hours practising.'

She smiled at him, but with all that talk about talking – the frisson between them had temporarily fizzled out.

Jo did not spend a comfortable night. She tossed and turned and asked herself what would happen if Ed/Penny/ RBC ever found out what she was up to, or what Charlie would think if – *when* – he learned the truth. But by the time she and Charlie met up the following day she had convinced herself she was doing the right thing. Charlie, Jo explained to herself, didn't realise that to get ahead everybody had to tell a white lie or two. Or seventy. He would be grateful to her in the end. When he was successful. She could picture him now, at one of her own dinner parties, seated casually between Sasha Joshlin and – she flicked through the giant Palm Pilot of her imagination, remembering all the people she would want him to impress. He would regale the table with stories about the time he interviewed Bob Dylan in New York, and they would notice the breadth of his shoulders, the laughter lines around his mouth . . . her mind began to wander.

The next day they met for lunch at a smart restaurant in Chelsea (Charlie's choice). She was keen to get straight to work, but she had to wait patiently while Charlie asked the waiter to explain at least five separate items on the menu before she could begin.

'Right then,' she said. She had provided Charlie with the all-important stainless steel notebook (and a pen, because he'd failed to bring one of his own). 'Are we ready? Now I think the most important thing at this stage is for you to remember not to say *too much*.'

'Talk the talk,' said Charlie, 'but not too much. Should I be writing this down?'

'I can't make that decision for you, Charlie,' she said seriously. She was in business mode this morning, playing the role she always found easiest. 'I can't make assumptions about how your memory works. But if you do write it down, for Christ's sake don't let anyone see it!' To her faint irritation, he put the pen down.

'Basically, Charlie, the less you say in these sorts of situations, the less they can throw back at you later. When

165

they ask what your vision is – and that's probably going to be one of the first questions they ask – *be vague*. Be enthusiastic, but be vague.'

'OK . . . So . . . what *is* my vision?'

'We'll come to that later. The point is artistic people aren't meant to be too specific. And certainly not at this very early stage. Concentrate on moods and impressions, and everyone will feel reassured. They'll know they're dealing with a pro. Plus they'll feel in a position to patronise you. It works perfectly for everyone.'

'Moods and impressions. I've got you.' Charlie nodded decisively, but he was confused. 'So, er. Give me an example.'

'OK.' Jo thought for a moment. 'Right. So Penny says, "Charlie [a major problem the name thing, but not insoluble, she would tackle it later] we're thinking along the lines of a big name intro. Maybe LA. Maybe New York. It's going to set the thing up. Make the audience realise they're watching something mega. Any thoughts?" What are you going to respond?'

Charlie looked utterly blank. 'Er . . . God. *Respond?* I'm not sure I understand the question. Can you ask it again?'

'Think of something vague. Something positive and vague. The important thing is, *sound busy and throw in some names*. That's all they're going to want to hear. Mood. Impression. Busy-busy. Big Names. Big Ideas. *Busy-busy*. So you say something like, "Sounds fab, Penny. I like it." And then immediately you've got to talk about time. You've *got* to sound busy. So you say, "I should warn you now though, we're going to have to structure things fairly tightly here. I've got a lot on the go. But, er – yeah. In principle – LA

166

sounds good." And *then* you've got to start talking content, OK? *Big Ideas*. So maybe you say, "I'm thinking . . . a good backdrop. The old Hollywood sign; it's so damn cheesy, we could probably have a bit of fun with it. Maybe we can stick someone in front of it. Someone who says MUSIC to us. Someone quintessentially Hollywood. Maybe Barbra Streisand –'

Charlie burst out laughing. 'I'm not saying all that rubbish!'

'Charlie,' said Jo sternly. ' "That" is *not* rubbish. "That" is raising money for a very important cause. People expect certain things from creative people. Look at Grey, for heaven's sake. D'you think he would have got that million-pound contract if he didn't look the way he did, and talk the way he did and behave like a pig –' She stopped suddenly. 'Isn't that awful? I've never thought of it like that before.'

'What about his poetry?' Charlie asked mildly. 'Isn't it any good?'

'D'you know, Charlie, I've no idea! I don't think I've ever read it.'

The food arrived but Jo was coaching so hard she barely ate a scrap. On she hammered. And on and on. Charlie listened with a mixture of fascination and intense confusion. 'Basically you've got to remember that they're the ones who need you, not the other way round.' [It simply wasn't true. He knew that.] 'Don't laugh too hard at their jokes. Preferably don't laugh at all. Talk *quietly*, so they really have to strain to hear you. And always be the one to bring the conversation to a close. That's very important. You've got to be one step ahead, make *them* feel under pressure . . .'

167

By the time the coffee arrived Charlie thought he'd heard more than enough. His head was in danger of melting. He told Jo to set him another question.

'OK,' said Jo. Charlie listened attentively. 'We're thinking pre-prod should be up and running pretty much right away. And then maybe a one–two-week shoot. When's the soonest you can zip off to LA?'

Charlie scowled in concentration. The idea that he should direct a documentary may have sounded absurd when she'd suggested it last night, but today – and especially after so much conversation, it was beginning to sound like a possibility. He would have been inhuman not to have been excited. And grateful. He wanted to reassure Jo that she wasn't mistaken in offering him such an opportunity. He was determined to get this right.

'Uh-huh,' he said seriously. But he had so many New rules to remember, and his attempts to sound 'contemporary' sent his accent to Australia, via Swansea and Peckham. 'I'm sure glad y'can – I can have time to respond to that inquiry. I can hop over, maybe Tuesday, so long as I'm back here Wednesday . . . The ultimate answer, if it is actually dealable with in this instantaneous – instant, yeah? Is basically yes. How long is a piece of string? That's something I can certainly come back to you on. Regarding that. Can I have a time check. Good God is that the time?' As he talked he could see Jo's expression change from hope to disappointment, to dismal, absolute confusion until suddenly she burst into laughter.

'Oh fuck,' he said. 'OK. Start again!'

But she was laughing so hard she couldn't speak.

'Come on! It's not funny,' He started laughing too. 'Ask

again! I just got – confused for a moment. I'm going to do it in my normal voice, OK? First. Until I get into the swing.'

'God,' she said, wiping her eyes. 'That was crap.'

NEW YOU RULE NUMBER SEVEN: How's it going, my New friends? Are you keeping up? Are you staying on top? Or is the STRESS of being PER- FECT beginning to GET TO YOU? Tough shit! 'cause believe me, it's only gonna get tougher!! That's right! The 'Nyouer' you are, the tougher it gets, and the COOLER you've got to stay! Yep! This one's all about MAKING MELLOW! So you've got phone lines FIVE on hold, deadlines FIFTEEN to meet by Wednesday, you haven't worked out for three days and your cleaner and your personal assistant (yeah, you heard me!) have BOTH just handed in their notice. So what? It may be FRAN- TIC out there, but it's still FUN, and a'rantin'-an'- a'ravin' ain't gonna impress no one!

A QUIET SELF-CONFIDENT DELIVERY

'Penny – Have you got a minute?'

'For you, Jo, I have a minute-and-a-half.' She tossed her pen onto her desk and looked up in a way to demonstrate playfulness. 'How can I help you m'darlin'? What's up?'

'It's such a silly thing –'

'You know I love silly things.'

'OK,' said Jo carefully. So Penny was in a good mood. 'But you may not love this silly thing. I mean it's so silly. It's about – Ed. Will you promise not to take offence?'

'Take offence?' The chirpy grin evaporated. 'He hasn't ducked out, has he? Tell me he hasn't dumped us in the shit –'

'No, no, no! Everything's fine. It's all looking *great*. He's absolutely up for it! Loads of ideas! No, no. Nothing like that!'

'So . . . ?'

'I wouldn't mention it except I've just come from a meeting with Des and I suddenly realised the whole thing's got a bit out of control. It doesn't matter, of course. But, Ed, well, you know it. He can be a bit tricky, and I'm just keen not to rub him up the wrong way where it's not *one hundred per cent necessary*. Especially now. Before we've even started.'

'I'm intrigued,' said Penny dryly. 'Since none of us has yet been allowed to meet him, what can we possibly have done that could already have caused him offence?'

'You haven't! Yet. But Des was going on and on this afternoon and, I don't know if you've noticed but the guy can't open his mouth without calling you by your Christian – first names –'

'I can't say I have. And your minute-and-a-half is running out. Where's this going?'

She took a deep breath. 'Ed . . . that is to say the man I call "Ed", and who you know as "Ed" isn't actually *called* Ed at all. Or he is called Ed. Professionally. But nobody *calls* him Ed. Except me. I call him Ed as a joke, really. It sort of developed because he's always so professional. I mean he takes his work so seriously. It's a sort of *boyfriend-girlfriend* thing. Do you get what I'm saying?'

'I don't have a boyfriend,' said Penny irrelevantly.

'No,' *Damn*. She should have seen that one coming. Penny never had boyfriends, only a succession of coke-fuelled, pretty-boy single-nighters, and she was a bit unbalanced about it. It was one of the reasons, unfortunately, that she so often liked to be unpleasant to Jo. 'But if you did. I mean that's not really the point. Do you see what I'm getting at?'

'So, basically you're telling me Ed isn't his real name?'

'*Exactly.*'

There was a pause while Penny absorbed this, and Jo watched her carefully. 'But I don't see,' Penny said with a faint frown, 'why that should cause me any offence?'

'Well,' said Jo. 'Because – well anyway if it doesn't, it doesn't. I'm just being oversensitive. Ignore me.' She turned eagerly back towards her desk. She was so relieved to have got the story out and for Penny to have believed her, she couldn't wait to get away again.

'So – hang on, Jo. Wait there a minute! What *is* he called, then?'

'Oh! Ha ha. Of course. Silly me. No. He's, er. He calls himself Charlie, these days. Just plain Charlie.'

'Charlie,' said Penny. 'Fine. Charlie it is.'

The negotiations taking place just outside Bonnyrigg, Mid Lothian, where Ed Bailey and his argumentative team of documentary makers were setting up to film Grey McShane's mother, as she hung out her eloquent washing, were only slightly more straightforward. At least (so far as anyone had checked) the protagonists were all who they said they were. But that may have been Ed's sole advantage.

It was to be an isolated day of filming – brought forward from the rest of the shoot because Grey had suddenly announced, and with two days' notice, that Mrs McShane only ever received visitors in her house on the fourth Wednesday of any month. It meant that if Ed wanted the mother in his documentary, this would be his only chance.

But the team had arrived at the small grey house on the small grey estate, as arranged, promptly at three o'clock, to discover that Mrs McShane was very far from alone. Grey (who'd chosen to spend the afternoon lying on his hotel bed, within comfortable reach of the minibar) had failed to explain that the woman he had identified as his mother didn't just 'receive visitors' on these special Wednesdays. She ran an open house. It was a point of principle for her, camera crew or no camera crew, that no one should ever be turned away.

'Ahv bin doin' i' tha long it's ni i Bonnyrigg tradishin,' she told Ed, who nodded enthusiastically without understanding a word. 'Ye as' tha silly coo a' th' visi'ors centa. Shy'll t'll ya!'

In fact, Rosemary McShane's traditional Wednesday afternoon openings had long been avoided by everyone except lonely, asthmatic Colin from next door, and her depressing sister Susie Dougal. But the rumour had spread that this Wednesday guests could expect something a lot more exciting than the usual forty-five minutes of tea and silence. And by three o'clock, the little Grey house was bulging.

It was eventually agreed that Mel would conduct her interview in Mrs McShane's bedroom. So, after the washing line scene had been shot they all squeezed in: Mel, Mrs McShane, Ed, Mike the cameraman and Sly the sound technician. While Ed rearranged the furniture so that the shot of Mrs McShane on her bed would also encompass a wealth of touching sociological detail, Beronica, the ambitious research assistant, was dispatched to negotiate for quiet with the glamour-hungry tea party downstairs. But Beronica, using her most engaging smile, must have been tactless because her request wasn't met with enthusiasm.

'Naboode ni t'll *me* whinta helme wittrin afore ne,' snapped lonely Colin.

'Aye, n 'y' cn siy i' agin fa me!' said Susie Dougal.

'Pardon?' Beronica looked in desperation from one to the other.

'Aye, asi, n 'y' cn siy i' agin fa me!'

'Ha! Sorry – It's Susie isn't it? Susie, I didn't quite catch that. Could you say it again?'

'*ASI*, AYE, N 'Y' CN SIY I' AGIN FA ME!'

'Yeah? . . . Fantastic!' She turned away before the woman had a chance to say anything more and after a few more unsuccessful attempts to communicate with the natives, decided to retreat upstairs.

Ed and the crew were fussing about, adding finishing touches to the set (the eighteen-inch Cinderella doll with real glass slippers, just *here*. The Bible – the *Bible!* – just *there*, the stacks of Mills & Boon romances, the peeling wallpaper, of course, and the pack of denture glue on the bedside table . . .) when Beronica reappeared. She looked flushed with the trauma of dealing with such disobedient, incomprehensible people.

'I'm having a bit of a problem,' she said, 'I *think* they're saying they want money but I'm not really sure. They seem a bit pissed off. Ed – sorry. Sorry, Ed. But could someone come and give me a hand?'

With a tight little smile which included everyone except Beronica, Ed slipped efficiently out of the room and within minutes the house was silent.

'What did you say to them?' asked Mel, when he came back.

'The truth,' Ed lied simply. 'If they were quiet we'd film the tea party. If they weren't then we'd have to leave.'

'What? Just pack up and go? Without even getting Mrs McShane?' Mel sounded incredulous. 'You'd never do that!'

Ed smiled. 'Ah, but they don't know me like you do, Mel.'

She giggled. 'You're terrible Ed.'

'OK,' said Ed. 'Nice and quiet everyone please. Are you ready, Rosemary? Feeling comfortable? Smashing. You look stunning. Absolutely stunning. And camera's rolling . . . Action!'

Mel couldn't understand a word Mrs McShane was saying and it was beginning to make her feel extremely uncomfortable. Her list of questions was coming to an end and she could only presume that they had been answered adequately. Ed had scowled so unpleasantly at the beginning, when, three times in a row, she'd asked the woman to repeat herself. So after that she'd given up trying. She'd stuck rigidly to the script he had handed her earlier, and since neither he nor anyone else was complaining she could only presume that it wasn't Mrs McShane's pronunciation but her own deafness which was the problem.

It wasn't. Ed couldn't understand her either. He was presuming that Mel could. Anyway, he was concentrating more on the bigger picture. His framing was perfect, he thought; and Mrs McShane looked and sounded exactly as she was supposed to. He would intercut this with a whole load of other stuff; shots of the estate, shots of local kids, local destitution, local law enforcement – and leave an overall *impression* of early home life. It was much more expressive than a straight interview, where every boring word was understood. In fact it was the sort of high-style innovation which post-millennium TV journalism was crying out for. It was the sort of thing, Ed thought quietly, that won awards . . .

'Tha' wa' en the vehicle wha' did 'im in,' Mrs McShane was saying, inexplicably (but affectingly) wiping a tear

176

from her wizened eye. 'Och, bu' I love tha' lad. But ye won' get me tekkin' aboo' tha'. Och, noo . . .'

'. . . And cut!' said Ed. 'Rosemary, that was fantastic. Really. Thanks ever so much. Well! That's us then! Done! We'll pack up quickly and get out of your hair.'

Mrs McShane looked disappointed. She said she thought they'd wanted to film the tea party. She said all her guests would be very put out if they went away without being filmed at all. Everyone looked totally blank, so she said it again, and then a third time, very, very slowly. 'Ohhh!' said Ed. 'Right! . . . Er, no. What a shame. No I don't think we're going to have enough time to do the tea party after all. I'm sorry about that, Rosemary. Maybe another time.' With practised ease, he bundled her out of the room.

'That was a bit mean, Ed,' said Mel (who understood better than anyone the yearning to appear on TV). 'They've been very quiet. They kept their side of the bargain.'

'Fine,' he said, fixing her with his ice-blues, and using his calmest, chilliest voice. 'If you're willing to personally underwrite the cost of Sly and Mike's overtime, and you're willing to personally guarantee that Grey a) won't have done a runner or b) spent the production's entire budget on alcohol by the time we get back, and you're willing to do all the negotiating with those people downstairs yourself – then great. We'll do it.'

'Well I –'

'Mel,' said Ed, sensing victory and wanting to come out of it seeming nice, 'You've got to realise that wherever we go with this *funny little machine here* [he indicated the camera with brotherly affection] people are going to want to get *involved*. Yeah? It's something about TV cameras. Don't ask me why, but they have a funny affect.

177

And if you want a career in this business you'll get used to it. We're here to do a job, not to temporarily satisfy the vanity of uncooperative passers-by. You have to be ruthless if you want to get the job done.'

So Beronica was dispatched to break the news to the silent and expectant party downstairs that their silence had been greatly appreciated at the time but was now entirely forgotten, and the camera crew packed up as quickly as possible and rushed off back to Edinburgh.

To everyone's relief, by the time they arrived at the hotel Grey had already passed out.

The day of the dreaded conference call arrived too soon. Jo, though you wouldn't have noticed it, was a nervous wreck. It had to take place in the early evening, due to the Los Angeles ingredient, and she had surreptitiously tried to arrange that she would be out of the office, sitting beside Charlie, when the call came through. But it had proved impossible. A horrible man called Steve, who represented Tribal Pilgrim (concert promoters), insisted on coming to the meeting in person and then poor square des@homeless said he wanted to bring along someone from Fz^z, which was a great nuisance, but nobody dared complain. Penny said Des and Steve were bound not to get on, and she needed Jo in the office with her, to dilute the atmosphere.

Ten minutes before the meeting was due to begin Jo was still whispering frantic instructions to Charlie over the telephone. Over the last three days Charlie had in fact learnt very fast. The more she'd talked, the less impressed by her little world he'd found himself, and yet the more possible it seemed that he could break into it, and achieve something she and his father might be proud of. There had been times when her suggestions had appalled him. (Even Jo, when confronted by some of her own directives, had been faintly disconcerted.) But after that first attempt, he'd got the gist of the system very quickly. Unnervingly quickly, in a way. It had made it all seem a bit facile . . .

'Come on, Jo. Off the phone!' Penny shouted, popping her head around the boardroom door and smiling tensely. 'They're on their way up, so get in here. *Now!*'

Jo looked across at her boss and gave a cheerful wave, a thousand times more cheerful than she felt. Charlie sounded much too confident. If he sounded confident then he'd talk, and the more he talked the greater the chance of his blowing their cover.

'And remember,' she jabbered, 'if they ask you something you don't know for Christ's sake *don't admit to it.* Try to sound disdainful, and duck the question. Better still, *come back* with a question. And try not to sound too posh. If you can. And – Oh God. If someone starts saying they already know, you just be cool with it, OK?'

'What do you mean?'

'Just – play along. People are always pretending stuff in this business. You shouldn't call their bluff unless you have a specific reason for it, OK? It wouldn't be fair. And if you start talking, for God's sake don't let them interrupt. It's a sign of weakness. And leave long pauses. It'll make them think you're thinking. And whatever you do, don't sound impressed, not by anything they suggest. And don't let des@homeless draw you into any of his stupid conversations about budgets. If the subject of budgets comes up just *go silent*. It'll make them nervous. And whatever you do –'

'All right. Shut up. Please. That's enough!'

'Yeah, but remember –'

'Jo, trust me! Go into the bloody boardroom or wherever it is you have to go and we'll talk again in a few minutes.'

'Good luck, Charlie,' she said. 'Just stay *cool*, OK? I love y—' *Ah!* Where the fuck had *that* come from?

She could hear his surprised silence at the other end of the telephone.

'Oh, shit, *Please!* Can we talk about this later?'

'We can talk about it whenever you like,' he said coolly. 'I'm going to hang up, now. Good luck.'

'I'm going to need it,' she said as lightly as she could. But she was furious with herself. Her unprompted declaration had clouded everything. She was going to find it hard to concentrate.

Jo headed towards the boardroom with a brave smile fixed on her face. She managed to greet Des like an old friend. She complimented Tim from Fz^z on the incredible deliciousness of his Northampton-based health drink. She said it was no trouble at all when Horrible Steve, forty-eight years old and dressed in rubber trousers, demanded non-alcoholic lager, which meant sending someone out to the off-licence. She agreed with Penny that it 'seemed a bit stuffy in here', and shared a group moan about the difficulties of air conditioning. She appeared entirely poised; just Jo, her usual, gracious, delicious self. But her mind was miles away.

. . . *The most important thing was to prevent anyone from talking to Charlie about his 'previous work'. If the subject of*

Ed's CV came up, there wasn't much she could do. She'd be out of a job. And Charlie – she dreaded even to think. She would tell him the truth one day. Very soon. After this. Very very soon. But the time had to be chosen carefully. When they'd finished the documentary. When he was the toast of London. When he understood about – success. She would tell him about the risks she took and he wouldn't just forgive her. He would be grateful. They might even be able to laugh about it together.

The sound of Lionel's voice on the speakerphone jolted her back to reality. Penny made the introductions. Poor square des@homeless, Tim from Fz^z, Horrible Steve, Jo and Penny in the boardroom, Innocent Lionel in LA, and Semi-Innocent Charlie in a top-floor flat in Parsons Green.

'. . . And Charlie, you know Lionel from RBC of course –'

'Hi Lionel.'

'Hiya – *Charlie!* You crazy guy!' Lionel chuckled. 'Nice name, by the way!'

'Yeah? – Thanks. I like your name too.'

'. . . And Charlie I think you know Jo,' smirked Penny.

Everyone laughed. Penny cleared her throat. 'Right then, I think we all know who we are. Let's crack on, shall we?'

They cracked on for a while before Charlie was called upon to say anything. Steve updated the group on the current situation; they'd now received definite confirmations from two 'major British acts' – a new Irish boy band called GEAR whose first and only single was currently at Number 17 in the charts (and falling), and Dyanne, a former soap star who'd had three top twenty hits within a month of each other, four years earlier.

Then Penny and Jo talked a little about related PR initiatives. The favourite of which at the moment involved

sending a dented can of Special Brew, some ragged finger-
less gloves and a roll-up cigarette to every features editor
in the country, along with a press release filled with 'loads
of statistics' about the homeless' plight.

'It'll get them thinking about the issues,' said Jo. 'Then
we whack 'em with the glamour!'

And of course Des was determined to give his local
kids/make-up artist initiative another airing. But this time,
instead of being met with Jo's tactful lack of enthusiasm,
it met with Horrible Steve. Steve was more than happy
to take advice from Top Spin on matters of celebrity
care (they were well respected for it in the industry),
but advice from Square Des, unsolicited and, it has to
be said, utterly impractical, was another matter. Steve,
who'd partied with a lot of rock'n'rollers over the years,
just couldn't be bothered with men like Square Des.

'Look, people,' he said, holding up a veiny, manicured
hand. 'I haven't got time for this. I don't know what this
guy's actually *doing* here, yeah?'

'He's from Meals For The Homeless,' said Penny quickly.
'Honestly Steve! He's the reason we're all here in the
first place!'

'That's as may be, but I've been liaising with a completely
different character at Homeless and frankly I'm unwilling
to sit around and make like a puppy while he tries to fuck
with my job. Either I'm doing it or I'm not doing it, OK?
If you want me on board then you're gonna have to leave
me to it. That's how I work, yeah? No fannying around. I
just get on with it.'

Penny jumped in to smooth things over. 'Absolutely. I'm
sure that's not what Des meant. He was throwing in a little
suggestion. Charlie, have you got anything to say?'

But Charlie, though horrified, stayed resolutely in character and said nothing.

Lionel laughed uneasily, 'Boy! When you English people do business you certainly say what you think!' Steve glowed sullenly, happy under the misapprehension that Lionel was paying him a compliment. And poor des@homeless turned bright red and looked as though he might cry, which moved Jo, in spite of all her private difficulties. She smiled at him, sneaked a hand round the back of her chair and gave his arm a squeeze. He looked absurdly grateful.

'So Charlie,' Penny said at last, 'we're all thinking along the lines of a big name intro, as you know. Maybe LA. Maybe New York. It's going to set the thing up. Make the audience realise they're watching something mega. Plus we can flag it prior to broadcast, so people can make a note in their diaries . . . What are you thinking?'

Long pause. Jo coughed. *OK, Charlie. That's long enough. Say something . . . Say something . . . Please. Say anything.*

'Hello, Charlie?' said Penny. 'Are you there?'

'. . . Yeah. Yeah, I'm still here . . .'

'Hollywood sounds nice,' said Des, to break the silence.

'Mm,' said Charlie. 'Timing's gonna be tight.'

'Well of course,' said Penny, smiling fatuously into the speaker. (She hadn't realised how sexy his voice was.) 'We can probably squeeze it into a couple of days. I was actually thinking –'

'This is meant to be a LONDON thing, right?' Charlie cut in. 'I mean, Northampton, *yes*. But for our purposes we need to emphasise the London thing.'

'Tim?' said Penny.

'OK by me,' said Tim from Fz^z. 'Fz^z is very much a health drink for the metropolis. An anytime-anywhere revitaliser for Big City People with Big City Minds; cosmopolitan, up-'n'-at-it. Basically it's *fun*. That's certainly where we're coming from on this. So, yeah. LONDON LONDON LONDON. Sounds good to me.'

'Too right,' said Horrible Steve. 'Good thinking.'

'Correct me if I'm wrong, yeah?' said Charlie, managing not to laugh, 'but London is a fantastic place to be right now –'

'You said it and I'm hearing it!' said Steve. 'Never mind "a", Charlie boy. It's *the* fantastic place to be. Why the fuck do you want to bother with LA?'

Charlie continued as if Steve hadn't spoken, 'So, I'm thinking we should make a feature of that. I'm actually thinking *let's do the Big Cliché thing!* Yeah? Big Ben! St Paul's Cathedral! Michael Caine and Barbara Windsor . . . BONKING, OK? On the top of a double-decker bus!' Jo bit her lips to prevent them from smiling, and stared hard at her notebook. Charlie was unrecognisable. He was perfect! Strangely awful, in a strangely familiar way. But spot on. And Penny and Des and Horrible Steve were enthralled. 'If this show is about London,' he went on, 'I want it to be about LONDON. Showing the world London can have fun and STILL remember to care.'

'Lionel?' said Penny. 'Sounds good to me, I must say. Sounds fantastic.'

Lionel was distracted. It wasn't his job to get involved in the nitty-gritty of the creative process and besides, an e-mail had just flashed up requesting his presence on the eleventh floor. He'd submitted someone else's idea for a celebrity-and-their-pets big money Q'n'A show which he was convinced could make his career. 'Penny, it sounds fabulous. I'm actually gonna have to leave you now, and for that I apologise. But you all sound pretty much on top of things over there. Charlie, I understand you don't want to get your hands dirty with all the production shallullah this time round, huh?'

'I wish I had that kind of time at my disposal. I'm –'

'Fine. I don't blame you. A guy called Dermott Svenson'll be contacting you. He's going to need to see a budget some time real soon.'

'We can get you that on Monday, Lionel,' said Jo.

'Uh-huh. Great. As I say I'm gonna have to go right now. I have a meeting. But it's been nice talking to you. We'll talk later. Good luck everyone. I think it sounds tremendous.'

He was gone.

One down, thought Jo. Four to go.

'I've got to head off myself,' said Charlie. 'Was there anything else or can we leave it there?'

'Just one more thing, Ed. I mean Charlie.' Penny giggled coquettishly. 'Or can *I* call you Ed?'

'Basically we've got five weeks till D-Day,' Jo quickly cut in, 'and I really think we should be up-and-at-it no later than next week. Charlie, can you manage that sort of timescale?'

'That,' said Charlie, 'is a good question. I'm thinking Thursday. Friday latest.'

'Fabulous,' said Penny. 'Steve? Des? Any thoughts?'

'Sounds great,' said Steve. 'And Charlie, we'll need to talk. It's for a cause I happen to feel strongly about, so I'm willing to bend a few rules, but you know it, I know it, I *am* gonna have to set boundaries. Let's hook up when you're back in town. Maybe grab a bite.'

'When do you think you'll be back?' said Jo.

'Ah – *well*,' said Charlie. The conversation was drawing

to a close and she could hear the mixture of amusement, relief and triumph in his voice. He was grinning and she felt dangerously close to giggling herself. 'Another excellent question, and one I can certainly get back to you on.'

'The, er –' She smiled idiotically. She realised she had nothing to say.

'*But how long,*' said Charlie suddenly and absurdly loudly, 'is a medium-to-short-term piece of string?'

With a violent snort, and a spray of spit that covered most of the table, Jo's self-control disintegrated completely. She leapt to her feet, apologising profusely, and rushed for the door.

'One of her coughing fits,' she heard Charlie saying dryly. 'Poor girl. Someone get her a glass of water.'

That evening she and Charlie met up at Soho House. Charlie wore his *fascistà* shirt from agnès b, and Jo brought along some cocaine, but then thought better of producing it, and it stayed in her pocket. They were flying high anyway, and they spent much of the evening congratulating each other fervently on their teamwork. They felt, for the first time, utterly, uniquely connected, in league together against the rest of the wicked world. To such an extent that Jo didn't have to pretend not to notice the two movie stars who, for well over an hour, were leaning against the bar directly in front of her table. She didn't notice anyone except Charlie.

Hours later they went back to his flat in Parsons Green. He made her coffee before discovering that the milk was sour and that neither of them wanted it anyway. They fell onto the chintzy sofa, snogging like teenagers again, both of them drunk as Lords, both of them fully aware and revved up for what was coming next when Charlie suddenly pulled back and said, 'So, er, did I dream it, or did you say something embarrassing about *love* earlier on this afternoon?'

She chortled. 'You dreamed it.'

'You're such a liar,' he said casually, and started kissing her again.

He was undoing some of the tiny buttons on the back of her Armani sleeveless polo neck, feeling slightly frustrated by them. It meant they paused for a fraction of a second; for just long enough to give Jo the chance to forget what a wonderful time she was having. Suddenly she caught up with her surroundings and realised that they weren't quite right. The chintz wasn't sexy. The coffee cups were still on the floor, they would get spilt, and the lighting was very harsh. Not, of course, that she had anything to be ashamed of. Certainly not. Not that she was a prude (God forbid!), she was a beautiful woman and a great lay – she'd been told it often enough. But she couldn't perform if the scene wasn't right. The scene was vital. Plus, damn it. She realised she was losing her nerve. She looked around the flat. *What was she doing here?* What she needed was a line of coke.

'Shall we have a line?' she said, with just the faintest edge of pleading in her voice. 'I mean of coke?'

He looked astonished. 'What, now?'

'Y-yeah. I mean. Not if you don't want it –'

'I don't want it. But if you do – please. Go ahead.' He watched her as she straightened herself up, brought out her little envelope, asked him for a mirror, rummaged in her jacket for a credit card. She looked very self-conscious.

'Do you always have coke when you fuck?' he asked curiously.

'I don't know . . . Yes. I suppose so. Usually.' She was looking through her wallet for a note. 'Bloody hell,' she said, trying to sound casual, wishing desperately that she'd never brought the coke out; that she'd kept it in her wallet where it belonged. 'You haven't got a tenner have you?'

'Oh for God's sake,' he said. 'Come here, Jo. Please. Forget the bloody coke.'

He lent across to kiss her again and she was torn: Coke? Kiss? Coke? Kiss?

'*Wait!*' she said. 'Wait! We're going to spill the coffee. And the lights are too bright. Charlie I know it's silly but I don't – *like* it when the lights are so bright. Let me turn them down, just a little bit. In fact, can we get off this sofa? There's something really tacky – I just don't like doing it on sofas.'

'Jo,' he muttered, stroking her cheek, looking at her tenderly, intently, willing her to relax. 'We can do it on the North End Road, for all I care. In the pitch black. In the pouring rain. We can do it on the roof, if you want to climb up there. We can do it in a dustbin outside Charing Cross tube station. Whatever you want. Wherever you want. However you want it. With or without cocaine . . .'

She decided to forget about the cocaine and they climbed up onto the roof, which was funny at first, but it wasn't quite as she had imagined. There were no stars in the sky, and then she grazed herself on the trap door, and the slates were slippery from so much rain, and though she gasped, as habit would have it, she felt cold and after a short while suggested they go inside again.

The sudden warmth of the flat, Charlie's clean, masculine smell and his strong arms around her as they half-stumbled back down the ladder together, made her

188

head spin, made her moan; the first genuine moan, it occurred to her briefly, since – well for years. She let go of the ladder and they climbed backwards, or Charlie did, holding her tightly, and they fell in a heap on the landing floor.

It was chaotic. The light was still too harsh, but she didn't care. He couldn't undo the Armani buttons so together they ripped them open. Seventy-five pounds down the drain. She didn't care. They somehow knocked the ladder off its perch and it came tumbling down, crashing over the bannister, nearly killing them. They didn't care.

'OK, wait –' he said suddenly. 'Jo. Have you been thinking about Charing Cross?'

'*What?*'

'Fuck Charing Cross. I'm just saying. Jo. It's early days. It's early days. If we'd gone to that dustbin it would have taken much longer.'

'You're talking rubbish, Charlie,' she murmured carelessly.

'Ah ha ha ha!'

'I'm so funny.'

'You're so fucking funny.'

'I am SO funny.'

'You are SO –'

'I AM SO . . .'

But neither of them was listening.

'Jo. This isn't funny. I told you. I'm going to come.'

'Charlie . . . Fuck! *This* isn't funny. This is – *astonishing* . . . Charlie! . . . So . . . Am . . . iiiIII! . . .'

At five in the morning, having worked their way steadily towards ever more conventional lovemaking locations, they had finally collapsed into bed. Jo, still exhilarated by lust and the discovery of so much unimagined passion, looked across at her lover, dozing lightly, and every angle of his face seemed to be perfect; the peaceful sound of his breathing was exquisite to her – and at last she understood what all the fuss was about. This, then, was what if felt like. It occurred to her that she had never been entirely convinced it existed before now. She had never known such happiness.

Charlie, there's something I've got to tell you.

Charlie, I haven't been entirely straight.

Charlie, I've got us into a bit of a stupid situation . . .

But she said nothing. When he opened his eyes all she could say was how happy she was and then they made love again and all night long she never could find a moment that was imperfect enough she was willing to interrupt it with reality.

Charlie, I've told you a bit of lie.

Charlie, I've presented the situation to you in a way that isn't entirely accurate . . .

It was only a faint shadow as they lay in bed together that night, but it would grow longer and heavier as the days went by, casting a blight over what would otherwise have been the most magical few weeks of her life.

RBC had requested that the emphasis in Charlie's documentary be more on the music than the homelessness. In fact (Penny and Jo were disgusted to learn) when it came down to it they didn't really want any visual references to Britain's homeless population at all. Which meant that apart from the London shots and a few prearranged interviews with the trickle of B-grade stars who were now committing to the concert, the bulk of filming would take place over just two days: the day of the concert and the one preceding it.

Jo, using information she'd gleaned from her time with Ed, managed to pull together an efficient producer and a cameraman, both of whom had spent the last ten years living abroad and were therefore completely ignorant of the newly-fashionable Ed Bailey's track record. It meant that Charlie (or rather she and Charlie, because she was giving a disproportionate amount of time to this one aspect of this particular publicity campaign) could spend a lot of time ingratiating themselves with the people that mattered. They lunched with Horrible Steve, in whose hands lay access to the backstage, and with a series of artists' managers and agents in whose hands lay access to the stars themselves.

Charlie's appreciative and innately, resolutely unaggressive manner proved to be quite a formidable weapon. One by one his victims would slope suspiciously to the lunch table, to sip at some mineral water and do battle, and one by one they would float away, disarmed and delighted. Charlie had no colleagues or previous experience to compare himself to. He was unaware of the true extent of his success, but Jo knew how difficult these people usually were. She watched in love-intoxicated amazement and ever-increasing respect as he continued, without a hint of cynicism, to soften some of the hardest hearts in the business. Horrible Steve was so enamoured he even offered, should Charlie ever return to his old singing job, to come to Fulham and listen to Charlie perform.

'I don't do pubs normally,' Steve said. 'My line is, if

you're still playing pubs in your mid-thirties, it's because you're crap. Real talent never slips through the net. Believe me. I've been in this business long enough. I know what I'm talking about.'

'Yes,' said Charlie mildly. 'You're probably right. But it used to be a laugh, didn't it, Jo? Used to be pretty packed, anyway.'

After the success of that conference call, Charlie had more or less reverted to his usual way of talking. Jo hardly noticed. She was so happy just being with him that when it came to much of what he said, she had lost her faculty for criticism. Anyway he had the job now. As long as Penny wasn't listening, there didn't seem to be any need for him to pretend. If people were sometimes disconcerted by his unfashionable speech patterns they didn't choose to mention it. And after a more successful shopping spree at the less expensive but equally subdued Muji, he certainly looked the part. Or almost. A cool eye might still notice that his body looked fractionally too relaxed as it lounged in those fashionable restaurant chairs, and his eyes didn't have the dehydrated look of a man who'd spent his adult life hunched over a computer screen, mapping out his career. It didn't matter. He was with Jo. He was with Top Spin. He was directing a relevant and morally appropriate documentary involving pop stars. He could do no wrong.

The days spun by. Penny made several snide remarks about Jo's selfless dedication to the Meals account, but Jo didn't care. Penny could have done anything, left a layer of Post-its over her desk so thick it took a year to work through them. Nothing, except her fear of discovery, could dent her exuberance. She was in love, and so was Charlie.

They spent most of their nights in Parsons Green. For

all of Georgie's embarrassing taste in chintz and Charlie's inability to buy lavatory paper it was a much more comfortable flat than Jo's. Also, Charlie was uncharacteristically stubborn about it.

'I spend all day with you cutting edge types,' he said. 'At the end of the day I need to get back to my roots.'

There had only been one argument. Charlie said he needed to go home to Fiddleford to check on his father, and Jo had wanted to come too. 'Seriously Charlie. We can't be enemies for ever. After all we both love you. We've just got to learn to accept each other.'

He'd looked at her warily. 'You always assume,' he said, 'that everything is *dealable-with*.'

'Yes! I do. Of course I do! You can't just *accept* things. If there's a problem, you have to solve it.'

'Some things aren't solvable.' He saw that she looked hurt and tried to repair the damage. 'I'm just saying – Jo, I'm just saying it's going to take time. However much you may want to patch things up between you, doesn't mean *he* does. He's an old man. I told you, he's set in his ways. He likes to let things fester.'

'But he shouldn't let things fester. That's what I'm saying –'

'And I'm saying he should be allowed to do what he bloody well wants.'

Their relationship was still so fresh, such a sharp retort was bound to wreak devastation, at least in the short term. The argument lasted just long enough for Charlie to return to Fiddleford alone, and for Jo to spend the weekend in her flat, picking up the four-day-old messages on her home answer machine (she was getting very remiss) and reinstating details of her beauty regime which had recently been alarmingly neglected.

There were two messages from Ed, the first sounding ironically apologetic, informing her he would be back in London 'for this wretched charity football match', and that it might be nice to hook up. 'I think we left things a bit unresolved. So maybe let's talk. Take care, Jo, yeah . . . ?' The second, left the previous night, sounded more irritable and, Jo thought, infuriatingly proprietorial. They hadn't spoken to each other in almost three weeks. He had no right to demand to know where she was. It wasn't any of his business. Not of course that it ever had been. They had always been scrupulous about that. Jo and Ed had been unrelentingly civilised with each other; no pressures, no promises, no expectations, not much of anything really, in retrospect. But she was glad he had called. She was fond of him, she supposed. And perhaps he was lonely. It was unlike him to call twice. She took pity and gave him a ring.

'So,' he said, having satisfactorily camouflaged his relief at hearing her voice. He'd missed her smooth, reassuring presence. After the last few weeks he needed someone to make him feel good again. 'What's up? Been busy?'

'Oh, you know. Hectic. Same as ever.'

'And the Meals thing worked out?'

'Yeah – You know. Sort of.'

'Who've you got directing it?'

'What? God. I don't know. It's all a bit up in the air, Ed. To be honest. But tell me about Grey. I'm longing to hear. Is he completely impossible? He must be. And is Mel behaving like a prima donna yet?'

'Bloody hell,' he laughed. 'They're both absolute fucking nightmares. I can't tell you . . .'

It was fortunate for Jo (though perhaps not for television journalism) that Ed so much preferred to talk than to ask questions. He talked for half an hour about the awfulness of the project he was working on, and about how it would all be worth it in the end, and about how he was 'quietly confident' of the quality of the work achieved so far. He was warming up to suggest that they meet when Jo, sensing danger, quickly brought the conversation to a close. She had to run, she said. She was already very late.

'But it's been lovely talking to you, Ed. Maybe we can get together when you get back. We'll both have more time.'

'Yeah. Sure . . . We should have a chat.'

'We should,' she said soothingly. 'We really should. Well –'

'But here I am, gabbing away as usual,' he said. 'You never even told me who was taking my place on Meals.'

'Didn't I? Look, Ed, I've really got to go. Will you call me? When you get back?'

'Of course I will.'

'I'd love that. And good luck with the football!'

'Yeah – Thanks.' His voice sounded rather flat when she hung up. He must be exhausted, she thought, and lonely. He'd obviously had an appalling few weeks. She realised how little she cared any more, and it made her feel terrible.

It was a reflection of what an unpleasant time he was having in Scotland that Ed had actually been looking forward to leaving his work behind that weekend. Unfortunately, what with Jo refusing to make herself available for him and then the football bringing such appalling humiliation, his weekend away hadn't really worked out as planned. The football fiasco was entirely his own fault. He'd been too distracted by Grey McShane to concentrate on pulling together a decent team, and the people he roped in were completely feeble. Worse than that, they were feeble nonentities. Worse still, the inordinate amount of morale-boosting cocaine he, Grey and Mel had been snuffling over recent weeks meant that Ed played very badly, even worse than usual. In fact he turned out to be the feeblest player in the team, and possibly in the whole competition.

The Head of Documentaries and Current Affairs at Channel Foremost, Tom, made it clear he felt insulted, 'I did get the impression,' he said, 'that you were going to organise some training for us.'

'Yes,' Ed said dryly, 'I think we might have benefited from some practice. Unfortunately we've all been so busy –'

'And what happened to all the marvellous players you had last year?'

'My apologies, Tom. Believe me, I'm as disappointed as you are. But, as you know, Grey McShane has been taking up –'

'Yes. Well, Ed,' he said, trying to sound jovial, 'I hope for both of our sakes you're a better documentary maker than you are footballer.'

'You know I am.'

They grinned at each other hatefully.

Ed decided not to turn up to the end-of-competition dinner, normally one of the best networking opportunities of the year. Instead he flew back to Edinburgh feeling very glum, and with the prospect of two more miserable weeks of shooting still ahead.

Or so he thought.

But three days later, after a surprisingly smooth afternoon in which Grey and his old schoolmaster, Mr Randolph, were filmed together sharing a bogus chortle about his not-very-naughty school days, things suddenly came to a head.

Strangely enough, until the day Beronica contacted him to organise an interview, Mr Randolph had known nothing of Grey's success. In fact he'd needed to look up old reports to be reminded of Grey's existence, and even then he couldn't quite conjure the face. The reports (over the top of which, Mr Randolph was disconcerted to note, someone had stamped the word DECEASED) seemed to intimate that he'd been rather a nice boy who'd fared reasonably well in his CSEs and liked playing rugby. An average pupil; decent but dull. Which obviously wouldn't do. At Ed's instigation, and Mel's relentlessly fatuous prodding, Mr Randolph was sporting enough to play along with a more palatable version of events.

'You had a quite extraordinary *native* intelligence,' announced the old fraud as, with Mel between them, and the camera behind, they pretended to peruse the non-existent Poetry section of the school library. 'Ha! It used to keep us all on our toes, I must say! Terrific! . . . And so amusing.'

'So you were individualistic even as a schoolboy?' grinned Mel.

'You see?' Grey turned flirtatiously to the camera. He tended to ignore everyone when the camera was rolling, especially Mel. If she asked him a question he would

197

only ever respond with a non sequitur, and always to the camera rather than her. Ed, having failed to persuade him to do otherwise, had come to the convenient conclusion that it was a good thing. Very arch, he thought. Very modern. And a very good way of annoying Mel. 'Even Mr Randolph here doesn't think much of this library do you Mr Randolph? It's a bloody disgrace!'

Excellent thought Ed. Some issues.

'You need to get in some comfy chairs –'

'Well, indeed,' said Mr Randolph. 'Unfortunately *funding . . .*'

'And a coffee bar, mebbe.' Grey's enormous hands sketched out a space at the other end of the room. 'Over there. How's a boy s'posed to take in all this fuckin' information without a wee bi' o' lubrication, for Christ's sake? Have you thought about that Mr Randolph. Sir? Have you ever put any thought into this library at all?'

Comparatively speaking it had been a very productive day. Grey had been, comparatively speaking, a paragon of malleability and good nature. And they'd got some shots of the school – nice and bleak, of course, and Mel had interviewed a geriatric former lollipop lady, who chuckled a lot about the funny – '*individualistic*, why yes!' – way he used sometimes to cross the road. The team had returned to the hotel in unusually good spirits.

To such an extent that Grey and Mel broke with well-established tradition and even deigned to join the rest of the crew for dinner. Grey, drearily plastered already, (he'd been glugging neat gin in the back of the crew minibus ever since breakfast) said he wanted to discuss the inclusion of an extra scene.

'There's a whole load of bloody stuff you still don't know about me,' he said.

'Well!' said Ed, quite delighted. It would be the first suggestion Grey had offered up in all the time they'd been in Scotland together. Perhaps he was finally beginning to feel engaged. 'Excellent! I think this calls for a mid-shoot celebration. After all we're still here, aren't we? I think it's going very well.'

Melanie snorted derisively. When she was beside Grey she'd taken to treating Ed just like she'd treated Barry Bald of the fleas-and-no-eyebrows, back at primary school. She sniggered unpleasantly every time he spoke. She looked haughty when he addressed her, and refused ostentatiously to laugh at his jokes – unless, of course her boyfriend wasn't beside her, or she was asking Ed to supply her with more cocaine. Grey was rude even when he was asking for cocaine. The two of them had formed an unfortunate league together against the rest of the group, and they huddled in his bedroom most nights, snuffing Charlie and muttering about the stupidity of everyone else. Not that Grey liked Mel much, either. She was just harder to shake off, and the ruder he was to her, the more adamantly she pretended to think it was funny, and the more firmly she glued herself to his side.

An hour later Ed was seated at the head of the table in the hotel's very smart restaurant, pouring the hotel's house champagne into six glasses. Dinner had been ordered and just for a minute or two everybody was pretending to be friends. 'I actually think,' he said, 'we can give ourselves a pat on the back. Between all the hiccups –' he left an ironic pause, and the three junior members of the team (sound, camera and poor, battered researcher) laughed with feeling '– we're getting some pretty special stuff up here. In bloody Antarctica. I must say I'm pleased. What do you think Grey? It's gonna be good, no? Pleased so far?'

Mistake. Stupid mistake. Ed had been under so much strain recently, and he was so relieved that the little shits had finally emerged from their bedrooms he wasn't focusing as efficiently as normal on the words coming out of his mouth.

'I think it's a load of bollocks, frankly. You know less about me now than you did before we started.'

'Oh!' Ed tried to look satirical, but it was obvious that Grey had only just begun.

'I actually think you're a lazy bastard.'

'Hey, take it easy,' said Sly the sound recordist, laughing nervously. 'We're meant to be celebrating!'

'Celebratin' what? That we're all engaged in a fuckin' *bonanza* of fuckin' *bullshit* that's about as factual as Peter-fuckin'-Rabbit? Ed, as a matter of interest, have you ever actually checked up on a single piece of information I've given you? Do you even know for sure my name is Grey McShane?'

'Grey!' Ed laughed nervously. 'Of course I do.'

'Do you know *for sure* that the "delightful lady" in Bonnyrigg was my fuckin' mother? Ask Mel. Mel, didn't I tell you my mother was dead? Didn't I tell you she died of alcohol poisoning in 1988?'

'I thought you said septicaemia.'

'Same bloody thing.'

'Ha ha.' Ed wasn't enjoying this. 'Don't be silly. She looked like you, Grey. Of course she was your mother!'

'How do you know?'

'Well – really. This is ridiculous. I mean, there has to be a certain amount of trust. Between us . . . Otherwise how does anyone ever know anything?'

'My point exactly,' said Grey. He took his glass of champagne, drank it in one and winced as it went down. '. . . Hey you, gorgeous girlee!' he shouted at a vacuous-looking adolescent in waitress uniform. He eyed her lasciviously as she lumbered across the room. 'Hello darlin'.'

She giggled.

'Say hello.'

She giggled again. 'Hello.'

He closed his eyes for a moment, as if savouring the greeting. 'Now, I want you to be as angelic as you look, my little . . . harlot. And bring me some gin. Can you do that for me, darlin'? And put some ice in it, would you. I don't like it when it's too warm.'

'OK,' said Ed, as the waitress trotted dolefully away again, 'Joking aside –'

'Ha!' said Grey. 'Who's jokin'?'

Ed sighed. He would be so happy when this thing was over. In the last few days and for the first time in his professional life he'd found himself wondering what possible career advantage could justify the hell he was putting himself through. 'So tell me,' he said with a patient smile. 'I must be being very dense –'

'*Ha!*' bellowed Grey. 'Now who's jokin'?'

'– But I'm not sure I understand what you're getting at.'

'Of course you bloody don't.'

Everyone waited. They watched him in expectant silence but then, as abruptly as he'd declared the war, he lost interest in it. A heavy, private gloom seemed to set around him suddenly. He looked distracted, absorbed in his own melancholy thoughts, and everyone breathed a sigh of relief.

'Well then,' said Ed dryly. 'I'm glad we cleared that up. So drink up, everyone! Two weeks down, two weeks to go! We're supposed to be celebrating!'

Grey didn't speak again until coffee, when he picked up the conversation exactly where he'd left it an hour and a half earlier. 'Which is why,' he said simply, 'I won't be doing this again after tomorrow. There's one more scene I want to do, and I'll tell you what it is when we get there. And after that I'm headin' home.'

Mel was the first to speak. 'But why? For heaven's sake what's wrong?'

'I'm fuckin' freezing up here.'

'So what? Grey, we all are.'

'Aye. And this gig is a load of crap.'

He wouldn't say another word after that. Everyone took their turn trying to reason with him but he ignored them all and one by one they gave up and went to bed. Grey stayed up drinking on his own until 6 a.m. when he was suddenly hit by boredom and treated each of them to a personal alarm call.

'Wake up you lazy bastard!' he bellowed happily into Ed's ear. 'Do a decent day's work for once in your life! I've got croissants down here. And fried eggs.' He was in quite a good mood. 'So hurry up. We're leaving in twenty minutes and if you're not careful Mel'll scoff the lot.'

In fact he was more cheerful during the ride to his wretched secret destination than Ed had ever seen him. And the more sullen his team-mates were with him the more cheerful he became. He was too drunk and much too incompetent to read the map properly, but he adamantly refused to tell anyone where they were going. So it took three hours to find the cemetery he was looking for, though it was only twenty-five miles down the road.

'Eh, Sly,' he grinned at the sound recordist, as they all clambered out into the cemetery car park and the miserable, drizzling rain, 'I'll bet you were getting a wee bi' impatient wi' me there, weren't you? Admit it now!'

Sly didn't reply.

'Ha!' said Grey casting merrily around the rest of the crew. 'He won't even speak to me now. Come on, Sly. Cheer up, lad. What a misery boots! We're here now. And just think, by this time tomorrow we'll be back in London and we'll never have to see each other again!' Sly smiled faintly and Grey clapped him on the back. 'See? So, come on everyone! Let's have a laugh! Now Ed,' he said, suddenly businesslike. 'This is the last thing we are ever going to do together, so I want it to be done properly. Can you manage that?'

Ed smiled tightly. He was only standing in this wretched cemetery because of the faint and fading possibility that he might yet be able to persuade Grey to change his mind about returning to London. He had no curiosity as to the reason why Grey should have led him there and, in fact, strongly suspected that there was none. Except to wind him up. Which Grey was doing, though he may not have realised it, extremely successfully.

'Grey, my old friend,' said Ed, 'I do everything properly.'

Grey ignored him. 'I want you to understand,' he slurred, 'that . . . this . . . is a very large cemetery. Have you understood that? A large . . . cemetery. And there's been many a time I've been lost in here. In fact I've never been here without getting lost. So it's very important, Ed – are you getting this? It's *very* important that you all follow me close behind.'

'We can do that,' Ed said patiently. 'But are you going to tell me a little bit about the place first?'

'No.'

'I mean what sort of significance it has to you . . . ?'

'No.'

'Grey,' Ed pretended to laugh, 'I will need to know, OK? Otherwise –' He paused, suddenly overcome by the pointlessness of the whole exercise. Otherwise *what*? Who cared why the bastard had led them to this fucking cemetery anyway? 'Otherwise – how am I going to know how to shoot it?'

'I'm tellin' you how to shoot it.'

'Grey, I hate to be rude. But it's really not your job –'

'Look. d'ya want it or don't you? Here I am. A fuckin' *poet* in a fuckin' *cemetery*. What more do you want? Are you goin' ta shut up and listen or shall we all just pack up now and head home?'

Ed thought about it carefully. What he wanted to do, what he wanted to do more than anything, was to lift his thin, white fist from the fleecy lining of his Time Zone donkey jacket, and slam it into Grey's face. He wanted to do it so much his arm started tickling and his head began to spin. For a second, or for a mere fraction of a fraction of a second Ed felt a rush of wild exhilaration course through him, the like of which he had never experienced. And then, as if with a mind of its own, his hand was suddenly emerging into the drizzle. *Back* and *up* it was flying, utterly focused, completely intent, clenched tight to deliver maximum damage . . .

But it stopped. For a frozen moment they gazed at it

204

hanging there between them, so tense and white and close to the end of Grey's nose, and then Grey burst into laughter.

'Och, for God's sake Ed. Do *something* with it. Don't leave the poor wee thing hanging out there for ever. It'll catch frostbite!'

The hand retreated to its fleecy covering and, barely missing a beat, Grey returned to business.

'We don't need Melanie for this,' he said. 'So you can tell her to fuck off back to the van. And Sly, as well. I'm not doin' any talking.'

'Even if you're not going to talk, we'll need sound, Grey,' muttered Ed. 'We can't do anything without sound.'

'Well I'm not doin' anything with it. Tell him to get back in the van. Sly! We won't be needin' you. Go and sit in the van!' He turned back to Ed. 'The rest of you can follow me until I find what I'm looking for and then you can buzz off, OK? And I don't want you talking to me and I only want Mike filming from behind.' He didn't wait for Ed's response. 'Right then. Let's go.'

Off he set with Mike, Beronica and Ed trailing obediently behind. Twenty minutes later, after an infuriating and apparently directionless ramble he suddenly came to a halt. 'That's Ma,' he said pointlessly, indicating an eight-foot marble angel with the inscription beneath: *Beth McCall, 1883–1890.* Moments later he was on the move again, laughing enthusiastically, his expensive black coat billowing elegantly behind him.

An hour after that, after the cold and dispirited little group had passed the minivan for the fourth time and there was still no indication of Grey's cemetery promenade either reaching a climax or drawing to an end, Ed and

Beronica decided to peel off. They were back in the bus, drinking coffee from a thermos, when Grey finally came to a halt in front of that small swelling in the grass. He stood there for a long while, saying nothing, breathing heavily. Suddenly he dropped to his knees, took his dark head in his great hands . . .

Back in the minivan Beronica salvaged yesterday's Dunkin' Donuts from the bottom of her bag. 'You see?' she was saying triumphantly, 'I knew they were in here somewhere!'

. . . And like a large wounded animal he rolled onto his side, curled his legs into his chest and slowly, so slowly, so very quietly, began to moan. He lay there for ages, until it was almost dark. The forgotten cameraman loitered a few feet behind him, bewildered, faintly revolted by such raw emotion, and completely terrified, too frightened even to turn his camera off, in case Grey heard it, remembered he was there and made him go back to the minibus, across the pitch black cemetery on his own.

NEW YOU RULE NUMBER EIGHT: You gotta treat HUMOUR like you treat your Gran's best tea set, OK? We're talking KID GLOVE CENTRAL, know what I'm saying? We're talking STEP AWAY FROM THE CAR WITH YOUR HANDS UP! True, if you can bring an ironic curl to a New You Lip once in a very while you'll reap the benefits, no question. But it's a dangerous business. Jokes about sex, farts, illness, perverts, women, children, and foreigners are gonna land you in the SHITBOWL! Yeah? And that's just for starters! So until you've learned the ropes, play SAFE and play SERIOUS. Just remember, there are more sacred cows out there than there are blades of grass to feed them on! Which means MOST THINGS AIN'T FUNNY!! Your new friends like to APPRECIATE humour but - get this - APPRECIATING HUMOUR is a club-class, jumbo-jet long haul FLIGHT away from actually LAUGHING!!! OK? And in a complicated world where we all want to look like we CARE (see New You Rule Number 5) and nobody knows exactly which cow is sacred, or exactly why, who's gonna risk it? Not you, baby! Your New friends won't be laughing. And - believe us - SOMEONE, SOMEWHERE is definitely gonna be taking offence!

THE MEMBERS' OWN DIRECTORY TO WHAT'S FUNNY AND WHAT'S NOT

The subject of Charlie's father was one of the few things in Charlie and Jo's relationship where friction and distrust still reigned. They tried to avoid discussing him, since it always seemed to end in argument. Charlie continued to return to Fiddleford Manor as often as he could, which was often; at least once a week, Jo stayed in London on her own and the General, for the time being at least, was allowed to foster his mostly-silent animosity unhindered.

And as the days flew by Charlie began to realise that the weight of his terrible grief was slowly beginning to lift a little bit. He was amazed by it, and incredibly grateful. After Georgie died he had imagined that he would never really feel fully alive again and yet here he was, less than a year later, in love, with a heart full of sadness but which could still sing, and which did sing, every time Jo walked into the room.

However, the depths of idiocy plumbed yesterday during his interview at a Soho café with the goofy young boys from GEAR had left Charlie feeling unusually depressed. It was his first interview for the Meals documentary and so he'd been more than willing to take advice. Jo, with kind intentions but forever the mind of a public relations girl, supplied him with a list of shamefully sycophantic questions and, in his enthusiasm not to let her down, Charlie stuck to them religiously. He sat in front of the boys while the cameraman adjusted the lights and watched them, slurping on glasses of latte, showing off to the unimpressed Soho locals on neighbouring tables and joshing neurotically about – well, about nothing; somebody's shoe size, somebody putting sugar in their tea. Midway through the interview, with a face cracking from the unaccustomed strain of false smiling, he realised he felt nostalgic for his old job at the mobile telephone shop.

'Of course we all know how much you care about the homeless,' he read. 'You've illustrated that just by being here.'

'That's right, Charlie.'

'But all-in-all are you having *fun*?'

'Fantastic fun, Charlie! It's hard work. Mega hard work. But it's our dream-come-true, isn't it? I mean, face it, it's everyone's dream-come-true! We are actually living a dream! So yeah! Sure it's fun. *Amazing* fun! And that's what it's all about, isn't it, Charlie?'

'Is it?'

'HA HA HA HA!'

So, for his audience with the sweet-natured but dim pop *divette* Dyanne, he decided to take a bolder approach. The Meals concert was still a fortnight away but she was releasing a new single that week and the day Charlie met her was her day for meeting the media. Charlie was to be the seventh interview of the afternoon and even she, who prided herself on her professionalism when it came to talking about herself, was beginning to feel the strain.

She had been the first and was sadly still the most

illustrious artist to have committed to the Meals concert, so Jo was especially keen that they make a fuss of her. They – that is to say Jo, Charlie, the cameraman, the sound man called Trevor, Dyanne and her manager, Leo – were all crammed into a chintzy, air conditioned hotel suite in the West End of London, making tense, bright conversation until everyone was ready to begin. Dyanne was complaining semi-flirtatiously because the sound man's hand had brushed against her breast while he was pinning on her microphone. 'I mean what *is* it about sound men and my breasts? It's always the same. They just can't keep their hands off of me!'

'You should see him when he gets near the boys,' said Charlie lightly. 'But we mustn't complain. It's one of the perks of the job, isn't it, Trevor?' Trevor smiled non-committally.

'Not funny,' muttered Leo, the manager.

'Call me a prima donna,' she went on, 'but it does get on my nerves though. I don't enjoy having strange men pawing all over my breasts the whole time.'

'Good job you're not a prozzie,' said Charlie. He noticed yet another shudder of disapproval pass though the room.

Jo offered an ambiguous half-smile; a subtle expression she'd perfected over the years, adopted for all jokes and other potentially dangerous situations, and glanced quickly around the room to see how the others were taking it. Dim Dyanne was giggling, which was disconcerting, but a relief. Leo, on the other hand, looked angry.

'I don't think a lot of prostitutes would appreciate that comment,' he said.

'But there aren't any in the room,' answered Jo, to her own surprise.

'That's hardly the point,' said Leo.

'You're too sensitive, Leo,' said Charlie mildy. 'You need to develop a thicker skin.'

'I'm not thinking of *my* skin.'

'Are we ready?' said Jo. 'Shall we get cracking then?'

And so Charlie began. He'd thought about what he was going to ask her for hours last night, as Jo lay sleeping peacefully beside him. What, he wondered, did people really want to know about Dyanne? She was twenty-five, white, quite pretty. She didn't have time for a boyfriend, or so the papers said, and she had a fantastic relationship with her Mum. After much thought he came to the depressing conclusion that people didn't really want to know any more than that. There was only one thing which set her apart from the rest of the human race, so far as he could see. It was all he could think of to ask her about.

'So,' he said. 'What's it like to be famous, then?'

Jo was standing beside Leo. She heard him click his tongue in disgusted disbelief, and even her love-blindness couldn't entirely protect her from a flicker of professional shame. It was not a sophisticated opener. But Dyanne didn't seem to mind. Once the cameras rolled – and quite often when they didn't – she tended to work on automatic anyway.

'Well,' she said with a professional stretch of her glossed lips, 'in some ways it's good, Charlie, and in some ways it's very bad. I do get tired of the press intrusions but then on the other hand I also get to wear some really sensational clothes!'

'Clothes! Goodness, I'd never thought of that! So are the clothes the best thing about being famous?'

She looked uncertain. 'I wouldn't say the *best* thing, no . . .'

'Oh. So what's the best thing?'

'Well – Obviously, I like doing things like this. For the homeless. That's very important. That's a very important part of the famous thing, I think.'

'That's the best thing about being famous?'

'Um – Yes.'

'And is that because you feel especially strongly about people sleeping on the streets or do you just really enjoy doing live performances?'

'Yes.'

'Which?'

'Well, both I suppose. I haven't actually done much live performance as yet, as you know. So I'm really looking forward to that. Really, really looking forward to that challenge. But basically it's actually something which disgusts me. I just can't believe that in such an amazing country as this, homelessness is still in such a . . . situation. It makes me so angry. I actually think it's obscene.'

'You really feel that passionately?'

'Don't you?'

Charlie shrugged. 'I suppose so. When I concentrate . . . But I must admit it's not something I think about often.'

Dyanne glanced uncertainly across at Jo and Leo, both of whom were looking as confused as she felt. Was this guy taking the piss? She just didn't know. 'Well you should, shouldn't you? Tony Blair should be ashamed of himself.'

Charlie laughed. 'But seriously,' he said, 'your first two singles did very well in America, didn't they?'

'They did, Charlie. They did very well.'

'Did they make you an absolute fortune?'

Behind him, Jo bit her lips and managed not to snort with outraged laughter. Leo's mouth turned white.

'Pardon?' said Dyanne.

'I was just wondering, because maybe it's a guilt thing. Maybe that's why celebrities like yourself feel so strongly about things like the homeless, whereas the rest of us just sort of shuffle along not really thinking about them much . . .'

'That's not right! Everyone thinks about them, don't they Leo?'

'Of course we do,' snapped Leo.

'I certainly do,' said Trevor. 'I feel terrible.'

'We all do,' said Leo. 'Except you. Can we move this thing on?'

'Crikey,' Charlie chuckled good-naturedly. 'What a bunch of liars.'

'He's only joking,' Jo said quickly.

Charlie ignored her. 'Dyanne, I hope you don't mind. Perhaps you'll think it's a bit cheeky but before the interruption . . . I was actually going to ask if you'd already donated any money to the Homeless charity?'

She looked astonished. Dumbstruck. 'It is cheeky, yes,' she said finally. 'But yes. Yes I can do.'

'How much?'

'Can we stop filming, please?' said Leo.

'She hasn't answered yet,' said Charlie. 'Give her a chance!'

'She doesn't need a bloody chance. She's doing you a favour!'

'Dyanne –' Charlie smiled at her confidingly. 'Can you ignore the barracking from the sidelines? . . . I can if you can.'

She laughed uncertainly. 'I suppose so.'

'All right. Good. Thank you.' He grinned. *'How much?'*

Dyanne's large, round, stupid eyes gazed at her interrogator in amazement.

'Dyanne,' said Leo urgently. 'Don't answer that. Dyanne! Listen to me!'

'No,' said Dyanne slowly, 'But he's right in a way isn't he?'

'That's enough! This interview is over! Dyanne, take off the microphone!'

'Because the funny thing is,' Dyanne continued obliviously, 'I get really annoyed when I see these celebrities preaching on, making out like they're so wonderful, but when you think about it I'm doing exactly the same thing.'

Charlie looked triumphant. 'You see?' he said. *'She* knows what I'm talking about!'

'You've got ever such sexy eyes,' she said quietly. 'Did anyone ever tell you?'

'Constantly,' said Charlie.

She leant back in her chair. Everyone waited. Suddenly her impassive face broke into an enormous smile. 'Isn't that terrible?' she said. 'Here's me, bullshitting away as usual. Cruising along nicely! And along comes a bloke with sexy eyes and all of a sudden I'm looking like a total wally!'

'Can we switch the camera *off*?'

'But if someone chucks me my bag . . .'

The cameras kept rolling as she scribbled out the cheque. After that, and after she'd made Charlie reveal its size to the camera – 'Go on! Tell everyone how much it is! It's the first decent thing I've done in ages, so I think I should be allowed to show off about it!' – the two of them relaxed into a friendly banter. And in due course Charlie, with kindly curiosity and the minimum of conscious effort, had managed to expose almost everything of her sweet but not terrifically interesting soul. In its own way it turned out to be an excellent interview.

When they'd finished Dyanne asked Charlie for his telephone number and Jo said, 'Yeah, that would be great. We live just near Parsons Green. You should look in on us some time.'

'Oh.' said Dyanne.

'Yes. "Oh",' said Jo.

Charlie looked from one to the other. 'So we *live* together now, do we?'

Jo looked faintly bashful. 'For the purposes of this con-versation we do.'

'Shame,' said Dyanne sadly. 'The best ones are always taken, aren't they?'

Meanwhile, in a screening room barely half a mile away, and before a roomful of sundry television executives and their minions, Ed was just coming to the end of a witty little speech about the difficulties involved in 'making television' about pathologically uncooperative alcoholics.

'As you will soon discover,' he said wryly, 'Grey McShane, who unfortunately couldn't be with us today, is not a man who sticks *religiously* to the facts. He talks in riddles. He delights in confusion. What I've tried to do here is to capture that essence, contradictions and all, and to leave you with the impression of a truly remarkable and complex creature; a very real and very modern genius. A man who doesn't depend on material truths the way the rest of us do. A man who can survive on ideas alone. Oh, and of course, the very occasional glass of gin.' He paused for the titter to subside. How little they knew. 'Sometimes infuriating. Sometimes . . . very infuriating. That's Grey McShane. Unquestionably a poet for our time.'

He was about to take his seat when, with a violent bang, the door to the screening room burst open and a familiar voice called out, 'Wait there Eddie my ol' friend. Wait for me and Mel! Don't tell me you were a-goin' ta start wi'out us?'

The small audience turned to see the poet of our time, lurching unquestionably towards them, filthy and unshaven, with a bottle of gin tucked under his arm.

'Grey!' cried Ed. The very man he'd decided against inviting. 'How lovely! And Mel, too! Goodness! What a bonus! I thought you two had gone off on holiday somewhere! Well! For heaven's sake, now you're here, *sit down*! We're just about to begin. How did you know –'

'How did I know?' said Grey, collapsing into a front seat and, in doing so, assailing the nostrils of everyone present with a stench of sweat and stale gin. 'How did I know? How did I know? That's a very good question. Mel, how did I know?'

'Grey. Have you met Tom Faulkner?' interrupted Ed. 'He's the guy who originally green-lit the project. So, er, – if there's anything in it you don't like, ha ha, he'll be the one to punch!'

'Hello there, Tom,' said Grey, stretching his legs out in front of him, setting the gin between his knees, and producing a small bottle of Angostura. 'Look!' he said slowly, mixing the two together. 'See? The red comin'

216

down there? Ed doesn't think much of it, I know, but I swear I think it's the most beautiful thing on God's earth. What do you think, Tom?'

'Fantastic!' said Tom. 'Absolutely ... *really* ... stunning.'

Grey squinted at the bottle more closely. 'You can't really see it in this light ...'

'Tom, this is Melanie Slater,' said Ed wearily.

'Hello again, Tom! Long-time-no-see! I'm so sorry we're late.' She kissed Tom on either cheek, turned to Ed and smiled unpleasantly. 'Small old world, isn't it? We only met at dinner last night.'

'Well,' said Ed, 'shall we begin?'

During the week that he'd been back in London Ed had seen no one. He'd bolted himself and his editor into a private edit suite and worked without stint, determined to salvage something brilliant from his Scottish debacle, and too nervous to announce his return to civilisation until he had. The only person he'd tried to contact was Jo. He'd left his third message on her voicemail only a couple of hours ago, inviting her in a casual, friendly sort of way to look in on the screening if she was passing. She was normally meticulous about returning calls, even unwelcome ones. So he didn't allow himself to worry. She was obviously away.

He settled himself into his seat and waited confidently for the show to begin. Tom was going to be delighted. What he was about to see, Ed Bailey knew, was *signature* Ed Bailey stuff. Ed Bailey at Ed Bailey's best. Against all the odds, he had created a working class hero to overshadow every working class hero in history; brooding, anarchic, enigmatic, a man who'd triumphed against greyness, against

217

prejudice and against incarceration. (Ed had had trouble discovering exactly where; there were no records of a Grey McShane having been incarcerated anywhere, and so, in signature Ed Bailey style, he'd fudged it with a stylish soundtrack; 'Who Let The Dogs Out?' and a souped-up montage of slamming gates and clinking chains, intercut with dramatic, *slo-mo* pictures of Grey, standing on top of Arthur's Seat in Edinburgh, arms outstretched and coat billowing, revelling in the freedom of the wind.) Even Grey at his most bloody-minded wouldn't be able to complain . . .

Sure enough, as the end music came up (credits to be added later) Tom leapt beaming to his feet. 'Well done, Ed!' he said. 'Bloody fantastic! Fascinating. Really . . . *uplifting* stuff. Nothing like your football, thank God.'

Ed tipped his head a little to the side and smiled. He could see other people getting up from their seats, making their way over to congratulate him. This, he thought, was the moment when all the pain could be forgotten, when he remembered what it was all about. He considered going over to make peace with Grey but quickly thought better of it. Even if Grey was pleased by what he'd seen – which he had to be, Ed thought, he couldn't possibly not be – he would still find something to be difficult about. Why ruin the moment? What did it matter what Grey thought anyway?

But if Grey had been pleased by what he saw he certainly wasn't showing any signs of it. He seemed to be frozen to his chair. He and Mel were the only people who still hadn't moved and for several minutes after the music had stopped they continued to sit, side by side, both, independently, too unhappy to speak. Mel looked up to see Tom making his way over. He was smiling, looking pleasant but confused.

'Melanie,' she could hear him saying, 'what a shame! And when you were so excited about it! He must have edited you out completely!'

'I guess he must have done,' said Mel numbly.

'And you had no idea? Well, that's obviously why . . . I'm so sorry. If I'd known I would never have mentioned the, er – screening.'

'Never mind,' she said bravely. 'Just so long as I get paid!'

Certainly not in full, he thought, but he wrinkled his nose and nodded sympathetically. 'Dear old Ed,' he said. 'You have to watch him, you know! He can be such a snake . . .' And then he turned to Grey. 'Well, Grey, you're being very quiet! What did you think?'

'Terrible,' he muttered. 'Absolutely bloody terrible.'

'Mmm . . . It's often a shock seeing one's self on television for the first time,' Tom said soothingly. 'But believe me, Ed's done us proud. It was excellent. I actually thought you came out of it very well.'

'But you don't know me,' said Grey solemnly. 'Excuse me.' He stood up. 'Come on Mel. I think we deserve a drink.'

They headed off to the nearest pub, but as she tripped silently beside him, Mel couldn't understand what his complaint was. Even she, in spite of her rage and disappointment, could acknowledge that Ed had done an amazing job. Grey had come out of it perfectly; the perfect fantasy of a modern genius; everything she had always wanted people to imagine she was fucking. What the hell was he looking so miserable about? They had to

219

drink heavily for another hour before Grey was ready to explain.

'D'you suppose Ed has any idea why I made him go to that cemetery?' he said suddenly.

'They didn't use it, did they?' she said casually. 'Probably too dark.'

'Fuck "too dark"! Does he think I like wandering around graveyards, getting my clothes dirty? . . . That man is a disgrace to journalism. He knows nothing! He's a disgrace to mankind.'

'I'll drink to that.'

'For Christ's sake! It's not even my real name.'

'Yeah?' Mel had her own disappointments to brood about. She wasn't really listening. 'It's a nice name, though.'

'Aye it is. It's why I chose it. Grey McShane was actually a friend of my brother.'

Through the fuzz of alcohol, Mel finally registered that Grey might be telling her something interesting. She forced herself to focus on his face. 'Are you talking bollocks again?' she said slowly. 'Because really, Grey, if you are I don't think this is the moment.'

'It's why they couldn't find any records at the prisons. It's why that stupid teacher didn't have a soddin' clue who I was.'

'Does Ed know all this?'

He shook his head and laughed. 'It's funny though, isn't it? Did ye not see how he got round it? The total absence of a single correct piece of information in the whole programme. Amazin' what you can drown out with a soundtrack, isn't it?'

Mel couldn't remember. She couldn't remember much about the documentary, in fact, except her own absence from it. 'So,' she said slowly, frowning in concentration, 'Mrs McShane? Who I interviewed? Was that –'

'Mrs McShane. Aye. I told you, the mother's dead.'

'So, in the cemetery . . . That was your mother? Or was it Grey – I mean the real Grey –'

'Och, *no*. That was Emily. That was *Emily*.'

'Who's Emily?'

'God, but we loved each other . . . Aye, we did.'

'She was your girlfriend?'

'She was fifteen when we put her there, can you believe tha'? *Fifteen* . . . And I was twenty-three!'

'I'm not really getting you, Grey. Why are you telling me all this?'

'I don't know,' he said blandly. 'Got to tell someone, haven't you? I thought I'd told Ed. I kept *tellin'* him to check his facts. But he's useless!'

'Actually, you told him *not* to, I seem to remember.'

'Aye. And he listened to that! He's a coward. He's fuckin' useless.'

'So, did you ever go to jail? Or was that a lie too?'

He nodded his head. 'Three months. Sex with a junior. Whatever they call it.'

'Fuck me!' she laughed. 'You're a *sex offender*! People aren't going to like that when it gets out.'

'Aye. And then I killed her.'

'Jesus Christ!' This wasn't funny. 'Grey, you're not being funny any more. I'm actually – You're actually freaking me out.'

'We'd both taken a load of bloody mushrooms, if you can believe it.'

'Should I?' she said, slightly hysterically.

'But I know how slowly I was going because I remember,

Emily was fuckin' around at the pedals, saying my feet looked like turds.' He smiled. 'And I was laughing so much I couldn't see a bloody thing. And then suddenly –' He clapped his hands in front of Mel's face and she leapt backwards, nearly falling off her stool. 'Wham! I can't even remember . . . Next thing she's dead and I'm in jail . . . Her parents told the police I was doin' her, so they got me on that . . . But you can't blame them, can you?'

Mel stared at him. She squinted at him. 'This is nuts,' she said eventually. 'You're not bullshitting, are you?' But she knew he wasn't. 'God, you poor sod.'

'Och. Never mind me . . . I wish they'd locked me up for good.'

She reached across and patted his hand. 'Don't say that, Grey!' she said kindly. 'Think of all the wonderful things that have happened to you since then . . . Your record deal –'

'For God's sake!'

'It may seem unimportant to you now. But give it a few months –'

'I've given it fourteen years!'

'– You'll feel better.'

'Och! Why'm I telling you? What do you know, anyway?'

But she did know, that was the thing. And his assumption riled her. What with his confession and her non-appearance in the show, Mel felt that the balance of their relationship had shifted in the last couple of hours and she suddenly felt inclined to stick up for herself, possibly even to patronise him slightly. He had no business to assume so much about her. What did he really know? What did anyone know?

'I *do*,' she said emphatically. 'Believe me. I do understand.'

He laughed. 'Aye. Of course you do, love.'

'No, I do.'

'Och, shut up, Mel,' he said blandly. 'You're drunk.'

'Grey,' she said carefully. 'Listen to me. *Listen to me*. I'm going to tell you something I've never told anyone before . . . Because I think it'll make you feel better. Do you understand?' He didn't reply. 'Because I think if we're going to be friends, I mean *real* friends, you need to know what sort of a person I am. I mean *really* am. Underneath the – bubbly exterior. Grey, have you ever been horseback hunting?'

'*Horseback hunting?* What the fuck's that? Of course I haven't.'

'Well I have. I mean I haven't actually participated, obviously. But I've watched. It's the most disgusting thing I've ever seen. It makes you ashamed to be human.'

'I'm sorry about that,' he said indifferently.

'I had a boyfriend who used to take me on day trips to the country. I won't mention his name because he's actually doing very well at the moment.' She paused, vaguely hoping that Grey would insist on it but he didn't. 'Anyway, we used to head off on these *coaches* – ha! – If you can imagine me on a coach! A bloody great gang of us, with banners and drums and God knows what. But it was a blast. You could get rid of all your pent-up aggression, get some fresh air, scream abuse at total strangers and still feel like you were doing something *useful*! And I'm not being smart, Grey, because believe me if you saw some of the stuff I've seen. Hunting is a truly barbaric sport. The little foxes are literally *torn apart* . . .'

Grey looked at her in vague, disinterested confusion. 'Mel, what are you going on about?'

'You know Jo's friend? The posh one? I haven't met him, thank God. He's called Charlie.'

'Charlie,' said Grey. 'He's a good man.'

'He had a sister. Actually he had a twin.'

'Aye. She died.'

'She did die. A year ago in December . . . Do you know how she died?'

'In a hunting accident.' Ah! She had Grey's attention now.

'An *accident*. That's *right*. Like you and Emily –'

'You fuckin' bitch!'

She shook her head. Perhaps she didn't even hear him. 'So, you see I do know what you're talking about. What I'm trying to tell you is, although of course I felt terrible about it at the time, I've managed to move on. It was an *accident*. It was just a terrible accident. If she hadn't been hunting in the first place. For Christ's sake if she'd been a better horse rider. If she hadn't been approaching the fence when she did. If she hadn't –' Mel shrugged, '– landed on her head. You see? Sometimes these things are just *meant* to happen. It's synchronicity. The fact is she shouldn't have been hunting in the first place . . . And *Emily* really shouldn't have been mucking around with the pedals of your car. You see? She knew you were on mushrooms, didn't she? The point is, Grey, sometimes bad things happen. Sometimes good things. And maybe that's what had to happen so you could be a better poet. Yeah? *Who knows? But you just have to move on.*'

Grey couldn't take his eyes off her. Suddenly he was

noticing details about her face he'd never noticed before; the strangely orange tinge to her skin, the glimmer of daylight which shone through the piercing of her right ear, the little pockmarks beneath her eyebrows where she'd plucked the hairs away, the yellowness of the white around her pale brown eyes . . . and all this time he'd thought she was pretty. A phrase he and his brother used to use suddenly popped into his mind. 'Good from far but far from good,' he muttered.

'What?'

He stood up. 'I don't think I can appreciate your angle on life, darlin',' he said. 'That was horrible and I'm going to try hard to forget it. But thank you for tryin'.'

'What?'

'We had a couple of good times though, didn't we? Maybe in the beginnin'? I don't really remember.'

'Well of course we did! We *do*! . . . Grey? *Grey! Wait!* Where are you going?'

But he was gone.

So this was what happened when you did someone a favour, she thought. When you tried to offer comfort. When you took a risk and confided a story you had never confided before. When you told the truth. This was how people like Grey repaid you. *These things happen*, she reminded herself. But she wasn't ready to move on. Not by a long way. She had never felt so angry in her life.

Early the following Saturday morning, and with just a week to go before the concert, Jo was lying in Charlie's bed, awaiting his return with sickly apprehension. Charlie, who'd gone to the corner shop to fetch breakfast, was due to be leaving shortly to see his father and Jo had finally decided it was time to tell him the truth. Over the last few weeks she had rehearsed every possible approach to the subject but now that it came to choosing one of them, they all sounded as feeble as each other. She no longer believed in her own excuses. There was no real excuse. She had exploited his trust, and there was a small chance he would never forgive her for it. But she had to take the risk, because the lying had become unbearable.

She heard the door slam, and Charlie whistling absent-mindedly as he came into the hall. She heard the clink as he dropped his keys somewhere he wouldn't be able to find them later, and she reached for a T-shirt. This was certainly not a conversation to be had from bed.

'I got you this,' he said, plonking a copy of the *Daily Mail* on the duvet and leaning down to give her a kiss. 'Because I know you want it really.'

'I don't want it!' she said, smiling. 'I have to read it every day at work. It's a disgusting newspaper!' She paused to scrutinise a picture of Jerry Hall (mum-of-four and still fabulous) in her swimsuit.

'Ah Jerry,' said Charlie mildly. 'How does she do it?'

'I'm not actually *reading* it!'

He sat down on the bed and kissed her again. 'Why are you getting dressed? I don't need to leave for at least an hour. I was just going to bring you some coffee . . . Please. Don't get out of bed.'

'Charlie,' she said, pushing him regretfully away, 'I've got to tell you something, and I think it's going to make you very angry.'

'I doubt it. I'm not sure there's anything you could do that would make me very angry.'

'I think there is,' she said.

He looked at her consideringly for a moment and stood up. 'Wait there. I can't take bad news on an empty stomach. I'm going to get some coffee.'

'No, Charlie –'

'I'm serious,' he said. 'I'll keel over.'

'This is serious.'

'Give me two seconds –'

Happy for the tiny reprieve, she turned distractedly back to the *Daily Mail*. How was she going to manage this? Couldn't she put it off, just for one more week? What if he really wouldn't forgive her? What if that last kiss turned out to be the last kiss for ever? . . . Suddenly she stopped. Staring out across the top of page seven was a full-length photograph of Mel, belly pressed to the floor, breasts and eyes pointed upward, face heavily painted and trying hard to look vulnerable. Beneath it, at a jaunty angle, was a smaller picture of Grey at some party. He was holding a glass of gin, grinning demoniacally at an unknown girl's cleavage. 'I Thought I'd Found Love But He Was A Millionaire Child Abuser' read the headline.

'Charlie!' she said. '*Charlie!* Jesus Christ! Look at this!'

Charlie rushed back and leaned over her shoulder to read the paper. 'Oh God, poor guy,' he said. 'What did he tell her for?'

'I knew there was something disgusting about that man.'

'He's not disgusting,' Charlie snapped. 'Don't be so stupid.'

'She was fourteen!'

'They were living together in her parents' house, for God's sake. He loved her . . . Anyway she wasn't fourteen. She was fifteen.'

'She says fourteen here.' She looked up from the paper. 'How come you know so much about it?'

Charlie looked slightly embarrassed. 'He told me. At Fiddleford last weekend. He turned up looking so pitiful, poor man. So I invited him in.'

'*What*? Grey McShane, a self-confessed – paedophile – is allowed to stay with your father and I'm not, just because I disapprove of hunting?'

'Come on, Jo.'

'Anyway, since when was Grey such a great mate of yours? What was he doing, just turning up uninvited?'

'He's not the first person to invite himself to stay with us,' Charlie said dryly.

Jo ignored it. 'I do wonder why you didn't tell me.'

'Well –' Charlie laughed. 'I mean, look at the way you're reacting. I didn't see much point.'

The thing quickly escalated into a row. It was so much easier for her to be angry than to continue with the conversation she had been planning. So, for the second time, he left for the country while they were still arguing. Jo flounced out of the flat pretending to be much angrier than she felt, and within moments of climbing into a cab, called Mel.

Mel was still in bed and hadn't yet seen the paper. She made Jo read the whole article aloud.

'Ha ha!' she cackled, 'that'll teach 'em, the bastards! See? *Nobody* fucks with me! How do I look? Do I look OK? Like a *journalist*, yeah? I look sexy, don't I? And strong? Sexy in a

228

strong way? Like that woman in – Sigourney Weaver. Like Sigourney Weaver . . .'

'You look fabulous,' lied Jo. 'But you've made Ed look like a complete prat.'

'Haven't I just? That'll teach him. I've ruined his career! Read that bit out again, will you?'

'Which bit?'

'Come on! The bit where I say his stupid documentary is a travesty. When I say the thing about losing respect for TV journalism. How many times do you think they actually mention him by name?'

'Mel, I don't understand. I mean Grey, yes. He dumped you –'

'He didn't! He did *not*! I dumped him!'

'OK. All right. Whatever. But what's Ed ever done to you? He's just given you an amazing break – What did you have to bring him into it for?'

'Because he's a journalist,' Mel said pompously. (She hadn't told Jo about her recent humiliation at Ed's hands.) 'And he didn't check his facts. He brings the whole profession into disrepute. He should be ashamed of himself.'

That was when it finally occurred to Jo how much trouble she was in. Penny would read this. And if she didn't she would soon read something else, because Ed Bailey, thirty-three, fashionable documentary maker and psychopathically ambitious man, had been publicly ridiculed and would now have to defend himself as loudly as he could. His reputation was on the line. One way or another Penny would soon work out that Ed Bailey, whom she thought was engaged on a documentary about a London concert, had in fact spent the last three weeks making a fool of himself, and an entirely different documentary, at the other end of the country.

Needless to say, at that very moment, in an £850,000 open-plan 'living space' in Fanshaw Street, Hoxton, Penny was lying in her white, cement bed, waiting for the little actor she'd picked up the night before to bring in the champagne and caviar kept especially for post-casual-sex occasions such as this. She was, of course, flicking through the *Daily Mail*, her laser eyes staying sharp for anything of relevance to her booming company, and sure enough, before very long, she had fallen upon the article in question. It confused her. Worse than that, it worried her. She forgot about the caviar and reached for the stainless steel notebook. What she needed was clarification at once. She didn't have Ed – (or rather Charlie's) – home telephone number, and she'd left his mobile number at the office, but she assumed, quite rightly, that after such a write-up, the man she thought she employed would be sitting at his desk, working hard to salvage his reputation. She called directory inquiries and got the number of his production company . . .

. . . 'How about lunch to celebrate? What are you doing now?' said Mel.

'Celebrate *what*?' said Jo. 'God, Mel! Why are you such a – You are so bloody irresponsible! You have no idea what damage you've done.'

'Jo! What's happened to your S.O.H. girl? Seriously. I'm getting *seriously* worried! Where are you now?'

'I'm in a taxi –' but she was distracted by the dreaded electronic beep. Somebody was trying to get through to her. Perhaps it was Charlie, ringing to suggest peace. Or perhaps it wasn't . . . She decided not to risk it. Just then the taxi swung left, and her cheekbone bumped against her telephone key pad. She was explaining to Mel that she was on her way to Peckham, which was a lie, when she heard Ed's voice at the other end of the line. 'Ed?'

'Jo? What are you talking about?'

'What are you doing? Why are you talking to me? I was talking to Mel.'

'That bitch!'

'Look – I really don't want to get involved in this. Can you get off the line please? I was talking to Mel.'

'Jo. I need your help.'

He sounded awful. She had never heard him sound so wretched. 'Oh God,' she sighed. 'Well what do you expect me to do, Ed? Why didn't you check the facts?'

'How could I? Where could I start? The stupid bastard didn't even give me his real name. He doesn't open his mouth without lying. He doesn't *understand* the concept of truth! I made it clear at the bloody screening, it was only ever meant to be an *impression* of a man. An impression! Can't they understand what that means? . . . I've already had Tom Faulkner on the line, threatening to pull the whole thing . . . I've got to think. I've got to come up with something or no one's ever going to employ me again.'

It was shocking to hear him so rattled. Ed – who was always so in control – actually sounded frightened. And she couldn't help it. Every kindly instinct in her otherwise perfect body made her want to help. 'OK. Ed, calm down. This isn't like you. It's not like you to panic. You've got to think of an explanation, that's all. Basically you've got

231

to –' In the background she could hear his other telephone beginning to ring.

'See?' said Ed. 'Oh Shit! What am I going to say? I've already had the *Telegraph* on, and *The Times* –'

'What did you tell them?'

'Nothing! I pretended I was the cleaner.'

Jo giggled.

'IT'S NOT FUNNY!'

'OK, listen. Calm down. Are you going to answer that telephone?'

'No!'

'I think you should.'

'What am I going to say?'

'Just what you said to me.'

'What did I say? I can't remember.'

'That . . . it was only meant to be an impression. That all your documentary has ever claimed to offer is a glimpse into the imagination of an artist . . . of a man who lives in a fantasy world. You've got to remember no one's actually seen it yet. So basically it's your word against Mel's. And to be frank that ridiculous photograph isn't exactly going to encourage people to take her seriously. Come on, Ed. Get a grip. *Answer the telephone.* And then call me back –'

'No. Wait. Stay on the line. I'm going to put it on speaker-phone.'

'Ed! For Heaven's sake!' Jo's telephone was beeping again.

'Please. I need your help.'

She sighed. 'Are you in the office? I'm coming over. Just – try to stay calm, OK?'

'Oh, Jo. I love you.'

'Don't be ridiculous.'

'I owe you one.'

'Answer the telephone!'

She heard him clearing his throat, taking a deep breath. 'Hello,' he said smoothly. 'Ed Bailey here. What's up?' Jo smiled. Amazing how he could switch it on when he needed to. Amazing and actually quite creepy.

'Charlie? Penny here. Is that you?'

FUCK!

'Wrong number!' shouted Jo, from her seat in the back of the taxi. 'Tell her it's the wrong number. ED! It's the WRONG NUMBER!'

'What? I can't hear. I've got the other line –' She heard herself being dumped unceremoniously onto the table. She was powerless to do anything but listen.

'Charlie?' said Penny. 'What's going on? Is that you?'

'Charlie?' said Ed. 'I'm afraid you've got the wrong number.'

'For God's sake,' said Penny. She sounded very ratty. 'Is that Ed Bailey or isn't it? Who am I speaking to?'

'Well you called me –'

'TELL HER IT'S THE WRONG NUMBER!'

'Is that Charlie? Who the bloody hell am I speaking to?'

'There isn't any Charlie here. Who's this?'

'It's Penny Corren. Top Spin Public Relations. What's going on? Can I speak to Jo?'

'Jo?'

'Is Jo there? Put Jo on!'

'No. Of course she's not here. What do you want?'

'I want to know what's going on.'

Suddenly Ed picked up his mobile. 'Jo? Are you still there?'

'No!' whispered Jo. 'No I'm not! Get rid of her! Tell her it's the wrong number!'

Ed turned back to the speakerphone. 'She's gone,' he said. 'You'd better call her on the mobile.'

'Are you,' said Penny, her voice loaded with sarcasm, 'at any point, going to be kind enough to offer me some sort of explanation? I have a newspaper in front of me here, which claims you spent the last three weeks in Scotland. I imagine that's why you've never been able to make it into the office?'

'What office? What are you talking about?'

'TELL HER IT'S THE WRONG NUMBER!'

And then the line went dead. She redialled but it sounded engaged. The bastard had taken the telephone off the hook.

A month ago she wouldn't have hesitated. She would have ordered the taxi to turn around. She would been there *already*, grovelling, ingratiating, saving her professional skin. But now there was Charlie to think about. She needed to talk to him before Penny did. She needed to explain everything, and not just over the telephone. Should she head straight for Fiddleford? Should she call Penny? Should she go and straighten things out with Ed? The taxi came to a stop outside her flat and she still didn't know what to do. In a blind and stupid panic she decided what she needed was an hour to think. She decided to go to the gym.

'So I thought after this I might try to do a documentary about hunting,' Charlie was saying cheerfully and with a great deal more enthusiasm than he felt, 'or maybe something about the end of British agriculture . . . foot and mouth ... That could be interesting ...' And the General was nodding kindly. They were in the library, playing an after-lunch game of chess, and Charlie had talked of nothing but his work since he arrived.

'I know it's pretty silly,' he'd said of his current project (and he'd said it more than once), 'but it's a step in the right direction. It's a foot in the door.'

'It certainly is. It certainly is. I think it's marvellous. Your turn.'

The General didn't much care for pop stars or television and in truth he was no more delighted by his son's new choice of occupation than he had been with his last. It all sounded terrifically second-rate. Not only that, he strongly suspected that Charlie wasn't happy. It was a case, he thought, of the fellow protesting too much. He'd never heard his son talk so frantically, or try so hard to impress him.

'Do you miss the singing much?' he asked tentatively.

'Oh crikey, no!' Charlie said emphatically. But of course he missed the singing. He missed so much about his old life. He missed the time he used to spend on the estate. He missed Georgie. He kept imagining how Georgie would laugh if she could see him now, in his subdued colours. But he felt he had no choice. There was his father to consider, who needed a son to be proud of. And there was Jo. Jo. Whom he loved. Who needed success like he now realised he needed the West Country air. It was something she had always been clear about. And he understood. He did. Or he tried to. Anyway, he loved her and if this was what he needed to do – ingratiate himself with idiots, mince about in mustard coloured trousers, chuckle quietly at jokes that weren't funny,

and always look sharp when 'social issues' were up . . .
he sighed.

Well it was worth it. She was worth it. He would not let
her down.

'It's your turn,' the General said again. 'And I should
leave that knight where it is if I were you.'

Charlie moved it anyway, as he always did, as his father
knew he would.

'Hm . . . Well. I fear you'll find . . . Ye-es . . . 'Fraid so,
Charlie. Checkmate.'

Which was when his mobile rang.

'I really think,' said his father, 'you might switch that
bloody thing off when you're in the house.'

Charlie ignored him. 'Hello?' he said. Which was a
shame. Because of course it was Penny.

He listened politely while she spat out her story, and his
fragile new life collapsed to the ground, and the woman
who had provided him with the only flicker of light in the
long, dark months since he buried Georgie was revealed
in her very ugliest colours. She was a liar. Their relationship
was built on lies.

'So where is she now?' he asked quietly.

'Yes! Where *is* Jo? I thought you'd know. I've been trying
to track her down since this morning . . . But you can assure
me absolutely that she's not with you?'

'No! I wish she were.'

'My God, when I get hold of that girl.'

'. . . What can I say? I don't know what to say, Penny.
But right now, if you don't mind, I'd like to get off the
telephone so I can think.'

'I dare say you would. And where does that leave me?
Right now you can consider yourself bloody lucky I've

236

chosen to believe your side of the story.'

'I don't have a "side of a story",' he said coldly. 'I'm just telling you who I am. It didn't occur to me you didn't already know.'

'Right,' said Penny. 'Yeah, *right*. But I can't help wondering what made you believe we'd want to hire you in the first place? I mean, if I understand you correctly you've done nothing. You're a total nonentity.'

'Well – I quite agree,' said Charlie reasonably. 'I mean obviously I thought you were mad. But then you all seemed so keen . . .'

Penny wasn't happy to be reminded of that. Joanna Smiley had succeded in making them all feel like fools. 'Well. As I say. You're bloody lucky I'm probably not going to sue you, Charlie . . . *Maxwell McDouglas*. Whoever you are . . .'

'Absolutely,' snapped Charlie, his patience finally running out. 'And vice versa. So if there's nothing else –'

'There's a lot else –'

'Then I'll call you when I'm back in London.' And he hung up.

'Doesn't sound good,' said the General kindly.

'No. Not good.'

'I find one can't trust modern people,' he said, shaking his sad head. 'They're all ghastly . . . Well! Perhaps you can do a bit more of the singing now? I was sorry I never watched you perform.'

With a brave smile Charlie left the room.

By the time the minicab carrying Grey McShane and his three large suitcases rolled up at the front of the house Charlie was a couple of miles away, riding over the same fences he rode the day he heard Georgie had died, and once

again, failing to draw any comfort from them. He felt angry
and ashamed and foolish and overwhelmingly lonely.
The Jo he loved, with all her warmth, her bravery, her
kindness, her sweet vulnerability – had been an illusion; a beautiful, perfect illusion, and without it he felt
utterly bereft.

The General, not surprisingly, sounded very cold when Jo
finally called. It was the first time they had spoken since
their argument.

'Charlie's not here,' he barked. 'What do you want?'

She asked him to tell Charlie that she was already on
the train to Tiverton and would be waiting for him at the
station within a couple of hours.

'You may be waiting a while. God knows where he is.'

'That's OK. I don't care. I'll wait all night . . . I don't
expect to come to the house. But I have to talk to him.
It's terribly important. You will tell him?'

She sounded nicer than he remembered; warmer, less
conceited. He was disconcerted to find himself feeling
very slightly sorry for her. 'It's none of my business,' he
said, 'but you might save yourself the journey. Whatever
it is you want to tell him, I think he already knows . . .
He spoke to someone called Penny.'

'. . . He what? . . . ' She groaned. 'Oh God . . . I'm
so sorry.'

'Well never mind that,' he said briskly. 'Look, I'll give
him the message as soon as he gets back.'

He hung up and headed out to the stables in search
of his son. 'That ghastly girl's just called for you,' he
said.

*   *   *

Charlie was on the platform waiting for her when the train pulled in. He hadn't wanted to be. He was infuriated when his father told him she was on her way down, and yet, in spite of everything, he couldn't just leave her there, waiting for ever while he never came.

Jo hadn't been expecting to see him. She hadn't really believed that the General would even pass the message on, so when she saw him standing there she thought, for a moment, that everything was going to be all right. With a surge of wild happiness, and a smile so broad she was almost dribbling, she elbowed her way out of the train and scrambled towards him. But he didn't move. He just stood there watching her, his hands in his pockets, his face as cold and detached as she had ever seen it.

'You shouldn't have come,' he said.

She stopped. Her smile evaporated. 'But I had to,' she said. 'I had to explain.'

'I didn't like to think of you waiting here so I came to meet you, that's all. I'm not very interested in explanations.'

'But you must be!'

'Why?'

'Because – because it's not the way it looks. It's –'

'You guys think you can talk yourselves out of anything,' he said quietly. '*Talk, talk, talk*. You never fucking shut up.' He sighed. 'Anyway. There's a train going back to London in seven minutes.'

'What? No! Please! Let me just tell you *why* –'

He smiled sadly and turned away. 'The other platform, I should think. But you'd better check.'

'Charlie, I'm so, so sorry. The whole thing was out of control and I didn't know how – I kept thinking somehow –'

'You should hurry,' he said. 'The train after that isn't for another couple of hours.'

'No, wait!'

'Go away, Jo. Go back to London. Where you belong.'

She followed him out of the station but he didn't look at her again. She followed him to his car. She pleaded with him as he started the engine. She was in tears as she watched the Land Rover drive away.

The Sunday papers contained several stories as a result of Melanie Slater's revelations. The *Mail on Sunday* had a nasty piece, and a large photograph of Grey huddled in the back of a minicab, as did the *Sunday Express* and the *News of the World*. A couple of the broadsheets also carried earnest articles about the responsibility of TV journalism and the *Observer* ran a damning half-page profile of Ed Bailey. There could be no doubt that his precious career was in trouble.

By the time Jo woke up on Monday morning, Channel Foremost had already issued a statement withdrawing its support from Ed's programme, and Ed had managed to wheedle himself a ninety-second slot on *Today*. He was putting up a fierce defence, claiming that his programme was not so much an example of shoddy workmanship as an example of a new and exciting television genre. 'Fictimentory' he was calling it. With a straight face. And for a while he managed to get away with it . . .

'I certainly sign up to the broader point you're making,' he was saying as her radio alarm clicked on, 'and in no way do I condone his actions on any level. But that really isn't the issue. The issue here, for me as a programme maker, is *choice*. Yeah? And freedom. The freedom to push back the boundaries of ordinary documentary making. My work has always tackled difficult subjects, I like to think with sensitivity and imagination. And as well you know, John, the problem here isn't my programme; the problem we're dealing with is the British media's knee-jerk reaction to all things modern and new. If they don't understand it, they just have to knock it. Frankly I'm not prepared . . .'

The interviewer guffawed. 'With respect, Mr Bailey . . .'

Poor man, thought Jo sleepily. Was it possible she had once admired him? Or had he changed? It all seemed such a long time ago. Then came the thud of realisation. She remembered the dismal state of her own relationship with the world and groaned out loud. There were forty-five angry messages on her machine; ten from Ed, thirty-five from Penny and not a single one from Charlie. She hadn't responded to any of them. She contemplated spending a second day in bed, but what would have been the point? He still wouldn't call. He would never, ever call her again.

She took a taxi to work, (it would probably be the last time she ever made the journey so she decided to do it in style) and on the way she called Ed. She'd spoken to no one since the situation had exploded, so Ed's reaction to her would probably be a good overall indication, she thought, of the level of trouble which lay ahead.

She opened boldly. 'Well done, Ed!' she said. 'Thought you put up a very good fight this morning . . . Not sure I understood everything you were going on about but –' Oops! Where had that come from? 'No, I thought you were great. Well done!'

'Oh it's you is it? I presumed you'd call eventually.' So indications were not good.

'Ed, I think I owe you an apology.'

'It's a bit late for that.'

'We need to talk.'

'It's a bit late for that, too. I've been advised by my solicitor –'

'Oh!' She heard herself laughing. '*Come on.*'

'I'm not actually prepared to get into a discussion about this. I'm currently talking to my lawyers and it may turn out that I have no choice but to take this matter to court –'

'But – we were supposed to be friends! Only the day before yesterday –'

'Yes, and the day before yesterday I didn't know –' He stopped. 'That was my *professional reputation* you were putting on the line there,' he said incredulously. 'I just – honestly, Jo. I am so disappointed by you. Words fail me.'

She could feel herself about to laugh again. 'Ed. Your reputation's – fucked, anyway. You did that yourself.'

'I'm glad you think so, Jo. However, the whole thing is out of my hands. I've said everything I need to say.' He smirked unpleasantly. 'So I suggest you have a word with Penny.'

Ed was threatening to sue everyone, it turned out; Top Spin, Joanna Smiley, RBC television, Melanie Slater . . . Penny could always reign in her temper when it mattered. That morning she reigned it in long enough to explain to Jo that things were not, however, as bad as they could have been. Ed had offered them a get-out. The way things stood 'with the Grey McShane debacle' she said, 'he realises it's unlikely anyone will be employing him in the near future'.

He needed to rehabilitate himself, and in order to do that he needed work. He was offering to withdraw all writs on the condition that he replace Charlie on Meals. What he needed to keep of Charlie's input would have to go uncredited, and Ed would be given full creative reign to knock together a documentary of his own in the five days that remained before the concert began.

'Obviously,' said Penny, 'I told him yes. Excellent. RBC and Meals need never know anything about it. Point number two. You're probably wondering why I'm not firing you?'

Jo didn't reply.

'Ed Bailey said he needed you as an assistant. His only other condition was that you were kept on.'

'Really?'

'He's obviously a very forgiving guy.'

'No,' she said, frowning. 'He's not. He thinks I'll be useful.

'Or perhaps he wants to rub your nose in it. Whatever,' said Penny. 'Frankly I don't care. We've got a shit load of work to do and I think you'll agree we've wasted enough time –'

'But I haven't said I agreed to his conditions.'

Penny laughed.

'And you haven't told me where Charlie stands in all this. What does he say?'

'Charlie?'

'It's his project.'

'Don't be funny.'

'If Ed hadn't messed us around in the first place we wouldn't even be in this situation.'

'So what?'

'None of this was Charlie's fault. It was *me*. It was *my* fault. So why should he be the one who has to pay?' Penny looked at her blankly. 'It sounds stupid to you. Of course. You don't know him . . . But the fact is . . . I'm sorry. I'm not going to let him down again.'

NEW YOU RULE NUMBER NINE: OK. Bottom line, guys: If you can't stand the heat, get out of the RESTAURANT and clear a space for someone who CAN! Cos there's TWO WORDS we can't stand at NYCO (NEW YOU CENTRAL OFFICE!!): that's NO and CAN'T!!! We don't want REASONS we want RESULTS! And as the great bard, W Shakespeare, once famously said, 'It's all about attitude!' He was right in 1066 and he's still right today! So get your POSITIVE heads on, boys and girls, and PUT ON THOSE OXYGEN MASKS!! We have EMERG-ENCY LANDING at Yes Can-Do City!

A YES CAN-DO APPROACH

Charlie had decided not to return to London immediately. His country responsibilities had been neglected since he'd been concentrating so hard on the pop stars, and there was no longer anything in the city to make him want to hurry back. While he immersed himself in work around the farm, the General and Grey McShane, who seemed to have settled in for the duration, spent Monday afternoon dissecting Grey's bad press. And there was a lot of it. For lack of a better diversion, and because all the papers had so many excellent photographs of him in the company of celebrities, the story of his fall from grace had become a great favourite. Nobody knew where he was hiding, which was frustrating for them because that Monday he was unquestionably the most hated man in Britain.

Not that it seemed to bother Grey. In fact he was on better form now than he had been for months. He sat at the large kitchen table, his enormous feet resting on a nearby chair, and a tumbler of whisky before him, cheerfully reading each of the articles aloud. A more unlikely friendship it would have been hard to imagine; the orderly, ambitious retired soldier and the shambolic sex offending drunk, but the two of them had taken a tremendous shine to one another.

'Poor old Charlie,' said Grey after one peaceful silence.

'Yes,' said the General. 'She's a dreadful girl. But time is a great healer.'

'Och, I don't know about that.'

The General chuckled. 'Of course it is, you bloody fool. Or it would be, if only one would allow it.'

Just then there was a knock on the door and a pretty blonde woman, wearing Nicole Farhi trousers and a golden sheen of moisturiser on her lips and cheeks, slithered gracefully into the room.

'Good Lord!' said the General. 'Who let you in?'

'I'm sorry to disturb you,' she said, with a harmless smile, 'but the front door was open. I'm Clare . . . I was actually looking for Mr McShane . . .' She cocked her head to the side. 'And I do declare I've found him! It *is* Mr McShane, isn't it?'

'Clare,' said Grey. He didn't stand up. 'Is it your habit to come barging into people's houses without knocking? It's very bad manners you know.'

'Ohh,' she said, 'ha ha.'

And the General melted. He wasn't accustomed to drinking in the afternoon, and she was extremely fragrant. He assumed, for no very clear reason, that she was a friend of Grey's, sent for to help Charlie forget about Jo. 'Well, sit down, sit down! McShane, move your great feet for heaven's sake. Why don't you let the poor girl sit down? James Maxwell McDonald.' He stood up to shake her hand. 'Charlie's father. Of course. How do you do?'

'*Lovely* to meet you,' said Clare, 'and I hope you don't mind me dropping in like this.' She turned a flirtatious look towards Grey. 'I've been searching for you everywhere.'

247

'Aye,' said Grey, indicating with a casual sweep the pile of newspapers spread across the table in front of him, 'I suppose you all have.'

'I thought you might appreciate the opportunity to give your side of the story. I mean,' she paused, looking appropriately serious and sympathetic, 'there's been some pretty negative stuff.'

'Wouldn't you like a cup of tea?' asked the General, feeling slightly confused.

'No thank you.'

'Where have you come from?' said Grey. 'On second thoughts don't tell me. I'm not very interested. So. Fire away. What do you want me to tell you?'

'Or maybe you'd prefer something wetter? We've been hitting the whisky I'm ashamed to say. Perhaps you'd like to join us?'

She put a hand to her tidy belly. 'Oh no,' she said. 'That's very kind. I'll just have some water, if I may.'

'Absolutely,' said the General. 'Only tap, I'm afraid. Can't be bothered with all that bottled nonsense, can you?'

She gave him a sickly smile and turned away. 'Grey – may I call you Grey?'

'If you want.'

'Do you think we could have a private chat?'

'There is nothing in the world I can imagine wanting to say to you,' said Grey, 'that I wouldn't want to say in front of the General.' He grinned. 'Unless you're feelin' frisky, in which case –'

'Oh!' cried the General merrily, his old cheeks shining with whisky and surprise. 'Ha ha ha. Oh I say! You are terrible! That's not funny *at all*. Please accept my apologies, young lady. Isn't he outrageous! Ha ha ha.'

She offered up another of her harmless smiles, and muttered something dishonest about being unshockable.

'I'm sure that's true, darlin'. I'm sure it is,' said Grey laconically and waited for her to begin.

'So –' She placed a small tape recorder between them. 'You don't mind if I use this?'

'Not at all.'

'What?' cried the General. 'Good God, McShane, watch out! She's a *journalist*! Do you realise? This young woman is a journalist!'

'Aye, I know.'

'Well . . . For heaven's sake! . . . They can be vicious, these people.'

Grey McShane grinned again. 'Aye, I know . . .'

'What newspaper are you from?' demanded the General.

'It doesn't matter,' said Grey firmly. He hadn't taken his eyes off her since the moment she'd walked into the room, and she was beginning to assume that he fancied her, which was a relief. It tended to make things simpler.

'I've always been such a fan of your work,' she began.

'That's nice of you to say.'

'So I was terribly sorry to hear about Phonix. There'll be a lot of disappointed fans out there.'

'Aye. Mebbe.'

'I take it you know about Phonix, then? I thought you might not have heard. They're telling everyone they don't know where to find you.'

'You should show them,' said Grey. 'I'm right here.'

'So, you know they've cancelled the contract?' she said, willing him to register surprise. He couldn't know, of course, because it hadn't happened yet. She was trying to make it happen, for the sake of her story. 'They announced it this afternoon. They're backing out of the deal.'

'What deal?' said the General.

But she didn't bother to reply.

'Aye,' said Grey. 'I imagined they would.'

'You didn't know?'

He shrugged. 'Well I did and I didn't darlin'. I did and I didn't.'

'So . . . What do you feel about that?'

'That's a very good question, sweetheart. A very good question indeed.' She waited. '. . . I'll have to think about that.' And then, more brightly, 'What else do you want to know?'

'Perhaps you feel let down?'

'Let down? *Let down?*' He burst out laughing.

'So you don't feel let down,' she said irritably.

'Oh God. It depends what you're referrin' to, darlin' . . . *Let down* . . .' He started chuckling again.

'But from what I understand,' she persevered, 'everything isn't completely decided yet . . . I mean, if you could just come out and explain yourself. Or deny it. Or *something* . . . everyone would probably sit up and listen. It's the *silence* that's confusing everyone, Grey. Don't you care that the whole country's marked you down as a pervert?'

Grey frowned. 'I don't know,' he said, 'sitting here in this lovely kitchen with my lovely friend, General James, and a pretty little lady askin' me piercin' questions, it all seems quite a jolly caper . . . I'm having a crackin' time . . .'

Crackin' time? thought Clare. *Jolly caper? How . . . inappropriate could this guy possibly GET?* 'Yes. But later,' she said earnestly, 'when the exhilaration of all this attention dies away –'

'Ha!' said Grey.

'Aren't you afraid you'll go back to –' she paused and dropped her voice to a confiding murmur. 'Grey, I don't know how else to put this without seeming insensitive – But surely you must have thought about it. Aren't you afraid you'll go back to living on the streets again?'

'Certainly not!' piped up the General warmly. 'Not while there's breath in my body! Mr McShane shall never live on the streets.'

'Well thank you kindly, General James. But don't you worry about me. I can look after myself.'

'And for the record, young lady, if Grey's a pervert then so am I . . . I've seen some *scrumptious* fifteen-year-olds in my time. What? Haven't you?'

'Not really.'

'Well my girl,' said the General, 'you haven't lived!'

Grey guffawed.

'Yes, but the difference is you haven't actually slept with a fifteen-year-old, have you?' said Clare.

'How do you know?' said the General.

'Anyway, she wasn't fifteen,' said Clare, 'she was four-teen. She was a *child*.'

'Is that so?' said Grey.

'Well, for heaven's sake if I'm wrong then *tell me*! This is an opportunity for you to set the record straight, but you're giving me nothing. You're behaving like a couple of schoolboys.'

'I've already set the record straight,' said Grey quietly. '. . . C'me on, darlin'. Stop workin' so hard. Have a drink with us and who knows? Mebbe I'll tell you everything you want to know.'

*   *   *

251

Outside, at the large front door, Jo Smiley switched off the engine of her Renault Clio and, after a brief internal struggle, lit up her twelfth cigarette of her early thirties, and her twelfth of the afternoon. She had run from the Top Spin office without bothering to tell Penny where she was going, taken a taxi back to the flat and immediately, with nothing but the clothes she was wearing, climbed into the car and driven West. Four hours later she was looking out at the cold October rain and trying to remember the last time she'd been sitting here, on that golden summer evening. Everything had been so simple then. It seemed like a lifetime ago.

Clare had left the door ajar so, after a moment's indecision, Jo stepped into the hall. She felt sick. 'Hello?' It echoed off the ceiling, just as it had the last time. 'Hello?' but nobody replied. She heard the sound of voices and followed it further into the house, through a second hall she'd never been into, and on, towards the kitchen. She reached for the door handle but her courage failed.

'. . . So, what you're telling me,' she could hear a female, vaguely familiar voice saying, 'is that if a girl looks physically mature at any age their basically she's asking for it, yeah?'

Grey bellowed with laughter. 'Very funny. Oh, very funny.'

'I'm not actually joking, Grey,' the voice said.

'Aye, but you should be.'

'Did I say that?' said the General unhappily. 'I'm not sure that's what I meant . . .'

'I'm sorry – General. Can I just get a name-check at this point? . . . Only forgive me for mentioning it but am I right in thinking your own daughter was recently involved in a

252

tragic accident? Because if that's the case, I mean if you actually lost a little girl of your own I can't help wondering why you don't feel more uncomfortable, harbouring –'

It was an outrageous question. 'You don't have to answer that!' Jo said angrily, bursting through the door. 'That's none of her business. She has no right to ask you that at all!'

Once again Grey broke into laughter. 'Saved by the AntiFreeze herself!' he said. 'Good God, it's like Piccadilly Circus around here. Doesn't anyone believe in ringing door bells any more?'

'Hello Clare,' Jo said coolly. 'I thought it was you.'

After quick and careful calculation, Clare jumped enthusiastically to her feet. She and Jo had shared a few lines in a few toilet cubicles over the years. They'd confided in each other various irrelevant intimacies which, under normal circumstances, would have meant they were friends, or allies, anyway; successful, good-looking sisters in a man's world. And all that. So she opened her arms and beamed.

'Jo! God, *hi!*' she said, stepping forward for a hug. 'How amazing! How fantastic! What the hell are you doing down here?'

'I wish I needed to ask you the same thing,' said Jo. 'I can guess exactly what you're doing down here because I represent –' She hesitated. Did she want to do this? Publicly, professionally defend these two ridiculous, unhelpful men? But she knew just how Clare intended to ridicule them; they were both such obvious targets. And whether she thought they deserved it or not (she was no longer sure) it was irrelevant. She'd come down here to help

Charlie, and Charlie cared about them both. 'I represent both of these gentleman –'

'Aye, that's right,' said Grey, with a mischievous gleam in his eye.

'And I think you should know that everything they have said to you this afternoon was *confidential*, and furthermore I think –' Jo indicated the tape recorder on the table, 'that we have that on tape. So there can be no question about that.'

'*Confidential!*' said Clare. 'Are you nuts?'

'Which means your reporting a word of it would be quite unlawful. As of course you know. So my advice to you –'

'Fuck your advice, Jo. I didn't ask for your advice. You haven't even been here. These guys never mentioned anything about confidentiality –'

'Aye,' said Grey suddenly, 'but we have now. Haven't we General James? Thank you, Jo. Now come an' have a drink so I can get a closer look at you. Something's changed . . .'

'What about you?' said Clare, turning to the General. 'Can I quote you? Or has all this been a total waste of my time?'

'Well . . .' He looked embarrassed. 'I must say I think Jo may have a point. It seems a bit unfair on Clare, but on the other hand if we *can*, at this late stage, suddenly wipe the board clean, so to speak –'

'We can,' said Jo.

'Then yes. Absolutely.' A smile spread across his face. 'But if you'd like to have a glass of whisky before you leave –'

There was nothing she would have liked less. She packed

254

up her notebook and tape recorder with flamboyantly rotten grace, and flounced angrily out of the house.

'Well! Thank you, Jo,' said the General reluctantly. 'I thought that was getting rather nasty, didn't you McShane?'

'It was,' said Grey. 'Jo arrived in the nick of time.'

'Next time, send them packing. Or call me – if you want to.' She looked embarrassed, suddenly remembering her position. 'I've actually come here to talk to Charlie. But if you need any more help . . . I know I'm not exactly your favourite person, but –'

The General scowled and said nothing. She was quite right of course. He would not allow her to charm her way back into his good books so easily. Certainly not. *Certainly not.*

Grey laughed. 'Oh, nonsense!'

She looked at him gratefully. 'You'll be pleased to hear your great friend Ed Bailey wants to take your other great friend Mel Slater to court about that article. He's very angry.'

'Ha!' said Grey. 'Well he should be careful. She's vicious. She's *ruthless*. She'll always win.'

'As you should know,' said Jo.

'Nobody gives Mel a piece of information they don't want broadcast around the world.' Grey winked infuriatingly at Jo. 'As well *you* should know . . . Which reminds me, General. When you're feeling strong enough there's something I need to tell you about that girl. She's actually a very nasty piece of work.'

'Oh goody goody,' he chortled. 'Is it racy?'

Since Charlie was not expected back at the house until after nightfall, Jo decided to go and look for him herself. The General loved nothing so much as giving directions; the more complicated the better. 'You'll notice a young beech wood to the west,' he said, 'head north, past the bluff. You can't miss it. And when you've crossed the ruined barley, you'll notice the pheasant coops. From there you can head north-northwest, beyond the hatcheries . . .'

'No, wait! I don't understand any of this. Can you start again?'

The General hobbled stubbornly off towards the library and came back with an ordnance survey map.

'Please,' she said, looking at it in horror, 'can't you just point?'

So, very unwillingly, and with plenty of barbed remarks about the uselessness of modern people, he sent for Sam, the farm hand, and asked him to show her the way.

Sam wasn't any happier about it than the General was. 'It'll be heavy going in those,' he said sullenly, indicating her hand embroidered Emma Hope slip-ons, which had set her back (though neither of them would have imagined it) exactly half of his entire monthly wage. 'It's bloody wet out there. I hope you can keep up.'

They set off through the rain at a cracking pace, which they maintained, in hostile silence, for nearly three-quarters of an hour. He pretended not to notice when she stumbled, and so did she. But she did keep up. Her sessions in the gym were not entirely useless. Halfway up a steep hill and just as they were approaching a large flock of horned sheep he suddenly came to a halt. 'See that gate over there?' he said, panting like a dog, and trying to hide it.

'Yes!' she gasped, equally exhausted, and equally determined not to let it show. 'Of course I do.'

'He's in the field beyond that one.'

But what if Charlie refused to speak to her? What if he wasn't even there? How was she ever going to find her way back again? 'I don't suppose you might come and get me again in an hour?' she asked his retreating figure. Very wisely, he pretended not to hear.

She found Charlie on top of a tractor in the middle of a vast, half-ploughed field. He was driving away from her, watching the ground as his tractor's blades turned up the soil in a neat path behind him. He was wearing the same stupid cork hat he'd been wearing the first time they met, and a Barbour jacket, and what looked like an old pair of chaps. And still her heart missed a beat. He looked so magnificently at ease, so absorbed, so utterly, peacefully self-sufficient. She stood still and gazed at him, unwilling to ruin the moment.

But he must have sensed her presence because just then he looked up.

'Jo?' She couldn't hear him. Was he dreaming? He watched in amazement as she clambered determinedly over the freshly made mud troughs towards him. Her pale grey satin skirt, her pale green (cashmere) cardigan were both so smeared with mud they looked more like army camouflage gear. She looked ridiculous, it occurred to him; and soaking wet and freezing.

It took her several minutes to cross the field and in that time he struggled with the desire to forget everything, to leap to the ground and run towards her. He'd missed her so much and now here she was, sodden, beautiful, getting closer every second – 'Look out!' he said – too late. As she drew level with him, her shoe caught on a rock. It sent her flying.

'Are you all right?'

'I'm fine,' she said, grinning at him, dragging herself to her feet.

But he didn't smile. He took off his jacket and held it out to her. 'You're shivering.'

'No, I'm fine. I'm just a bit cold.'

'So – here. Put it on.'

She couldn't resist. Her whole body was shaking. She'd never felt so cold in her life. 'Thank you. I'll give it back in a minute. Just let me warm up.'

'You should have worn a coat.'

'Yes I probably should.'

'It's almost autumn. It can get very cold.'

'Yes. So I've discovered.'

He didn't say anything. He didn't know why she was here. He wished she wasn't. He wished she would go away. Why was she standing here, not saying anything? Making him feel –

'I've been trying to talk to you all day, but you've switched off your mobile.'

Charlie didn't reply.

'Actually I came here to apologise . . .'

'Fair enough,' he said.

'. . . You've forgiven me?'

He shrugged. 'Would it change anything?'

'Well, we could –'

'Because if you're apologising for the lying, which I presume you are, then there isn't very much of our relationship left. So far as I can see everything was lie. From the beginning to the end. *Everything* was a lie. So what's left?'

They looked at each other silently, their regret – and

Charlie's anger – too overpowering, for a moment, for either to speak.

'It's not the only reason I came,' she said eventually. 'I came because although I know I can never make up for what I did, even though I always meant to tell you and it was never ... I never planned ... Part of me always thought you'd be pleased.'

'What exactly do you want?' he said coldly.

'I wanted to warn you that Ed is trying to take the credit for all the work you did. He's making Penny hand over the documentary as a condition for not suing us all. But he's crazy! You've got to come back to London and fight. You did so much brilliant work. He's got no right –'

To her astonishment, Charlie started to laugh.

'No! Listen to me! This isn't about us. This is about your *career*. For God's sake, forget about all the stupid things that have happened between us. You've got to think about yourself. You're so talented and Ed's such a –'

'Jo,' he said. 'Shut up. Please. You're wasting your time. I don't want anything to do with it.'

She couldn't understand. Here she was, asking nothing in return, only trying to put things right; jeopardising her own career, willing to be taken to court to help him back onto the ladder, and he was telling her not to bother.

'I know you can't believe it,' he said, 'and I know your world is full of impressive, exciting and wonderful people all doing extraordinary, useful and probably amazingly important and interesting things ...'

'Not really,' she said dutifully, but it lacked conviction.

'The fact is I'm not like those people and I never will be.'

'*Of course* you are. It's just a matter of –'

'Will you *look at me*! Bloody hell, Jo. I represent everything they – *you* – despise.'

'How can you say that?'

'Because it's true. And Jo, I don't care.'

She laughed uncertainly.

'I *like* my big house and my decadent Highland cows.'

'So do I – in a way.'

'And I perfectly like the way I speak – which you
don't. And the way I dress – which you don't. And I
like hunting foxes – which you don't. And I like listening
to – Meatloaf.'

'I love Meatloaf. All my friends love Meatloaf!'

'And I probably want to send my children to boarding
school –'

'Oh, come on Charlie –'

'And I think people on cocaine are bloody boring –'

'That's –'

'And I like jokes about *farts* –'

'Oh.'

'And foreigners –'

'Now you're just being silly.'

'Of course I am. I know I am. That's exactly the point.
Look – I'm sorry, Jo. It's too late. I'm trying to put this
as politely as I can, but please,' he started the engine, 'go
back to London, and leave me alone.'

She dropped Charlie's jacket where she stood, and slowly
turned back towards the field of sheep. She didn't even
notice they were following her. She left the gate open and
kept walking, with the sheep not far behind – past the
beech wood, past the bluff, past the beech wood again,
through two fields of ruined barley and then past the

bluff one more time. An hour and a half later it was growing dark. She was completely lost and frozen to the bone. Half an hour later still, after climbing a fence that seemed distressingly familiar, she looked up to see the shadow of the beech wood once again, and the fight deserted her. She collapsed onto the ground, buried her head in her hands and began to cry, loud sobs that shook her frozen body but which sounded feeble against the relentless, pouring rain. For the first time in her life she thought –

No! Can't do.

And there was nothing left inside her, not a flicker of spirit in her entire body which was able to advise her otherwise. She sat there for some time. When she looked up again it was pitch black. She could hear the sheep somewhere in the distance, and the rain, and then suddenly, just a few yards behind her, she caught the flash of a torch and footsteps. Somebody was singing . . .

> *Oh, the grand ol' Duke of York*
> *He had ten thousan' men,*
> *He walked them up to the top o' the hill*
> *An' he walked them down a—*

'G – Grey?'

He jumped. 'Who goes there?'

'Who goes there?' she said. 'I'm not a fucking highway-man!' And then she started laughing, and her whole body started to shake again, and she was retching and laughing and sobbing at the same time, and the flood of tears were burning her frozen cheeks so much they hurt. She couldn't stop.

'Hey,' he said. 'Jo –' He crouched down to look at her. 'What the hell happened?'

'Nothing!' she sobbed. 'Nothing happened! I'm completely fine.'

He helped her to her feet. 'Come on girl,' he said. 'Let's get you back to the house.'

'No!' she said. 'I can't go back there! What if I see Charlie?'

'Charlie's still working,' said Grey. 'You won't see him . . . I'm gonna take you back so you can change into something –'

'No!'

In the end he led her back to her car instead. After several minutes of negotiation by freezing torchlight, it was agreed that he would sneak into the house to fetch some of his own clothes and that they would then head for the local pub, where she could change and get something to eat before driving back to London. He wrapped his coat around her and virtually carried her most of the way back to the house.

Surprisingly the village pub was packed full. Jo fought her way to the lavatory with Grey's bundle of clothing and Grey headed for the bar. It didn't take long before somebody recognised him. In fact it didn't take long for Grey to realise why the pub was so busy that night. Within minutes he was surrounded. By the time Jo returned, wearing a pair of Grey's Prada trousers held up with a piece of string, and a jersey which reached her knees, the room was alight with camera flashes. Grey was pressed up against the bar, reporters were shouting hostile questions at him and an angry crowd jostled to be closer to the drama. Jo pushed her way through the rabble and managed to reach him just as the landlord arrived.

'Mr McShane?' He had to shout to make himself heard.

'That's me,' said Grey gloomily.

'I must ask you to leave. As you can see, you're not welcome here.'

'My friend is very cold,' he shouted, indicating Jo. 'She's been out in the rain these last five hours. Couldn't you just give her a drink?'

'I won't ask you again.'

'But –' Grey laughed in exasperation. 'I only want to buy her a drink!'

'Do I need to call the police?' asked the landlord. 'Hop it!'

The press people elbowed each other aside to capture his humiliation. One of them thrust a photograph of an eight-year-old girl into Grey's face. It was a picture of Emily, taken many years before he ever knew her. 'Is this the girl you were having a sexual relationship with?' he said.

Slowly, Grey took the picture. The room fell silent, waiting, willing him to acknowledge that it was –

'Don't say anything!' said Jo, suddenly coming to her senses. 'Don't say a bloody word. Come on! Let's get out of here.'

'You do that,' said the landlord.

But Grey ignored them. He gazed at the picture for a long time. 'That's Emily,' he said quietly. 'But she was fifteen. She didn't look like that –'

At which point the place erupted. Someone threw beer at him. He didn't retaliate. He handed the photograph back. It only enraged people further. Someone kicked him. He still didn't retaliate.

'Leave him alone!' shouted Jo.

Someone slapped his face. And he just stood there, taking it.

'*Leave him alone!*' screamed Jo. 'She was *fifteen*! Didn't any of you bastards get laid at fifteen?'

A middle-aged man lunged at her and Grey stepped in to intercept. It was the first time Jo had seen him move. He was holding the man by his wrists, asking him, unrealistically (but politely) to leave Jo out of it, to calm down, when his wife joined the fray.

'Get your filthy pervert hands off my husband!' she shouted. Things were getting totally out of hand. The landlord stopped congratulating himself on his authoritative demeanour, stopped imagining his shiny face on the front of tomorrow's newspapers and started worrying about insurance claims. By the time the police arrived Jo and Grey were both soaked in alcohol, and a fat man with a smoker's wheeze was holding a broken glass to Grey's face.

The police escorted Jo to her car first. 'I'll call you!' she shouted above the jeering crowd. 'I'm so sorry!'

'Aye,' he said bleakly. 'So am I, darlin'.'

'What will they do with you?'

'Don't you worry about me! I'm sure these fine gentlemen will give me a lift to the General's house.' He turned to the two surly looking policemen on either side of him and smiled. 'Isn't that right?' Though they despised him as much as anyone who'd seen the stories in their newspaper that day, they had no choice but to acquiesce.

'Thank you, Grey,' Jo shouted. 'Thank you a million times.'

'Och, never mind that, darlin'! Thank *you*! You're an angel. Thanks for stickin' with me. I won't forget it.'

*   *   *

Looking at all the front page photographs the following day, three thoughts occurred to Mel; that she had no idea McShane knew the Maxwell McDonalds so well, but that it didn't matter because nobody would ever believe a word he said ever again; that her friend Jo was looking slightly mad and decidedly rough around the edges, and that Ed, whom she'd wanted to suffer from her disclosures as much or possibly more than Grey, seemed to be getting off rather too lightly. Ed's career was not in ruins, as it should have been by now. In fact, when she called his production office, she discovered that Ed was 'out on location, and would be unlikely to return any non-"Meals" related calls for at least a week'.

Think positive, she said to herself. Think . . . YES CAN DO. *Think* . . . YES! Why not? The only question remained, which of her feature editor friends would be likely to pay the most for her story?

There had only been one message on her answer machine when Jo got home late the previous night; it was from Jessie, telling her she'd given birth to an 8 lb 4 oz baby girl called India. 'Gerald's on cloud nine,' she boomed. 'India's beautiful and I'm baby-blissed out. Never been so happy! I know you're frightfully busy, but will you come and pay homage when you get the time? Loads and loads of love – Oh God, did I say? My brain's turned to mashed potato! It's *Jess!*' She was still roaring with laughter when she hung up.

The other news had been delivered by courier. It was a letter from Top Spin telling her she was out of a job.

NEW YOU RULE NUMBER TEN: So you've made it!! Give yourself a pat on the back! How's life looking from up there? Pretty good, hey? Pretty damn good. We know it . . . One final word, before we let you loose on the world. It's a LONG WAY DOWN and if you fuck up, your New friends sure ain't gonna be picking up the pieces. No Sir! They're gonna pick up the jobs you left behind, more like! So be vigilant! Stay busy! Sound nice! And remember INTEGRITY is a USEFUL word (look it up, guys!) but like most things you'll be saying from now on, it DOESN'T actually mean ANYTHING!! So don't go wasting precious time THINKING!! We've done the thinking for you. All you've gotta do now is BELIEVE . . . Be Rich! Be Happy! Get out there and ENJOY!

BELIEF!!

Grey's courier delivery arrived at Fiddleford a couple of days later. He was lounging at that kitchen table, discussing the day's headlines with the General and distracting Charlie from his depressing examination of estate bills when they heard the knock on the front door. Grey went to answer it.

After the nasty scenes two evenings earlier, when reporters had followed Grey back from the pub and then hammered relentlessly on every door into the house until daybreak, Charlie had decided to lock the gates at the bottom of both drives. He'd posted Sam at the back drive (much to Sam's annoyance) with instructions to be ruthless about turning people away. This, amazingly, had been their first interruption since.

'We should have put Sam on the job after Georgie died,' the General said suddenly. 'We would have been left in peace.'

'Mm,' said Charlie distractedly. 'It's quite a haven here, isn't it? . . . Dad, have you thought any more about holiday cottages? I've got some quotes here for converting the stables, plus the lease comes up at Stower Hill at the end of the year, and there's Stower Cottage still lying empty. We could let it out on a short lease or we could hold back, because I think if we're going to make it worthwhile we need –'

'The stables are much too close to the house,' said the General. 'We'll have ghastly self-confident people eating crisps and wandering across the lawn in tracksuits.'

'No we won't.'

'They'll be knocking on the door asking to use the "toilet" and of course by then the hygiene people will have made it illegal to pee behind a tree.'

Charlie looked faintly bored. He'd heard it before.

'Almost certainly the worst idea you've had yet, Charlie. Anyway I was thinking McShane might rather enjoy Stower Cottage for a month or two. Especially if he's going to lose that marvellous arrangement with the recording people. Which he seems to believe he is . . .'

'Aye,' said Grey, walking in at that moment, 'and I was quite right.' He dropped the courier's letter onto the kitchen table and sat himself down again. 'I must say that's a bloody relief. I never was a great fan of poetry.'

'Well – *marvellous*!' said the General. 'Why don't you stay with us for a while? We've got a cottage going spare. You could set yourself up there. Don't you think, Charlie? Wouldn't that be fun? He and I can fume over the news-papers together . . .' He glanced nervously at his son. 'And I'm sure Grey could make himself useful around the estate . . . After all what's the point in having these bloody cottages if one can't give them to one's friends?'

Charlie sighed. 'Dad – it's lovely having Grey here, and as far as I'm concerned he can stay as long as he likes – but we can't just *give* him the cottage. We've got to get an income from somewhere, and if the threat of ghastly people on the lawn rules out holiday cottages –

although I'm sure we could persuade them to use their own lavatories – we'll have to think of something else. Or sell something else. We lost £20,000 last year.'

The General looked very depressed and slightly angry. 'Don't be vulgar, Charlie. Poor old McShane hasn't got anywhere to live! What are you going to do, hand him over to those vultures out there?'

'Don't you worry about me,' said Grey. 'I can look after myself . . . but if it's not too much trouble –' He sounded uncharacteristically diffident. 'Could I maybe stay here a week or two longer, while I get my head together so to speak?'

'*Of course!*' burst out the General. 'Please! Hide away here as long as you like! Keep us company! I shall be furious if you leave before Christmas.'

Grey still had a lot of money left over from the Phonix deal. They had not asked for a return of any of the original £250,000 advance, and would be unlikely to, given the terms of his contract. To Charlie and his father's great embarrassment, he announced he wanted to pay them for his keep.

'Are you mad?' said the General.

'But I can't stay here if you don't let me pay and to be frank it's the only place in the world I want to be.'

'It's out of the question,' said the General. 'What do you think I am? A hotelier?'

'I don't really know,' said Grey mildly. 'Whatever you fancy. But I've got cash and I need a place to hide. And you need cash and you've got a place to hide. I can't relax if you won't let me pay my own way.'

'Good *God*!' said the General, his old body shuddering with disgust.

Charlie chuckled. 'Mind you, if he's planning to stay until Christmas . . .'

'I should certainly hope he is,' snapped his father defensively.

'I can forget my troubles in here,' said Grey.

'Except you keep reading about them in the papers,' said Charlie.

'Aye,' he laughed. 'But it's like reading about a parallel universe. I'm the most hated man in Britain,' he said (not without an element of pride). 'And here I am, sittin' here. Peaceful as a Sunday evening! . . . If I pay the rent, you can get someone in to do Sam's work while he's guarding me.'

Eventually they relented (or rather Charlie relented and the General was overruled). Charlie had been on the verge of hiring in extra labour to make up for Sam's absence anyway, and it didn't seem unreasonable to him that Grey should pay for that. The General was delighted that Grey had agreed to stay, and Charlie was pleased, not so much by Grey's presence as by the extraordinary effect it had on his father, who'd talked and laughed more in the last two days than he had in all the time Charlie had known him.

In fact, he talked so much it became impossible for Charlie to concentrate. With the deal struck, Charlie collected his papers and retreated to the library, leaving Grey and the General free to attend to their new obsession (undiminished in spite of the fact that reports of Grey's disgrace were already beginning to slip towards the back pages). Tabloid newspapers were something of a discovery for them both, since the General had rarely ventured beyond the *Telegraph*, and Grey never bothered to read a newspaper at all. So while Charlie sat in the library weighing up the pros and cons of developing the marginal land above the bluff into grant-sponsored broadleaf woodland, the increasingly irresponsible General and his strange new friend tested each other's knowledge of celebrity trivia, about which both were fast becoming exceptionally well-informed.

They discovered that Grey was not the only figure to be damned by the newspapers that day; there was an ex-employer being sued by his fat secretary over remarks he'd made about her chocolate intake; there was an 'It' girl who'd been quoted as saying something fatuous about the poor; there was an author who'd suggested that rape wasn't the worst thing that could happen to a woman; a pop star who'd had breast implants when she should have been breast-feeding her baby . . .

'Appalling!' said the General, examining a picture of the non-breast-feeder as she fought through a barrage of photographers to get into her house. 'She'd do better to be staying here with us. Don't you think McShane? They all would! Sam could look after the lot of you!' Grey thought it was a magnificent idea and it soon developed, or at least so they thought, into a serious proposition, something (once they had agreed the details) they intended to present to Charlie at dinner, as the brainwave that could save the estate. The house could be offered as a refuge to anyone under popular attack, they agreed, regardless of what they might have done.

'Except murder,' said the General.

'Usually,' said Grey, 'but not always.'

'Well, anything too exceptionally hateful.'

'Aye. We can do it on a case-by-case basis.'

271

But the devil was in the details, of course. Because it transpired that the General would have problems admitting anyone 'too ghastly', and Grey insisted on refusing entrance to anyone fat, Welsh or Chinese. They spent a lot of time arguing (because the General had always fancied oriental girls), a lot of time refusing to accept each other's House Rule modifications, a lot of time in silence, scouring the papers in search of new potential candidates to squabble about.

'Here we are!' said the General after one such silence. '"My Hell with Drug Pusher Boss". There's a ghastly girl here who says her poor boss force-fed her cocaine while she was working on a – Oh! I say! McShane, do you know about this?'

Grey leant across the table to have a look. 'My goodness,' he muttered to himself. 'There's no stoppin' her, is there?'

Mel, who'd posed for the photograph and written the article herself, was claiming that during her weeks in Scotland Ed Bailey had (albeit briefly) transformed her from an 'ambitious, fun-loving girl who loved a challenge', to a 'sad and pathetic drug fiend'.

'He used to have stashes of cocaine in his room, [she wrote] *because he let me see it one day and I remember thinking "the police would have a heyday if they saw that!" . . .'*

'Och, she's terrible!'

'. . . Once he'd got us hooked there was always the unspoken threat. If we didn't perform as he wanted, he would withhold the drugs. I felt so used. It was like slavery. It got to the point where I didn't even want to come out of my room. In the end Grey and I just looked at each other and I said "Enough!", and the documentary shoot was cut short. Ed offered us more cocaine

if we agreed to stay but I just couldn't carry on . . . It was the best decision I ever made.'

'General,' said Grey quietly. 'There's something I need to tell you. Somethin' I should a' told you some time ago, except I just couldn't stand to bring you more suffering. But I've been sitting on this particular piece of information, turning it round and round in my head, wonderin' what I'm to do with it. And I still don't know for sure, but all I can think is – in your position it's something I would definitely want to be told . . .'

The first thing Ed knew about Mel's most recent act of sabotage, he was setting up for a Meals interview with SHAZZ-i, a promising young rap artist from Birmingham whose first single was due to be released in a month's time.

There was no doubting that the line-up for this Homeless concert was pathetic, actually quite embarrassing. But Ed was coming at it with the usual yes-can-do approach. He'd been through Charlie's footage and discovered, with a mixture of irritation and relief, that there was plenty to plunder, in spite of the low calibre of the celebrities involved. He now believed, as he always believed mid-project (the more fervently, the less likely it was to be the case) that this project was going to be the Big One. He believed, as he glanced across at SHAZZ-i, legs flopped apart on his swivel chair, head nodding moronically in time to his own music, that this documentary, this study of budding talent and philanthropy juxtaposed, was going to be the one to strike his critics dumb for all time.

So SHAZZ-i was already miked-up and ready to spout. Ed was in his element; rescued by his own brilliance from the very brink of disaster, and back on the job of making masterpieces once again. He took a final look at his TV monitor and sat down on the chair beside his subject. 'OK,' he shouted. 'We're gonna have to lose the music, guys, yeah? Are we ready? . . .'

And then Beronica burst in, followed closely by a couple of WPCs.

Of course Ed assumed they'd come for SHAZZ-i, for reasons it would have been embarrassing for him to explain. He looked across at his subject with an expression of weary, street-wise empathy, but SHAZZ-i didn't seem to pick up on it.

'Mr Bailey?' said WPC Theakston.

'Yes.'

'Mr Edward Bailey?'

'That's right. What's up?'

'Perhaps you haven't read your newspaper this morning?'

'We're actually working under a very tight deadline here. We don't have time to read newspapers. We don't actually have a tremendous amount of time to spare at all, so if you and SHAZZ-i have something to discuss –'

'I haven't fucking done nothing! Fuck you!' said SHAZZ-i indignantly.

'Right,' said Ed enthusiastically. He turned back to the WPC. 'I hope you guys have got a bloody good reason to be in here, because if I get a sniff of police harassment I will not hesitate to switch that camera on, yeah? And the next thing you know you'll be watching yourselves on the six o'clock news . . . So step carefully. That's all I'm gonna say.'

Next thing Mr Edward Bailey knew, he was under arrest.

His flat had been searched an hour earlier, and cocaine had been discovered everywhere; in the top drawer of his desk, in the top drawer of his wardrobe, on the coffee table in his sitting room, underneath his bedside table. Not only that, they had a witness willing to testify that he was her supplier.

Mr Edward Bailey was led away in handcuffs. He rose from his swivel chair with great dignity, it should be noted. He bade farewell to his documentary team, to SHAZZ-i, and to SHAZZ-i's publicist, apologised for letting them all down and left the studio with his head held high. He didn't believe it at the time. It took months of unreturned telephone calls before he began to acknowledge it, but that was the moment when Ed Bailey's name was officially relocated in the minds of his professional peers, from the 'What's Hot' section, to the 'What's Oh-So-Not'. By the time he'd reached the studio door, Ed Bailey was already an irrelevance.

Mel was in the bath when the policemen arrived for her. She assumed they'd come to talk more about Ed Bailey, or possibly even to thank her, or congratulate her. So she buzzed them in with a tremendous flurry of flirtation, and while they made their way up to the third floor, came to the conclusion that it would be droll to receive them in nothing but the small towel she was already wearing. (She thought she might even get an article out of it afterwards; *They Couldn't Take Their Eyes Off Me: Are The Police Institutionally Sexist?* Something along those lines. Or better still, *Are The 'Pigs' Institutionally Chauvinist!?!!* Very witty.)

'So? How did it go?' she asked enthusiastically as she threw open her flat door to welcome them in. 'Did you get him?'

PC Donne glanced distractedly at her luscious thighs and quickly looked away again. 'Get who, Madam?'

Her lusciousness was obviously confusing him. 'Ed Bailey of course! Come on in, anyway. Do you fancy a coffee?'

But PC Donne did not want coffee. He wanted to know what she was doing the weekend before the weekend before last Christmas.

She said she had absolutely no idea.

'I was probably drunk, somewhere. Ha! I normally am! God knows! What are most people doing on the weekend before Christmas?'

'I meant the weekend before that. The weekend of 12th.'

'I don't know! Crikey! Same bloody thing, I suppose.' But she suddenly felt very naked, and very scared. 'Why are you asking me?'

He said she might prefer to go and put some clothes on.

Jo's parents had gone off to Eastern Turkey on another of their self-improvement jaunts, and Jo had spoken to no one since returning from Fiddleford late on Monday night. Now it was Thursday afternoon, the day after Ed and Mel had been carted off to their respective police stations, and it was the first day Jo had managed to get out of bed. As yet ignorant of the fate of either of her friends, she had so far spent the day in her pyjamas,

gazing morosely out of the sitting-room window. She
thought obsessively about Charlie, about how she'd let
him down, how for the sake of a career in a public
relations firm, she'd thrown away the chance to be with
the only decent, honest, uncorrupted human being she
had ever met – and about what a stupid mess she'd made
of her entire life.

Perhaps, after twelve years of being too busy to do it at
all, she now had too much time to think. Because after
three miserable days of self-scrutiny she had started to
hate herself; her petty ambition, her petty snobbery, her
vacuous social conscience, all the millions of little lies
she'd had to tell every day of her gilded life, in order to
keep being Jo Smiley. And on top of that the mortgage
was due on her flat in two weeks time. She needed to find
a job. The thought of it, the thought of being breezy and
enthusiastic about nothing, and phony and ingratiating –
actually the thought of ever having to leave her flat again,
filled her with nothing but dread.

There were a lot of old messages on her answer machine
which she hadn't yet bothered to listen to properly. She'd
heard most of them burbling in the background as she'd
lain in bed, too listless to want to hear from anyone –
except Charlie. So it was with a great effort of will and
almost no curiosity – since she knew that none was from
him – that she finally settled down to make a note of who
had called.

Most of the messages had been left on Tuesday; boring,
facetious messages from her successful intimates, wanting to know what lay behind the newspaper pictures
of her and that day's devil incarnate, Grey McShane.
But news of her own downfall had obviously travelled

fast, because on Wednesday the calls had reduced to a trickle and by Thursday her telephone wasn't ringing at all.

There were three messages from Mel; two left on the Tuesday, bossy and irritable, asking what the hell was going on between Jo and Grey, and wanting to know why Jo never called her any more. The last had been left late on Wednesday afternoon. She was whispering – something about Grey and the police, but her voice was muffled and Jo couldn't make out everything she said.

'You've got to get hold of Grey and ask him what the fuck he's . . . He'll probably tell you . . . load of lies but please, I've got . . . fucking police in my sitting room . . . Talk to him. Tell him . . . off my fucking case. Shit! Bye.'

She called Mel's flat but there was no answer. She called her mobile, but it was on voicemail. She paced up and down her empty, silent sitting room wondering what to do next. Calling Grey was the obvious answer. She wanted to call him anyway, but what if Charlie answered? Worse still, what if he didn't? She was facing the horrible prospect of getting dressed and driving over to Melanie's flat when the telephone rang, and she jumped out of her skin.

She stared at the telephone suspiciously, thinking of all the hundreds of people she didn't want to speak to at that moment, or possibly ever again. But what if it was Charlie? What if it was Mel? What if it was Charlie and he hung up when the answer machine clicked in? She picked it up.

'Hello? Is Charlie here? I mean Jo. Jo here. Hello?' She hadn't spoken for three days. Her tongue felt clumsy and, after so much thinking, the words that came out were getting dangerously jumbled with the only thing that was occupying her head.

'It's Lionel, Jo.' He sounded cool and sarcastic and slightly patronising. 'I gather you've got us all into something of a situation.'

'Lionel?'

'RBC,' he drawled. 'I kind of wish I could forget you so quickly.'

'Oh.'

'How're you?' But he didn't really wait for an answer. 'OK,' he said briskly. 'So let's bring you up to date. Penny tells me that Ed Bailey, as opposed to Charlie McDouglas-Dougall, was arrested on drugs charges yesterday afternoon, 2 p.m. London time.'

'*Was he*? . . . Wow! Poor guy . . . God! What a bloody mess! What a bloody mess we've all made of everything . . .'

'Uh-huh. OK. So now we have exactly forty-six hours until this gig kicks off. What do you suggest?'

'What do I suggest?'

'What do you suggest.'

'But Top Spin fired me!'

'I'm aware of that. However, you got us into this situation and unless you prefer to settle it in court – and Jo believe me that's not gonna be cheap – you'd better come up with a solution. Because no way am I losing my job over this.'

He was beginning to sound agitated which made her suspect, in a detached way, that he hadn't been nearly as calm as he'd pretended to be when the conversation began. For some reason this struck her as extremely funny and she heard herself starting to giggle.

'Oh. Excuse me. I must have missed it. Did I say something funny?'

'No,' she said, trying to pull herself together. 'No, not at all.'

'This is no joke.'

'Of course it isn't. Sorry.'

'I understand you're the only one with any sort of relationship with this McDougall character –'

'Maxwell McDonald. He's called Charlie Maxwell McDonald.'

'Ya. Whatever.'

'It's just it's a bit rude. Not to get his name right.'

'Sure. We need him back on the job.'

There was a silence while Jo took this in. 'You've *got* to be joking! . . . You can tell Penny –' Jo stopped, momentarily so outraged she was lost for words. 'She *dumped* him! I mean *She* dumped *Him*! Last *Saturday*! She honestly thinks he's going to come crawling back now? After the way she treated him?'

'I actually think he'd better,' said Lionel. 'For your sake as well as mine. So call him. And call me when you've spoken to him. Because this is no joke, Miss Smiley. This is RBC. And people tend to stop seeing the funny side when the people at RBC get angry.'

At Fiddleford meanwhile, Grey was just then ambling into the library as if he owned the place. He sat himself down in the leather armchair opposite Charlie's desk and waited for Charlie to look up. Charlie pretended not to notice. He had been skulking in the library all day and most of yesterday, burying himself in estate work, not even coming out to eat. This was Grey's third attempt to engage him in conversation since he'd first told them about Mel; the fourth since he'd rescued Jo from beside the beech wood, and it was (Charlie noted) his boldest, most determined approach yet.

'I know you're busy,' he said at last. 'And I know you think it's none o' my business.'

Charlie didn't reply.

'But you're bein' a pillock.'

'Well, I suppose it takes one to know one,' said Charlie mildly.

'That's exactly my point.'

'Grey, I know your intentions are friendly but I really have got a lot to do.'

'Och, for God's sake, don't be so damn pompous. I haven't come to talk about Mel if that's what you think. I wouldn't dream of treadin' on your toes or trying to imagine what you're thinkin'. All I'm saying is I know you have your argument with Jo, but don't go mixing it with your feelings for Mel. It's not fair. She's a good girl, Jo is. She's a good girl.'

'Ha! And this from the man who told me she was made of antifreeze!'

'Aye and I was wrong! Come on, Charlie. You know it as well as I do! It's only your pride speaking. You're too bloody angry. You're not thinkin' straight.'

Charlie looked at him thoughtfully. 'Was there anything else?'

Grey sighed and stood up. 'No,' he said sadly. 'Mind you, I thought you were smarter. She loves you. And whatever you may be tellin' yourself right now, I don't believe in your heart you can be in any doubt about it.'

Grey crossed the room and slowly closed the door behind him. He returned to the kitchen, where the General was waiting impatiently to show off his newest discovery (a fascinating magazine called *OK!*), and Charlie returned to his work.

Or tried to. But he couldn't concentrate. Grey was wrong. Jo didn't love him. Jo loved herself. She loved her job, her successful friends, her clutter-free flat; she loved agnès b, and important cities, and clever men who didn't laugh too loudly. What did he have to offer her? What did he have that she could possibly want? Grey was wrong. He turned back to the papers in front of him. *Grey was wrong.* All Charlie wanted was a bit of peace, and the chance to get the estate working again. He didn't want to have to think about Jo, or Mel, or London, or bloody TV documentaries ever again.

Except it wasn't possible. Images kept coming to him: of her stumbling across that ploughed field, her face, so absurdly determined, so unreasonably filled with hope; and then, afterwards, after he'd turned her away, of her completely lost in the blackness; miserable, cold, terrified . . . He longed to call her, if only to hear her voice, if only to check she was still OK. Again and again he needed to remind himself of how ruthlessly she had let him down.

Twenty minutes later Grey was back again. This time he knocked first. He opened the door a few inches and poked his head into the room.

'I just talked to her, if you're interested. I called her up.'

'You did?' said Charlie, trying hard to sound irritated, unable to suppress the hope from his voice.

'She's been fired from her job. And the American fellers are taking her to court because she's too proud to ask for your help.'

'Help with what?'

'They need you back doin' the show.'

'Ha!' Charlie burst out. 'The only decent thing to have come out of all this was my escape from that fucking show.'

'Apparently Ed's been arrested.' Grey continued stubbornly. 'Which is a bloody good joke.'

Charlie hesitated. He needed to know, just this once, just to set his mind at rest. 'But she's OK is she?' he said. 'She wasn't ill – after all that time on the hill?'

'She's fine, Charlie. She's just fuckin' miserable.'

'Right.' It sounded very detached. 'You know, I've been looking into the possibilities of this refuge idea, Grey,' he said deliberately. 'I actually think it might be worth a punt. There's nobody else doing it . . . I'm just wondering who we need to talk to for advice.'

'And she never knew about Mel. I just told her. Just now. She never knew a bloody thing.'

Charlie said nothing and a moment later Grey closed the door again.

Jo hadn't wanted to tell Grey about the RBC crisis but he'd sounded so sympathetic and she hadn't spoken to anyone except Lionel for days. She made him promise not to tell Charlie, but now, four hours later, she couldn't help wondering . . .

Did he know? Perhaps Grey was telling him right now, at this very moment, and he was having a good laugh

283

about it. Perhaps he and his father were laughing together, rubbing their hands together, congratulating each other on her downfall. The minutes ticked silently by and with each one she plunged deeper into despair. Was it possible he had forgotten about her already? The telephone rang. It had to be Charlie. She leapt to answer it.

'Lionel here. RBC. You didn't get back to me.'

The disappointment was so overwhelming that before she had time to think, she'd hung up on him.

So he rang again.

'I take it you didn't have any luck with McDougall?' he said dryly.

'He's getting back to me.'

'Perhaps you should give me his number. Maybe it would be simpler –'

'No!'

'What?'

'I said *no*. He's already got enough on his plate.'

'What the hell is the matter with you? D'you have some kind of death wish I don't know about? Jesus, Jo. You seemed like such a together person when we met. Just give me his number –'

'No! . . . Piss off!'

'*Piss off*? I don't think you fully appreciate the gravity of this situation. We're not just talking about filing a civil suit here. We're talking about fraud. We're talking about you facing a spell in jail. OK? Wake up! So give me the guy's number, and we'll see if we can't make some sense out of this thing.'

But she burst into tears and hung up again.

She was lying in a heap on the floor, trying to ignore the insistent ring of the telephone, trying to ignore Lionel's hectoring voice on the answer machine, when she became aware that someone on the street was shouting her name.

'Jo . . . JO! . . . Where are you? Come to the fuckin' window, will you? Better still, open the fuckin' door! Jo! JO! I can't remember what fuckin' number y'are! Open the door! It's freezing out here!'

She pulled herself off the floor and peered furtively out of the window. It was Grey of course. And he'd seen her. In her pyjamas. With no make-up and eyes puffed up like tennis balls, and crows' feet that hadn't been moisturised for days. And a boil on her chin, and hairs beginning to sprout where the arch beneath her eyebrows used to be. Not that she cared any more. Apart from Charlie, Grey was probably the only person in the world she would have been pleased to see. Without thinking, she ran down to the ground floor to let him in.

'Grey!' she said, throwing herself into his arms. 'Is he all right? How is he? Oh God, what am I going to do? They want to send me to prison!'

They heard a slow click on the floor above and looked up to see Jo's front door closing gently behind her.

'Keys?' said Grey.

'Inside.' She sighed limply.

'Shall I kick it in?'

'N-no. We can call a locksmith.'

'Y'see?' laughed Grey. 'That's more like the Jo I used to know! Still just a bit too fuckin' sensible! Oh well. We'll have to make ourselves comfortable out here then.' He brought out a pack of 555s and the two of them sat down on the stairs for a smoke.

'So he knows?' she said eventually.

'Aye.'

'But he isn't coming.'

'If it's any consolation I think he's being an arsehole.'

'But you can't blame him. Not after everything that's happened . . . How is he? I mean about Mel?'

'He's not talking.'

They fell silent again.

'I can't bear to imagine what he must be going through. I just – can't even imagine it.'

'Aye. He's very brave.'

And then she cried again, slow, fat, helpless tears. 'I've never really lost someone I care about. But a *twin* . . .'

He put his arm around her and said nothing, because there was nothing to say. They sat there silently for a while and then, without thinking, she suddenly said, 'Tell me about Emily.'

He withdrew his arm. 'There's nothing to tell. You read the papers . . .'

'Yes. But they painted you so black. There must be more to it.'

'Why?'

'Because I know you! You're not evil. You're a wonderful man. One of the kindest men I've ever met.'

He laughed. 'You're embarrassin' me,' he said, but he was obviously pleased. 'I'm no angel.' He hesitated, as if he were on the brink of saying much more. 'But I'm not the fuckin' devil, either. We were in love. Or *I* was in love,' he amended heavily. 'That's all there is to it.'

'But *why*?' she said. 'Why someone so young? Didn't you *realise*?'

'Of course I bloody realised.'

'So what made you . . . ?'

'She was the Saturday girl where I was workin'.'

'. . . *Yes* . . .'

'It was just the men all the rest of the week. She used to cheer the place up.'

'What did you do?'

'I worked the petrol pump.'

She laughed, but he didn't seem to mind.

'Now of course the job doesn't exist. You have to do it yourself.'

'Usually, yes.'

'Shame that.'

'I suppose so.'

'Drivers have to exit their vehicles whatever the weather.'

'Yes.'

He shook his head sadly. 'So we went on like that for months. Her comin' in, the Saturdays; flirting around with us – nothing else.' He smiled. 'But the other lads were jealous. Because she was *beautiful*. Golden blonde hair. Beautiful – *round* – beautiful, *round*, laughing eyes. Och, God. She was always laughing . . .' He stared ahead of him. '. . . I suppose I was twenty-three, twenty-four. I don't remember. I was staying with Mum, and the drink was finally killing her off. The poor cow had fallen out with everyone. There was no one else around to take care of her . . .'

'Is that why you got together with Emily?' Jo asked. 'Because you were lonely?'

'Mm?' Grey looked at her distractedly. 'Oh God no . . . At least I don't think so . . . Maybe I was. I haven't really thought about it.'

'So? . . .'

'So she used to come in every Saturday, bright and cheerful and full o' the joys of spring. She used to light

287

up the whole place . . . She had this voice, this soft, sweet voice . . . och, fuck.' He swallowed. '. . . So full o' hope an' life, an' – certainty . . . that the world was a friendly place. It was the most beautiful voice . . . And then one day she came in an' she wasn't laughin' any more. She wasn't talking. Her eyes were all –' He frowned. 'They were all puffed up like she'd been cryin' for a week. But she wouldn't talk and she wouldn't talk. All Saturday she wouldn't let us hear that voice . . . So eventually I thought – I went off an' got us a couple of those Babychams. D'you know them?'

Jo shook her head.

'Disgusting stuff. But the girls tend to like them. Or they did . . . And we went and sat on the wall at the back and I opened the bloody Babycham and she took one smell of it and vomited all over the floor.' He shook his head. 'All that time I'd been holding back, thinkin' she was too bloody young. And she was *pregnant*. Can you believe it? The boyfriend had told her to sod off of course. She was bloody miserable. It broke my heart. I would a' done anything to see that smile back on her face. I would a' taken the kid off her hands and raised it myself.'

Jo smiled. 'But you didn't.'

'And then poor old Mum kicked the bucket. It must have been about a week later. And we lost the flat and Emily said they were looking for a lodger. She lived with her parents. So I moved in. And I still hadn't laid a finger on her. Oh God. It was driving me mad. But I couldn't. Not when she was carryin' the next man's child.'

'It doesn't make it impossible.'

'Aye but she was *delicate*. And she was very emotional. I didna want to upset her.'

'So what happened to the baby?'

'She lost it. Five months in. The magic mushrooms were meant to cheer her up. That's funny, isn't it? We snogged the first time that afternoon.'

'You mean you never actually –'

He shook his head regretfully. 'She was in that much of a state, poor lass. Never laid a damn finger on her.'

'But I don't understand,' said Jo. 'Why didn't you say? Why didn't you say to the police when they arrested you?'

He shrugged. 'I was responsible. I couldn't fight the grievin' parents. It wouldn't have been right.'

She took a moment to absorb this. 'And when the newspapers were writing all that stuff about you? When they cancelled the recording contract? When they were attacking you in that pub? *Why didn't you say?*'

He looked at her as if she was stupid. 'It was none of their bloody business.'

'I think,' she said, after a long, long pause, 'I think we need a drink. In fact, I think I've needed one for days.'

Grey left Jo with a couple of extra cigarettes and headed off on his own in search of an off-licence. If he spotted a telephone box before the lynch mob spotted him, he said, he would call for a locksmith at the same time.

But only a couple of minutes later, just as she was feeling cold and lonely again, and beginning to panic that Grey might never come back, she heard him shuffling on the doorstep. Still in the process of lighting one cigarette from the other, and squinting to keep the smoke from her eyes, she hurried across the hall to let him in. 'So, you didn't manage to spot the telephone at the end of the street?' she said, chuckling through the smoke. 'It's over there – CHARLIE!'

'I just saw Grey.'

'Oh. Good.'

He stepped into the hall and they stood there for a moment, gazing at each other. He took a drag from one of the cigarettes and passed it back again. 'So, I'll do this documentary, Jo. Because I love you.'

'You do?'

'But after that I'm going back to Fiddleford.'

'And I love you.'

'All this nonsense about "careers". I finally worked out what I'm going to do.'

'I really, really *love* you!'

'Before it's too late.'

'What?' said Jo impatiently. '*I love you!* Before *what's* too late?'

'Before Dad hands over what's left of the estate to every waif and stray who tips up to stay with us.' He told her about the plan to turn the estate into a Disgraced Persons refuge.

'Charlie . . . it sounds great. Can't we talk about it later?'

'Oh? What do you want us to talk about now?'

'Well – You know. Us. And love. And things . . .'

He smiled at her, a delicious, lazy smile. 'I thought you'd be pleased,' he said. 'I've decided to "concentrate on my strengths", as you so cleverly put it. I think it's an excellent idea. Don't you?'

'Well – I mean there's certainly a hole in the market,' she said glumly, unable to take her eyes off his lips, longing to move the conversation on. 'Of course, you'd have to charge a bomb to the people who could afford it. But with discriminatory pricing of some sort,' she found herself getting interested, 'maybe rural leisure activities at extra cost, therapists on call, a few very carefully orchestrated financial deals with approved publications . . . You'd need to build a gym –'

'I don't suppose,' said Charlie, 'after we've done this television thing you'd fancy taking a job at Fiddleford? There's a cottage going spare . . .' But upstairs the telephone had started ringing again. She looked distracted. '. . . Do you want to answer that?'

'Not much. It's only Lionel, trying to send me to prison.'

It was a flimsy door and he forced it open with the first kick. They burst into the room just as the answer machine clicked in, 'Jo, you silly cow. Mel here. I've been released. No thanks to you. They didn't exactly have much to go on, thank God. Due to the fact that the only evidence comes from a proven pathological liar who can't even tell the truth about his own name. And because I'm innocent. Obviously. Anyway, I've decided to write an amazing book about it. And so far, I have to say, you're *not* coming out of it very well . . . Jo I know you're there so you can bloody well pick up . . .'

Charlie stepped towards the telephone.

'Melanie?' he said. 'Charlie here . . . Yeah. I want you to forget the book, OK? . . . Shut up . . . I'm telling you . . . to *forget* the book . . . If you write anything about my sister, anywhere at all – or anything about Jo, come to that, I'll –' He hesitated. 'Kill you,' he said, simply, and he realised he meant it, too. He hung up.

There was a movement from the corner of the room. Charlie and Jo looked up to see Grey, his feet resting on the fascinating, primary-coloured chaise longue, his head thrust forward. He was studying Charlie.

'Well spoken,' he said.

'Grey! How did you get in here?'

'I didna' want to disturb you,' he said. 'You left the window open.' He stood up, padded across the room towards the kitchen and opened the fridge.

'So,' he said, pulling out a bottle of champagne. 'Have you got some good news you want to share with me?'

'Grey, *please*,' said Charlie, 'just this once. Will you bugger off?'

'OK, OK. I'll take a bath. If that's OK with you, Jo. Only I can't hang around outside. I'll get murdered.'

Charlie waited for Grey to close the door, and then he turned to Jo. 'Where were we?'

She smiled at him. 'You were offering me a job.'

'Yes.'

But they were standing absurdly close to one another. It was impossible to concentrate. She cleared her throat. 'It, er, yes. It sounds very tempting. Especially after what happened to, er. Y'know . . .'

'What?'

'The – Grey . . . In the pub . . . Horrible.'

'Or shall we get just married?'

'What?' It brought her to her senses.

'Then we could put Grey into the cottage. Because frankly I don't see him ever moving on. And Dad'll almost certainly want to follow him . . .'

'*Charlie!* I mean I love you and everything. But marriage? It's – Marriage is just a bit –'

'Say "old-fashioned",' he said, 'and I'll die of boredom and withdraw the offer.'

She laughed. 'I was going to say "a bit embarrassing".'

'Is it? Not for me. All right, silly idea. Forget it –'

'Oh.' She sounded disappointed. 'But it might be fun.'

'It would be fun,' said Charlie. 'For a bit, anyway.'

'Shall we do it?' She grinned at him. 'Why not? We could give it a try!'

'But a serious try.'

'An incredibly serious try.'

They paused, just for a second, to gaze at one another, to revel in their own wonderful good fortune. He bent to kiss her, she put her arms around his neck, their lips were just a millimetre apart . . .

'Excellent,' said Grey, striding out of the bathroom. 'About bloody time. Right then . . . So, who's goin' to break it to the General?'